Publication: 15th June 1992

THE
M

James Hamilton-Pa~~~~~~ ~~~~ ~~~~~
the Whitbread First Novel Award in 1989 and was also
nominated for the Whitbread Book of the Year. He is
also the author of the autobiographical *Playing With
Water* and a second novel, *The Bell-Boy*. A Newdigate
prize-winner, he has also published two collections of
verse. His new book is a non-fiction work on the Ocean,
Seven Tenths.

He divides his time between Italy and the Philippines.

James Hamilton-Paterson

THE VIEW FROM MOUNT DOG

VINTAGE

VINTAGE
20 Vauxhall Bridge Road, London SW1V 2SA

London Melbourne Sydney Auckland Johannesburg
and agencies throughout the world

First published by Macmillan London Ltd, 1986
Vintage edition 1992

1 3 5 7 9 10 8 6 4 2

Printed and bound in Great Britain by
Cox & Wyman Ltd, Reading

ISBN 0 09 979110 2

for
Ann, Shelley, Matthew and Alice Masters

Contents

Author's Note

It is unreliably reported that the Cynic philosopher Chimerides, whose dates are unknown and whose very existence is doubted, was exiled to the salt marshes of Meddo (Asia Minor) for the excessive venom of his political criticisms. There he is believed to have written a series of essays which he sent home to a friend in Athens under the title *Letters from Mount Dog*. This was a sarcastic reference to (*a*) the unremitting flatness of Meddo and its environs and (*b*) the nickname of his own philosophic school, members of which were decried as snarling fault-finders. The essays were obviously written in defiance of his judges and detractors, the implication being that, no matter where he might be obliged to live, his very contumely would always afford him a lofty view.

It is a great loss that these essays of Chimerides survive only in fragments quoted by contemporaries – a perverse sentence here, a surly phrase there. He must certainly have been more than a sublime curmudgeon, estimable though that would be. His acrid reproof, 'Belief is merely a failure of doubt: beware', is justly celebrated for its elegant scepticism, and this centuries before Pascal, Schopenhauer, Nietzsche, to say nothing of Wilde.

Precisely because of modern scholarly opinion to the contrary, I am more than ever convinced that Chimerides existed. Faint whiffs come down to us of the awe in which his brilliant crabbiness was held: difficult people may become legends but they do not become myths. Whatever the case, one or two of the stories in this volume were written in the foothills of Mount Dog, whose summit stands ever before me as inspiration and challenge. Naturally, the higher I climb the more I shall come to doubt Chimerides ever lived. But even if he did not I honour his putative memory, worthless though it is. Or, rather, my own memory of his memory, now failing.

Multiply & Rule

His Most Serene Highness Sultan Yussuf Masood Ammar had enjoyed quite a lot of his state visit to Britain. He knew perfectly well that occasions of this sort were intended to be politically useful before they were pleasurable, not least because there is generally more agreement between culturally dissimilar nations about what is of mutual advantage than about what constitutes pleasure. Nonetheless, there had been several moments when he was grateful that members of his entourage – notably the Royal Photographer and the Royal Diarist – were present to click and scribble the records which on their return to Jibnah would be worked up into a scrap-book bound in green kid. He had watched a racehorse he was told he owned win the Derby; he had shamelessly overeaten at various banquets; he had been graciously permitted to blow up a mouse-coloured tank on Salisbury Plain.

But what had made the Sultan's visit were the trains. There were alas no railways in his country which, thanks to the provision by a munificent Deity of vast mineral wealth beneath its sands, had recently moved from caravans to state airline more or less overnight. Accordingly advisers and senior diplomats had made sure in advance of his trip that the Sultan would spend plenty of time on trains, and the highlight of the entire visit was the granting of his special request that he might be allowed to sit with the driver of the night express to Edinburgh.

After that, little in the last week of the visit made much impression on him with the single exception of an informal afternoon spent at Buckingham Palace at the Queen's personal insistence. The Sultan vaguely perceived that unlike his own Palace of a Thousand and One Rooms the Queen's palace was not very sybaritic – an impression reinforced by taking tea with her in a drawing room full of family photographs, a portly dog asleep on a cushion, plates of sponge cake and back numbers of *Horse & Hound*. However, he did notice a table covered with the day's newspapers, and his attention was further caught by a three-inch headline reading 'Queen Hosts Despot'. During tea the wife he used for state visits, an ex-air hostess from Harrogate, engaged the Queen in lively if one-sided conversation while he edged back towards the table and surreptitiously read some more. Under the guise of looking out of the window at a very orderly garden full of guards disguised as gardeners and gardeners hoping to be mistaken by photographers for guards, the Sultan put his cup of tea down on the newspaper in question and, by squinting sideways and downwards and taking frequent sips of tea, read an article about himself describing some sort of desert Yahoo rolling in money and wallowing in gore. The Sultan was far too exalted to feel hurt and far too pragmatic not to be quite certain that the gore of usurpers and pretenders was always much better spilt than one's own. He did, however, feel a little jab of apprehension, something to do with the way the domestic press of another country could print such things as gospel while back home the idea of calumnies like that even leaving somebody's typewriter, still less being set up by compositors, was unthinkable. Was he, then, two people? Was he simultaneously beloved shepherd of his desert flock and pariah-sovereign of the international community?

Thoughtfully he dropped a half-scone buttered side down on the page and, holding the bottom of the scone, turned the page with it. Here the headlined article which had begun with banners and continued with trumpets fizzled out in two column inches. Idly the Sultan's eyes drifted on past the buttery transparent stain spreading from the other side down to an article about the double of the lady behind him. He read in astonishment, bent now over the open page, all pretence at looking through the window gone. He couldn't believe his eyes. Here was a woman, a commoner, a nobody, capitalising on

2

what the newspaper claimed was a close likeness to her Monarch. Well, he thought, things were certainly organised rather differently back home. The physical characteristics of his own family were pronounced, the Ammar nose being striking in itself but in combination with the Masood chin unmistakable. Occasionally in some desert village a child would appear whose features bore a peculiar resemblance, but in such cases an exquisitely wrought damascene blade would fall regretfully but not over-apologetically and the child's family be presented with a lame white camel in traditional acknowledgement.

'Your Majesty,' said the Sultan, turning to interrupt an account by his wife of the dowry system in Yorkshire.

'Your Highness,' said the Queen gratefully. 'More tea?'

'Thank you, but I am puzzled by an article in this newspaper. This may come as a shock to you but there seems to be a woman daring to impersonate you. Can this be true?'

'So it would appear, although we are assured it is not impersonation as such.'

'You do not *mind*?'

'It's not clear there's a great deal one could do about it even if one did. It is peculiar, isn't it, since you mention it. Apparently the lady in question is always being asked to open fêtes and that kind of thing, despite everybody's knowing she is not myself and her insistence that she would never pretend to be. Don't you think that's interesting? It implies, does it not, that if one's parish priest happened to resemble the Archbishop of Canterbury there would be more cachet in being married by him than if he merely looked like everybody else's parish priest?'

'Exactly,' said the Sultan uncertainly.

'Or suppose,' said the Queen, warming to her thesis, 'suppose one had an imitation Rolls-Royce made by, well, a Japanese company, for instance, a vehicle which *very closely resembled* a real Rolls-Royce but which had on the radiator a badge declaring it to be a Honda.' The hush which traditionally fell whenever the Queen spoke took on an attentive edge at this bizarre fancy. 'The question is, would it be accorded the same degree of *respect* as if it were the genuine article?'

Everyone pondered this for a moment before a crusted old equerry ventured an opinion, it being tea-time and the moment of the day usually reserved for informal conversation of a democratic variety when almost anyone might lay claim to having had a thought.

'That would depend on whether Ma'am were in it or not.'

This excited a murmur of agreement. Even the Sultan found himself nodding, although, truth be told, he was completely lost by the conversation's sudden philosophic turn.

'An excellent point, Bertram,' conceded the Queen. 'One had overlooked that. Very well, then' – a mischievously speculative look came into her eye – 'supposing, supposing it was not one*self* inside the vehicle but the lady who resembles one? Now, then.' She sat back in triumph and took a large bite of sponge cake.

'Humpf,' said the equerry, emboldened by the intellectual cut and thrust. 'A fake Queen in a fake Rolls, y'mean?'

'Not exactly,' said a clear voice. 'They're not *exactly* fakes, are they? It's not Her Majesty because this lady doesn't claim to be, and it's not a Rolls because it plainly says "Honda" on the front. Or am I being stupid?' – and the Sultana giggled a little, just as she once had whenever facing a hundred and twenty strangers wearing a yellow lifejacket and miming the automatic fall of oxygen masks in the event of a sudden loss of cabin pressure. 'That's not proper deceit, is it?'

Other voices began to join in. Forgotten wedges of sponge cake punctured the air to make debating points.

'I say, now, hold on,' said a plain-clothes detective masquerading as a page boy. 'If that's not deceitful, what is, I should like to know? It's like this painter fellow comes up to you and says, "Here, cop a look at this picture I've just done of my girlfriend. It's pure coincidence she happens to be the spitting image of the Mona Lisa." To my mind he's being deceitful on two counts.' He held up two fingers and knocked each down with his other hand. 'One, he's pretending his portrait's original when it was da Vinci's idea all along and, two – most important of all – he's pretending his girlfriend's as beautiful as the Mona Lisa.'

The discussion continued in this lively vein for nearly twenty minutes before the Sultan's own private secretary managed to divert the company's attention back to the forgotten monarch who was sitting on a spindly gold chair, gold-trimmed white robes about his feet, the Masood chin on his chest. From the moment he left this palace until the moment he once more set foot in his own he was observed to be thoughtful. After the long flight home and once in the Royal Bath-Chamber, however, letting the residues of travel soak off his body in a huge glass chalice filled with his favourite mixture of rose-water and

Harrods bath salts, he began taking decisions. His first was to summon the Minister for State Planning, who arrived down below within half an hour in an air-conditioned Cadillac and was ushered into the royal presence.

'I want a railway,' announced the Sultan without preamble. 'It should go from here in Jibnah down to Hafoos. Later we might make a branch line to Rifa'aq.' He swished some greenish foam decisively. It became apparent that he wore all his rings in the bath, for they clicked on the glass sides of the chalice.

'Certainly, Highness. It is a wonderful idea. Do you wish this project to fall within the portfolio of my own humble ministry?'

'No,' said the Sultan. 'Excellent as you no doubt are where overall planning is concerned, railways are highly specialised affairs. We need a Minister in charge who really understands trains. I recommend a man named Reg Burnshaw. You'll find him in England. He is an absolute authority on the line between London and Edinburgh.'

The Sultan dismissed his Minister, changed into a magnificently embroidered robe with a gold-handled ornamental dagger at his waist and roamed thoughtfully through the royal apartments trailing a confused scent of roses and verbena. Night had fallen. Beyond the windows designed by a firm of Italian architects to imitate the shape of the opening in a Bedouin tent lay the small desert capital of Jibnah, neat avenues of mature date-palms (transplanted by airlift from an oasis three hundred miles away) radiating from in front of the Palace. The beacon revolving on the control tower of the newly built international airport some distance away intermittently lit one corner of the night sky, and the Sultan knew that if he went and looked through the windows at the back of the Palace he would see another corner of the sky suffused with the flickering orange glow of the burn-off flares at the Zabul gas-fields sixty miles away over the horizon. He stepped out on to the balcony breathing in the smell of mimosa, baked earth, urine, freshly cut grass and petroleum fractions. It was the unmistakable smell of his Sultanate; it was good to be home.

But a thought was troubling him somewhere at the back of his mind. Some days ago a doubt had been sown by a phrase. 'Queen Hosts Despot', indeed. Still, one could never be too careful. He took another decision and rang for his personal servant.

'Do we have any old robes in the Palace, Mehdi?'

'No, Highness.'

'Are you sure?'

'Certain, Highness. There is nothing old in this palace, Highness, except the traditions of your subjects and the allegiance we owe you.' He said this very gracefully with his nose touching the rug.

'I see. Then bring me a camel-driver.'

'A camel-driver, Highness.' It was a flat repetition.

'Well?' said the Sultan, sensing difficulty.

'*Any* camel-driver, Highness?'

'More or less. About my size.'

'But young, of course,' said the prostrate Mehdi, 'and fair of countenance.'

'Not necessary at all,' the Sultan said impatiently. 'I don't care what he looks like as long as he looks like a camel-driver.'

'Highness, I hear. Now, this instant. But', came the voice as it retreated slowly over the priceless half-million knots, 'it may not be easy.'

'Why not? It is a simple enough order.'

'If Mehdi dare presume, Highness, it is your Highness's own fault in being so prompt to make manifest the gifts of Allah the Bountiful to all men that today camels are a rarity in the city. Now, if you had asked for a *taxi*-driver, there are a thousand at this moment sitting in their ranks with the air-conditioning on, reading Egyptian paperbacks.'

'A camel-driver, Mehdi, at once.'

Mehdi withdrew.

He reappeared forty minutes later escorting a magnificent old man whose lined and hawk-like face the Sultan barely glimpsed on its way down to the rug. Around him on the floor lay a spreading puddle of tattered brown robes. The peculiar scent of camels became apparent. The Sultan looked at him speculatively for a moment, but then his heart failed. His own power was such that at his behest damascene blades lifted and fell; but all of a sudden he had not got it in him to make this dignified old man stand up and take his robe off. He could not even dismiss him to another room and likewise order the clothes off his back, not even if they were immediately exchanged for the most sumptuous in his own private wardrobe. In all probability the camel-driver had never removed his robe since the day he put it on. How long ago? the Sultan wondered. Three years? Five? How often *did* camel-drivers change their garments? And, anyway,

6

how did they do it? He could not imagine a naked camel-driver but he did remember a boyhood visit to the Gulf where he had had hermit crabs explained to him by an English tutor. Perhaps camel-drivers were the same. When the time approached for a change of outer wear maybe they looked around for something suitable and then, under cover of darkness and when they were sure no one was watching, quickly slipped out of the old and into the new. The Sultan experienced a brief imaginative flash of something coiled and tender and pink and then came back to earth.

'A thousand greetings, O loyal camel-driver,' he said. 'I wished merely to see again something familiar from before the day when Allah opened his riches to us. Go with peace and a suitable gift which Mehdi here will be glad to bestow on you.'

His subjects retired; the Sultan fell to brooding. The newspaper articles he had read in Britain had given him various ideas, all of them fuelled by a growing sense that in these turbulent times he ought to be better in touch with things outside the Palace. There had been one or two awful reminders lately of what happened to rulers who went on living feudally in a world where yesterday's illiterate Bedouin now read inflammatory Egyptian paperbacks. All that talk in London about disguises had reminded him of the old stories they used to tell of kings dressed as beggars and even of beggars dressed as kings. He had lately heard that one or two modern rulers had resorted to such things the better to guide their people's destiny. It had been the plan, therefore, of His Most Serene Highness Sultan Yussuf Masood Ammar secretly to don a humble disguise and prowl the streets of his capital incognito. Yet it was turning out to be infernally difficult. The embarrassment he had experienced at the thought of ordering an old man to undress had extended itself to the explanations necessary to stop Mehdi gossiping, the Palace guards shooting, the general uproar on discovering what purported to be an unescorted camel-driver smelling of roses and verbena trying to leave the Royal Apartments. It was hopeless. How *did* they do it in the stories?

The difficulty in even finding a camel-driver was also significant. If they were now that rare, it would scarcely be an act of self-concealment to slink in rags about streets busy with air-conditioned limousines and pedestrians who did their shopping in Bond Street and Saks Fifth Avenue. And where did one go nowadays to hear the murmurs of discontent, the ranklings of ingrates? The Sultan had no idea but he suspected there might not be any cafés and souks left, having been transmogrified by Divine Will into drugstore soda fountains and hypermarkets. Truly the whole thing needed thought.

A year or so passed in which the wealth of the Sultanate increased while the spirits of its ruler declined. Pragmatic he may have been in straightforward matters involving damascene blades, but the Sultan was rapidly wearying. He was not an old man by any means – somewhat under fifty – but he was finding the relentless pace at which everything changed confusing and exhausting. Each evening when he stood on his balcony sniffing the familiar breeze he thought Jibnah had grown a little. How could he ever have been so foolish as to imagine he could find a camel-driver in this city? he wondered. It seemed years since he had even seen a camel. Now there were endless Daihatsu showrooms and Lear Jet shops. In his boyhood and youth – well, until only a few years ago, now he came to think about it – camel-meat was on sale everywhere and very good it was, too, hanging up on hooks in the markets so that you could see what you were buying. Now, he gathered, there were only air-conditioned supermarkets whose meat counters sold Australian mutton, Argentine beef and unnaturally huge, tasteless chickens, all of it bundled up in plastic film and stiff with ice.

The burdens of State, though, were really getting him down. His days, albeit ever shorter on ceremony, were ever longer on being pestered for decisions and having to meet excruciatingly boring foreigners claiming to represent excruciatingly boring corporations. Awesomely keen to help the Sultanate develop, they were, as if they had just discovered within themselves gushing wells of altruism. To these the Sultan preserved a grave and passive demeanour except that he was unable to stop himself smiling as each of them inevitably said: 'It is clearly in the interests of the country, Your Highness.' They flew in on Concorde and stayed in the Jibnah Otani or the Oberoi or the Meridien, drove madly around ministries the next day, like as not seeing close relatives of his and leaving behind a spoor of glossy brochures full of half-truths written in a quaint businessman's dialect; and then, full of mint tea and self-esteem, they would roar away the day after that heading for Jeddah, Tokyo, Frankfurt and Los Angeles on their restless mission to help countries develop.

One morning the Sultan cracked. It was bound to happen and it was just plain bad luck for his visitor to have had his name down in the Royal appointments-book on that particular day. He was the Sales Director of a vast and prestigious West German corporation which produced water desalination plants and he had just made a glowing pitch to install one at Manduri on the coast.

The Sultan had listened abstractedly.

'Tell me, Herr . . . er, Schönau, did you fly in last night on Concorde?' he asked when it was over.

'I did, Your Highness.'

'I see. Well, you woke me up,' the Sultan told him simply, 'so I don't want your water thing.' His guest fought for words. 'Besides,' the monarch went on, 'have you been to Manduri?'

'Oh, yes, Your Highness. It is quite undeveloped, ideal for—'

'I used to go there as a boy to collect shells. I had by far the best shell collection in the country, did you know that? No; well, even today it forms the core of the collection in our National Museum here in Jibnah. My English tutor taught me how to classify them, and we did it together. It was fun,' he added, staring reminiscently at a little flag on his desk. 'We lived in tents. Lots and lots of tents, all different colours. Tents for me and my brothers, tents for the Scottish nannies, tents for servants and guards and everyone. That was at Manduri. And now you want to build a huge water factory all over it? Well, you shall not. Today I give the order to make Manduri a National Conchology Reserve. And next time, Herr Schönau,' the Sultan added in what might have been a whimsical attempt to soften the blow, 'I suggest you fly Lufthansa. They have no Concordes.'

This sudden impatience with businessmen coincided with an equally complete exasperation with politicians, be they local ones, visiting Arab heads of state or – in particular – American Congressmen. Sometimes it seemed as though he had spent much of his adult life kissing hairy cheeks and being lectured on the Sudan question, the Egyptian impasse, the Libyan dilemma, or the Syrian problem. Increasingly the hard-edged world of his youth was dissolving into an international slurry of détente, vetoes, UN votes, peace initiatives, OPEC summits and Gulf crises. What was it all for? he wondered. Why couldn't people be a bit calmer and quieter as they had been before God was so good to his little Sultanate? It was wonderful indeed that the sands of the desert concealed a commodity which other people wanted, but why should that be any different from having a racing camel that somebody wanted, or a daughter, come to that? If they offered a good price and you were willing to sell, then that was that; you sold. If not, you hung on to your camel or daughter until someone happened by prepared to offer more. That surely was the essence of all business, always had been, and he couldn't for the life of him work out why something so simple should be inflated into matters of such hopeless complexity. . . . He began leaving meetings early complaining of indigestion; then he took to avoiding them entirely, nominating Prince Bisfah and Prince Ashur as his proxies. Not that he had much confidence in his two eldest sons. Bisfah was seemingly unable to drive his red Italian cars along even the most deserted road without careering off among the dunes in search of the only boulder for miles to crash into, and Ashur. . . . Well, Ashur. The Sultan had once discovered that Ashur's nickname at Harrow had been 'The Queen of Sheba' and that was not something a father forgot. He wondered if the Queen of England had known when they had last met. Hadn't one of her own sons gone to Harrow? If so, he might well have told her. The Sultan's cheeks burned. Maybe she had known all along and even as she had so graciously presided over the sponge cake she had been thinking *That's the father of the Queen of Sheba*.

The one thing which cheered the Sultan up was his new railway. Having to contend with none of the traditional obstacles to progress such as shortage of funds and recalcitrant labour, it had progressed rapidly and there was now a regular high-speed train service between Jibnah and Hafoos, a small provincial town at the foot of the Jebel Ahmar, that great escarpment of red sandstone which leads to the stony and waterless high plateau, one glimpse of which through a helicopter's tinted and juddering windows makes oilmen wonder how on earth their mortgages can be taking so long to pay off. As often as he could, which was nothing like often enough, the Sultan would sit high up in the driver's compartment of the giant French-built locomotive and thunder across the desert at a hundred and eighty miles an hour. Beside him sat his Minister of Railways, still keeping in practice as the Sultanate's premier engine-driver. Since Reg Burnshaw's bewildering translation from British Rail locoman to Minister and private engine-driver to His Most Serene Highness Sultan Yussuf Masood Ammar the two men had become very close and the Englishman was proud of his pupil. He now allowed the Sultan to take the handle for the tricky banked section – a miracle of engineering, incidentally – at Wadi Shaduf, and the time was not far off when the monarch would be able to start practising shunting. The only thing which secretly troubled Reg Burnshaw was the lack of passengers. He had endless rolling stock at his disposal: elegant dining cars, sleeping cars, couchettes and carriages, all of them air-conditioned and all of them practically empty. The Sultanate's population – barely two hundred thousand people – preferred either their Cadillacs or their Cessnas for travel. Rail was somehow not very chic unless one could commandeer an entire train for one's family, and the choice of route was so restricted it seemed hardly worth it.

'You wait till we get the branch line going,' said the Sultan happily. The branch line as projected was to climb slowly up the escarpment for sixty miles in a series of breathtaking panoramic curves before reaching the plateau. Then there was to be a single flat-out straight all the one hundred and fifteen miles to Rifa'aq, a tiny oasis not far from the border. There was nothing in Rifa'aq, certainly nothing worth building a railway to; but there again, as the Sultan reflected, it's not the destination but the journey which counts. He remembered his old English tutor telling him that, and he had been absolutely right; the man had obviously been a genius, and if he were still alive there was no honour and dignity his ex-pupil would not have heaped on him.

Apart from the railway, however, there was not much nowadays to brighten the Sultan's eye. He began indulging in an activity which more than almost any other must be the mark of civilised and melancholic man: he took to spending long hours in the bath. Lying there in his capacious glass chalice, big toe comfortingly inserted into the hole of one of the gold taps, he was struck one day with an amazing realisation. *He was fed up with being Sultan.* That couldn't be right. He poured some more bath salts in and swirled them around with his brown beringed hands. Not fed up with *being* Sultan exactly, just fed up with having to *act* Sultan. It was then he recalled something else from that tea-party in Buckingham Palace over a year ago. That woman in the newspaper. . . . Well, why not?

It was difficult. Indeed, to anyone without his limitless financial resources it would have been almost impossible. The rise and fall of the damascene blade in small villages over the last decades had scarcely helped, but a cadet branch of the family was unearthed in South Yemen. Arrangements were made with the finest plastic surgeons money could procure. The secrecy was awesome, the threats terrifying, the results astonishing. One afternoon the Sultan's private Boeing landed at an airport in Italy and taxied to a remote corner of the field. A car with smoked windows drew up and a man wearing dark glasses hurried up the steps of the plane. The Boeing immediately took off and sped southwards. Once it was over the Mediterranean the Sultan was introduced to his double.

He had expected to find it uncanny, instead of which he found it absurd. Since he was quite certain he was himself he could see little resemblance in the man standing opposite him. He looked like any other handsome Middle Easterner with a sensibly shaped nose and chin. It further annoyed him that everybody else thought it was hard to tell them apart. The fellow was clearly an impostor, and for a moment he wondered whether to call the entire thing off and bring Faroukh el Damm, the Sultan's private executioner, out of semi-retirement to keep his hand in. It would, after all, never do to get the public executioner to do it in the Maidan: from a distance the crowd might easily mistake the victim and it could trigger off an unseemly power struggle. But then fresh memories came to him of meetings with businessmen, of Islamic fundamentalists with bushy beards and wild eyes, of OPEC ministers talking about quotas, and his resolve hardened.

To his surprise the ploy was extraordinarily successful. After several months' indoctrination – a tedious period for the Sultan when his double traipsed around the Palace of a Thousand and One Rooms aping the way he walked and repeating everything he said – the subterfuge was subjected to limited public gaze when the pseudo-Sultan took his place on a reviewing stand. All the man had to do was hold himself gravely at the salute while a succession of dun-coloured land-rovers bowled past, but he did it beautifully. He even fooled the Sultan's High Command, who all privately agreed afterwards that they had not found him so alert and well informed for years. The Sultan himself remained in his bath and began drawing up the first National Railway timetable. It did occur to him, though, that it would be safer if both he and his double were not to live in the same palace. An irreducible number of essential people was in the know, of course, but sooner or later the Sultan's apparent ability to be in two of the thousand and one rooms at once would arouse comment. He commissioned plans for a summer palace to which he could retreat, and in a remarkably short time a simple white pavilion was standing exactly in the middle of the site where a German corporation had once had visions of building a desalination plant. To this secluded coastal residence the Sultan moved one night with a skeleton staff and a concubine. At some point in the previous months his Yorkshire wife had become confused and was still paying visits to the Royal Bedchamber far away in Jibnah; there seemed no reason to suggest she stop.

This moving away from the capital, this abandonment of the Palace marked a turning-point in the Sultan's life. He became far less anxious, less preoccupied; he put on a little weight. He had commandeered a generous slice of the National Conchology Reserve for his new private residence and in it he lived a life of such freedom as he had not enjoyed for years. Screened from the eyes of Manduri's tiny population by quick-growing conifers and slow-chewing sentries the Sultan began to enjoy himself. He sent back to Jibnah and spent a happy morning unpacking all his old shell-books. He sat on the floor of his bedroom in a pair of khaki shorts smelling the pages in wonderment that the grains of sand which fell out of them were from that very shore beyond the verandah and had lain in fragrant darkness since his own boy's feet had scuffed them there and his own boy's hands had shut them in. He stared at his large jewelled fingers and thought about time and Mr Munson and Nannie MacWhirter and sighed. Well, from now on he was going to have a lot more fun.

He still had to go back to Jibnah now and then, of course. There were things involving the family which could not be left to an outsider (remarkably few things, he noticed) and likewise things involving the State for which he was reluctant to delegate responsibility. For most daily purposes, though, the fake Sultan drove about Jibnah in a perfectly genuine Rolls-Royce exciting quite unfeigned obeisance. Both of them thought about this and each in his own way marvelled.

Another year passed in which the pseudo-Sultan took over almost all executive power and had grown so familiar with the role he was playing that for days on end he could forget it was a role. To all intents and purposes he *was* the Sultan, and the irony pleased him. So did his new life-style, which was a great improvement on what he had been used to in South Yemen. He liked the perks and trappings, the sumptuous robes, the arcane protocols, the guards with scimitars in their belts and Berettas under their embroidered tunics. He enjoyed the parades with camels wearing kettledrums slung from their humps, he liked bugles and jet aircraft in formation overhead. He liked banquets a lot and he loved concubines very much indeed. In the early days he was even quite amused by playing monarch with the jet-set businessmen and politicians. Many of his decisions were fairly arbitrary; several were positively quirky. He unexpectedly welcomed a delegation of Jehovah's Witnesses, gave them full permission to build a large and costly Kingdom Hall in Jibnah and, when it was finished, confiscated it without compensation. He gave the Witnesses a day to leave the Sultanate and converted their Hall into a braille school for blind Imams. People openly thanked God that the Sultan had regained his old spiritedness.

But abuses of power may herald a growing disenchantment with it as much as a craving for more of it, and so it was in the case of the pseudo-Sultan. After making sure that nobody in his own family could ever conceivably lack for the odd ten million dollars and after indulging himself royally at – apparently – nobody's expense he, too, began to grow restless. The real trouble was that life in Jibnah was dull. Whatever he wanted, *almost* whatever he wanted, would instantly be brought him; but that was not the same as being able to wander around the world looking for nothing in particular but indulging his fancies with somebody else's platinum American Express card. Jibnah was the conservative and provincial little capital of a conservative and provincial little sultanate, and the pseudo-Sultan felt himself inhibited from asking for certain things he quite wished to toy with. For example, he dearly wanted to try cocaine ever since talking to the American ambassador's son, but he was far too embarrassed to ask. He also longed to learn how to water-ski, but the idea of having to flounder about in front of lickspittle aides pretending to be overwhelmed by His Most Serene Highness's God-given skill was enough to deter him. Why could he not practise in private with just a single motor-boat driver who could instantly be rendered headless at the slightest suspicion of a snigger? But he couldn't: security was obsessive and Court protocols inflexible. Besides, vague memories came to him of *Paris Match* pictures from the fifties, grainy black-and-white photos of playboy monarchs such as King Faroukh being towed around behind boats in places like Monaco wearing dark glasses and looking like portly beetles. That was not the figure the pseudo-Sultan wished to cut for himself.

After sunset he would often stand on the Palace balcony as the Sultan had before him, made introspective by the evening breeze, which seemed nightly to contain less mimosa and more exhaust-fumes. The city, until so recently a shady little oasis scattered with flocks and tents and houses like whitewashed cubes, had grown so that one of the shopping malls now ended abruptly at the airport's perimeter. Bad planning there, he thought and wondered if the odd head shouldn't roll, but then his attention was redistracted by the sight of listless knots of European *Gastarbeiter* making their way slowly up the boulevards in front of the Palace, sweeping the drifts of crumpled petrodollars into little piles and setting fire to them. A great sense of unease and thwart came upon him.

It was inevitable, of course, that he should have hit on the same solution and that it should then have seemed so obvious. No need to tell the Sultan; much better not, in fact, since he was by all accounts becoming more and more reclusive and would now only talk with any interest about cowries and winkles. Using the same methods by which he had himself been so successfully recruited, the pseudo-Sultan quietly introduced a second pseudo-Sultan into the Palace of a Thousand and One Rooms. It might have been thought such a move would lead to complexities unimagined since the death of Feydeau. Not a bit of it. Most of the Palace staff were desert fathers who had been retainers to the Sultan's family since birth and tended towards age and forgetfulness. A few of the more alert ones below sixty wondered at their monarch's extraordinary energy and slight departures from habit and custom but reflected that the Masood Ammar boys always had been headstrong and gave it no more thought. The Sultana from Harrogate marvelled at the efficacy of the tablets compounded of ginseng and dried scorpion venom which her husband had begun taking. Even the Sultan, when he paid a surprise visit to the Palace to look for a scrapbook he had once made, noticed nothing on running into his second double. His original double, fortuitously out of town for an important meeting with the son of the American ambassador, heaved a sigh of relief when he heard. That was one of the really wonderful things about conservatism, he reflected: it never wanted to *know* anything. Just as long as things looked right, with the correctly dressed people coming

15

through the right doors at the right time of day and uttering the same prescribed formulas, things *were* right. What did it matter whether somebody were actually the person he purported to be? As long as whoever it was acted in character and looked the part there would never be any end to the motorcades and the cheering crowds. With all that dead weight of conditioned reflex working in one's favour the only real enemy was one's own disenchantment, the deadly tedium of the puppetry, the awareness of dwindling days.

At the last count there were eleven Sultans. This figure happens to beat by three the present number of Queens of England but is one fewer than the Presidents of the United States. They are easily outnumbered by the twenty-seven current Popes. All the Popes are interchangeable, as are the Presidents and the Queens; but one of the Sultans loves driving trains.

The Moon as Guest

Nobody could remember how it had started – least of all Anding whose leg it was – since it had been with him so long. It had been named over the years: 'varicose ulcer' or 'that time the chip of wood flew off and stuck in when Clody was chopping'. The health worker called it 'a chronic sore', but by none of these terms could Anding recognise an old friend. When he thought about it with the near-affection due to the utterly familiar he could imagine he had been born with it. Not exactly as it was at this moment, of course, since its appearance changed from time to time. Its phases were varied: sometimes it wept, sometimes it bled, sometimes it shrank to a dry pucker surrounding a black borehole, and now and again it rotted a bit and smelt as at present. Essentially, though, it was resident as this hole on the outside of his right leg about three inches below the knee. In so far as it had to be allowed for at all times, but chiefly when negotiating public transport or the bamboo settles at home, Anding thought of it as he would any of his limbs: somewhere between an appendage and an inhabitant, something whose absence in other people he had begun to notice.

'I can't sleep with that smell in the house,' his wife told him. 'It's disgusting. It attracts flies and keeps people away. Haven't you noticed how few of our friends actually come into the house nowadays? They hang around the doors but they won't come inside because of the stink. That leg of yours has taken over my whole house.'

'I can't smell anything,' said Anding truthfully, 'although he certainly looks as though he's coming up for one of his wormy times.'

At fairly long intervals there would recur a period lasting anything up to a month when the presence of small creamy maggots could be noticed as they burrowed around in the necrotic hole. Tatang Petring up the track, who was by far the best barefoot doctor in the area, had told him this was an excellent sign since it meant all the green stuff was being eaten up and only clean uninfected tissue would be left whereupon the wound would quickly become smaller. And it was true the maggots came and went beneath the papaya poultices which Tatang Petring applied, but so, too, did callers at the house come and go. Anding was a fair man and came to think his wife was probably right. Certainly there were a lot of flies about.

What did not go was the wound itself, undoubtedly a black miracle, a medical mystery. Although often enlarging and deepening to the point where the bone could actually be seen by anybody interested enough to look (mainly small children and Tatang Petring himself), the wound appeared to be self-limiting in some way. The maggots did their bit, the wound grew huge and deep but quite neat: a light pinkish-grey smooth wet crater with bone at the bottom and with a slightly raised crusty rim – and anyone who knew anything about Western-style medicine or Eastern-style ways of death predicted that Anding would soon run a tremendous fever and his leg swell up and go glossy black, and at that point unless it were cut off entirely he would be done for. Yet this never happened. The health worker would procure some unmarked capsules in a twist of paper, and Tatang Petring would leave off the papaya poultices and instead apply grated palm-heart tinctured with ordinary kerosene, and within a week the wound would be half its previous size, the skin around it a glowing healthy brown.

At this point Anding used to worry about its disappearing entirely and would stop taking the capsules. It would be like murder, doing away with a companion as constant yet as varied as this one. His friend did not in the least incapacitate him but merely made him courteous when dealing with furniture or dogs (which were fascinated by the smell) or those small children always apt to bang into legs. Little boys particularly were wont to dash off suddenly in pursuit of their chafers, which instead of droning in tight circles above their heads at the end of lengths of thread would somehow escape and blunder away, trailing their moorings. Only the other day a child had smacked into the leg, bounced off and plunged away through the goats rooting among the banana plants at the side of the track.

'You smegma!' Anding shouted half-heartedly after him and wondered if he hadn't heard a faint 'sorry, sir' amid the crashing of sticks and goat-bleats. For it was on behalf of his friend that Anding felt annoyance: it was no way to treat a companion. The question of pain never entered into it.

And that was one more extraordinary thing. Almost regardless of which phase it was in or what was done to it Anding scarcely ever experienced his wound as painful. Occasionally his whole leg would ache but, then, so did everyone else's after about forty; it was called arthritis and was an unbidden but not unexpected guest who would come one day and take up residence in someone's body and not leave until that person was dead. That was the thing about wounds and diseases: they, too, had lives of their own which they had to live, and it was in their nature to have to depend on the bodies of people and animals in order to do so. Tatang Petring had told him that years ago, and Anding had long since had enough experience to confirm its truth. Sometimes one of these visitors might be accompanied by a companion of its own – it might be fever or pain. Such happened not to be the case with his own wound, which had turned up all by itself (perhaps on that wood-chopping day, perhaps not) and required a home. True, it had had certain consequences: discomfort when lying on the floor at night, inconvenience in that he always had to be on the lookout for stuff that would serve as bandaging to hold Tatang Petring's treatments in place and, if Lerma were to be believed, a disgusting smell at the wormy periods which messed up their social life. But never actual pain.

'He's not going to go away, is he?' Anding asked Tatang Petring one day.

The doctor considered silently.

'No. He wants to stay. He likes you. Sometimes it looks as though he's going to take over more of you and sometimes as though he might move out altogether. But he never does either, does he?'

'It's strange,' said Anding, who was still then thinking in terms of his wound's apparent indecisiveness.

'Not a bit,' Tatang Petring told him. 'Look at the moon. That comes and goes at seemingly odd intervals, all the time on the wax or on the wane, but you couldn't say the moon was vague, could you? It's always in exactly the right place. It's just a question of understanding its habits. When you understand things as they properly are they almost always turn out to be regular in some way. Look at women's periods; or better' – Tatang Petring hurriedly skipped over one of the greater mysteries whose very irregularity accounted for a large percentage of his patients' visits – 'the tides.'

'They're both connected to the moon,' said Anding. 'Everyone knows that.'

'Perhaps your leg is, too. We don't know.'

Both men contemplated this possibility.

'If *madness* is,' pursued Tatang Petring, 'why not wounds? It doesn't matter if it's your spirit that's wounded or your leg. Perhaps everything's connected with the moon in some way. Meanwhile, how is he?' He began unwrapping the strip of old T-shirt which this week was tied about Anding's leg. It had part of a legend printed on it in faded blue letters advertising a paint company. Underneath lay an amorphous lump of pus and poultice, and beneath that Anding's old friend.

'He's going down a bit for food,' the doctor said at length after close examination. 'He's growing now so he needs more nourishment.'

'Ah.' To study the outside of his leg Anding craned down and bobbed his knee inwards at the same time, a movement which in the early days had felt awkward and even slightly painful when prolonged but which now had become an entirely natural posture like squatting or bowing or kneeling or any of the other contortions human beings ritually adopt from place to place; there was indeed an element of obeisance in his gesture. 'And then?'

'Well, what do you do when you eat a lot?'

'Fart, usually. Sleep?'

'You *shit* a lot. Eat a lot, shit a lot; it's natural. So he's going to shit a lot of this greenish stuff. That's when the worms come along to clear it away.'

'That's the bit Lerma says is smelly.'

'Of course,' said Tatang Petring. 'Did you ever have shit that wasn't? Though wound-shit doesn't smell quite the same as ours.'

'By all accounts it's a lot worse.'

'Depends on your point of view. Think how bad your own shit might smell to him.'

They both looked at the wound.

'I hadn't thought of that, certainly,' said Anding. Then he asked: 'So what are you – or we – actually *doing*?'

'You mean to the wound?'

'Exactly. If he's living his own life in his own time, why are we treating him at all? Why all these leaves and herbs and things?'

Tatang Petring looked up at him in surprise. 'Isn't that obvious? I'd have thought that was obvious, myself.'

'Not completely,' said Anding humbly.

'When you have guests in your house . . . in the *old* days when you used to have people who stayed overnight, did you ignore them and just leave them to fend for themselves?'

Anding studied the palms of his hands very closely, 'Of course,' he said. 'I see now.'

'Well, just as when friends stay we can never be sure we're giving them exactly what they want most at any moment because there are codes of politeness for guests as well as for hosts, nor can I be quite certain that I'm making him' – he indicated the wound – 'as comfortable as I can. We can only try. I sometimes worry about the flies, though.'

'How?'

'Occasionally my dressings make it quite difficult for them to reach the wound. Suppose, now, that those flies are *his* house-guests.'

'Goodness. . . . We're driving away his friends just as Lerma says I'm driving away ours.'

'I'm not saying we are. I'm just saying we might be. Medicine's extremely difficult; there's so much we don't know yet.'

For a long time afterwards Anding had brooded about this conversation and had come to a barely identifiable conclusion that somewhere, in a way which he did not at all understand, there was definitely a suggestion of rightness about it all. Once you had grasped the essential correctness of things the only course which remained was learning how to live with them as they were. Viewpoints. The more viewpoints you saw things from the more sense they made . . . well, the less they seemed open to the slightest change.

So now when Lerma was complaining about his friend's smell

he was patient. Quite truthfully he did not himself notice it, and when from under the edge of leaf or bandage a maggot would rumple itself aimlessly away across the brown bumpy expanse of his calf Anding would tuck it back underneath with an offhand solicitude, an abstracted courteousness which quite precisely was unable to notice the reaction of wives, house-guests, casual passers-by. Dogs, small children and Tatang Petring were, Anding did comprehend, about the only creatures yet able to see how interesting and proper the notion of a body-guest was.

'Let them wait,' he said of the others to himself while going to and fro about his business, chopping firewood here, feeding the pigs there and walking up the track to chat with Tatang Petring daily. 'Sooner or later somebody will call on them.' And spotting the piercing yellow of an oriole looping up to its nest in the crown of a coconut-tree felt a blaze of happiness which made him chuckle at a point a few inches above the head of a passing child.

Nard for the Bard

Lost in the immense gloom of a great forest was a small clearing where the sun might break in to bring extraordinary treasures to light. Feathery tufts of palm made moiré patterns behind each other and against the blue of the sky; the delicate arms of porphyryngias were raised to bestow a benign shade upon the humbler glyptopod. On every side vines restrained the frothing tonnage of vegetable life which otherwise seemed likely to break loose and balloon skyward, lifting with it the rest of the forest from the face of the earth. Amongst this foliage glowed flowers and fruit of every kind: bells and cups, cynths and calices, sprays and single blooms like solitary gongs mingled with pricklefruit, quinsicums and the scarlet orbs of the tart *tabitabi*.

To one side of this clearing stood a hut made of fronds like a woven basket set upon timber legs. And in this hut, all by himself, lived the Poet. Many years ago he had come from a distant country, a cold grey place inhabited by a cold grey people little moved by Art but much interested in Commerce. Hither had he come, a wanderer, a solitary in search of he knew not what except that it would thaw the chill from mind and marrow. For, truth to tell, his first book of poems, *Nard for the King*, had not been well received in his native land.

Then he had curled his beard and put upon himself traveller's raiment. 'For,' he reasoned, 'while it is little to me that I am unappreciated, it is everything to my Soul that it should be able to feed on beautiful things. Here there is only ugliness and

23

meanness since the cold grey North has crept into these people's hearts and locked them in ice.'

For a while he trudged the world, and the world rewarded him with wonders and delight. In love and gratitude he spoke his verse in dusty squares and village lanes; in bazaars he raised his voice among gold-capped minarets, and the desert wastes heard his songs. At length, meagred by hunger and worn out with travel, he wandered into a library where, having first ascertained that it held no copy of his poems, he found a map of the country he was in. It was rather old and still had the word 'Unexplored' printed across many a region of the interior.

'That', mused the Poet, 'is where I must go. I have lived too long among the known. A hundred cultures have I seen' (this was, of course, poetic licence) 'and sundry domestications of the earth. And always where the hand of man sets its imprint a strangeness vanishes, a uniqueness is lost, an otherness is made the deadly same.'

So saying he drew a line across the map with decisiveness and was engaged by the Librarian in a short conversation before making his way to the market-place to find bearers to carry his few necessities. Then he recurled his beard, gathered his tatters about him and taking up his leather pouch of manuscripts set off on his last journey.

On the tribulations which beset him there is no need to dwell. At the end of the time it took to write four sonnets and an epithalamium he pushed his way through a clump of stinging millefoils and limped into the clearing. And in that instant he recognised his home.

Time passed, and the Poet moved through intensities of vision. At dawn he would rise to watch the night's distillates tremble their dewdrops along the edges of leaves as the first rays of the sun pierced the upper branches. Nearby there ran a shallow stream whose laterite bed was home to sly brown elvers and translucent prawns which a quick eye and a defter hand might net. Across this each dawn shimmered the first gauzy dragon-flies like scattered dream-residues, which would vanish as the heat hardened into broad day. At noon he ate a simple meal of fruit and rinsed his mouth in the crystal runnel before retiring to his hut, doubtless to write. At dusk a light breeze would spring up and lemon-censers spill their fragrance on the air which with the aromatic popping of peppernut husks would bring the Poet forth, stretching the cramps of creativity and yawning in the cool of the evening.

And thus in simple splendour he passed his days. Sometimes he was a little lonely. 'But', he told himself, 'I have my Art, and all Art demands sacrifice. If I have renounced companionship, I still live in a world of Beauty and Love,' since the love he lavished on his poems was indeed that of a parent for its child. Nevertheless, at dusk sometimes a young and slender-limbed creature – as it were some shy and gentle faun – might be glimpsed flitting from the undergrowth to the rude hut wherein the Poet glowed and burned and gave off sparks in his solitude.

Now, there was a Headman whose village lay some way off in the forest and in whose bailiwick the Poet was living. Sometimes when the sun was high and smothered the clearing with its heat this man would trudge through, now carrying a great bundle of wood on his head, now with merely a bow and a knife but with his body streaked with sweat and the bright blood drawn by cruel whipthorn. Often the Poet would be so entranced by his Art that, lost in inward vision beneath the emerald tent of a clump of sagathy plantains, his eyes were blind to the Headman's weary progress past his hut. But at another time he would spring up and bid the Headman rest awhile.

'I fear,' he would apologise on such occasions, 'that I have little enough to offer your body by way of refreshment, so simply do I live. But your mind – ah! that I can refresh. I have just this moment made the most exquisite ballad, and there should be a fragment of ode lying around somewhere from last night.'

Then he would read to the Headman in a strange and beautiful voice. And it was as if his words were so attuned to the Nature from which it seemed he had drawn them that the very leaves shivered and the twigs like silver tuning-forks responded to his pitch until the whole glade rang softly at his words. Even the insects' mechanical clamour grew hushed. Shard and carapace ceased their husking; mandibles in mid-munch froze; locust heads with many-faceted eyes swivelled to where this music came.

The Headman sat as if enraptured. 'Oh, you have spoken truly', he would say in a soft voice when the last hum had died away. 'You have once more spoken the Truth, my great and good Friend.'

And the forest exhaled its long-pent decaying breath, the jewelled birds dared try again their own small voices. For the Poet had spoken of things which other men cannot see but which on hearing they know to be true; and this recognition makes them inexpressibly sad yet eager to hear more as if it were a cure for unacknowledged wounds. And the Poet knew of his power and whence it came. 'Wherefore', he said to himself when the heaviness of night lay on the forest outside his hut and the fireflies inside tangled their shining paths in the thatch overhead, 'I hide myself from the world and formulate medicines for its pain. I am not a Prophet in the wilderness, for I herald no one. Also I foresee nothing. Yet am I a Seer, for I see everything as it is.'

Since he was not a stupid man, either, he saw that part of the reason for the Headman's visits had to do with a supply of gin, the last remnants of which the Poet still had laid by him from the day of his arrival, having known of no good reason why plain living and high thinking should be any further penalised. Thus grew up between them that agreeable companionship which may be distilled from grain and words. And each was much the better for it since under its benign influence the Headman could forget he revered this foreigner as a shaman while it would quite slip the Poet's mind that he sometimes thought of this native as marvellously dignified.

So tireless sun and patient moon swung each other about the sky in a literary device known as tachychronia, signifying the rapid passage of time. And dawn preceded dusk and vice versa until the day came when a hardly audible sound like a memory of thunder hung breathing about the forest's distant rim. It rose and fell on the breeze so that at times it was not there at all but then took its place once again behind the jungle cries of insect, bird and beast. Some days later it had become almost constant, and when the Headman appeared, bowed beneath trusses of viridian gourds, the Poet having bade him rest and refreshed him as usual with verses and gin asked him what it might mean. 'I fear', he added, 'that dreadful disasters, storms and earthquakes such as never before must be shaking the land about us. And yet the ground whereon we sit is curiously unmoved.'

The Headman, too, had heard the sound but was equally uncertain as to its cause. His village had spoken of the roar of floodwaters since it bore some resemblance to that caused by the river in spate with the coming of the monsoon. Days later still the noise had grown more menacing, and amid its now constant growl were to be discerned irregular pantings such as wild beasts make when rending prey. This time the Headman was more informative.

'A messenger has arrived by boat. He comes from the King. The King in his wisdom, caring only for the greater well-being of his subjects, has contrived a brilliant plan to make us all rich. Maybe you as well' – he gave a reassuring bow to the Poet. 'For, although you are a foreigner and a wonderful teacher not like us, yet still you sojourn in the King's land and may receive of his benison.'

'But I am already far richer than I deserve.' The Poet looked round in bewilderment at the familiar yet ever-changing beauty of his domain. 'I need no other wealth. The King is, of course, too good,' he added politely. 'But what is his brilliant plan?'

'He has sold the forest', announced the Headman, 'to strangers like yourself from far-off lands. They have bought all the trees and now they are cutting them down. Those are their remarkable machines which you can hear even as we speak. They say they can make a field this size' – he pointed at the clearing – 'in the time it takes us to cook rice and *banban* and of it make a sweet-sap pudding. Whereas it would take my people with their axes fourteen suns to clear this ground for our slender purple cassava.' And with that the Headman left, his head dazed with Progress and the benefits it promised to shower on his hitherto moneyless folk.

But the Poet was filled with anguish and with rage. For a further two whole days he listened to the inexorable tide of engines encircle his beautiful world and watched in love and pity the trees put forth their young leaves, the spiders spin their sticky threads, the elvers in the crystal stream lave their slippery ribbons in the current. All was as it ever had been, and all was changed for ever. He alone of those myriad creatures to whom the clearing was the universe knew it and could mourn their end before they ended.

Then on the third day at dawn the Poet arose and addressed his domain with bitterest tears:

'Is it not I who have brought this down upon you? Is not the fault mine? For at last they have tracked me down, my cold compatriots: they pursue me and my kind even to the uttermost ends of the earth. I took upon myself an exile's life that I might court the Muse in her natural halls, and even so did she come to me. Where before was silence we have made enduring music; we have wrought marvellous songs. Out of nothing have we spun our webs of words and hung them up to ensnare with gentlest Art the unhappy souls who chance by. We have magnified the beauty of the world whose outward sign Creation is and lo! the hearts of men grow greater in response.

'Now they, those countrymen of mine whose blood is salt with the driven spume of grey and Northern seas, whose hearts are cold with Nonconformist zeal and will not be warmed except before the twin fires of self-righteousness and greed, they have tracked me here so they may lay waste my Soul.'

And the clearing was hushed as he paused and it seemed as though the uneasy rumble of vile mills had drawn a little closer.

'Is it not I who have brought this down upon you? Oh, my lovely elverines, beloved *tabitabi* tree, is not the fault mine? My error lay in thinking them indifferent. Yet, though many years have passed, they have not forgotten me, hidden in your midst in populous solitude. What other motive could they have, thus to track me even to Paradise itself and encompass me about with hateful engines? Even now they steadily abolish Nature who for so long has cherished me secretly in her bosom as a pearl in a precious setting. What other motive could they have but vengeance? Is not the world already full enough of Swedish furniture? Lives there a man who would not see a shaggy, ancient hardwood tree stand in living majesty rather than in the office of some executive? Who, looking at such a noble giant, thinks only of a heap of desks? No, the fault is mine, the fault is mine.'

Thus spake the Poet; and he ceased, weeping. And the clearing heard his words and the forest trembled, for it knew that, although in matters of detail he slightly erred (the logging consortium which had gained the Royal Warrant being, in fact, Japanese), in essence he was accurate and once more spoke a Truth. So the Poet retired to his simple hut heavy-hearted and, with the world's encroachment ringing in his ears, began his greatest work: an Elegy such as had not been before or since and written as though his very eyes had shed every one of the *lacrimae rerum*.

Meanwhile by devious routes the reputation of this stranger living in the land had reached the ears of the King.

'Seemingly,' he told his Chamberlain, who had actually brought the news himself a month or two ago, 'there lives in a

28

distant region of Our Kingdom a Poet with the gift of Truth and Beauty. We find this hard to believe, for such parts are commonly lived in by displaced zoo populations and dreary savages. Wherefore would a Poet seek Beauty and Truth in such a place? Nevertheless, it is Our wish and Our command that a poem from this man's pen be brought that We may judge with Our own eyes the truth of these astounding claims. *Selah'* (which, being interpreted from the language of that land, means 'Hurry').

But the Chamberlain groaned inwardly; for, although it was his pleasure and his pride to do his Monarch's bidding, he was wont to do it comfortably at Court and had not the slightest desire for arduous travels to howling outposts. Nonetheless he went; and towards the end of quite excessive tribulations through lands which would not recognise his ebony stick of office, sumptuously inlaid as it was with rubies, onyx and the clearest amethyst, he came upon the Headman, who undertook to guide him through what remained of the forest to his final goal.

They found the Poet deep in composition of his Song of songs beneath the cool pavilion of umbrageous sagathy. His Elegy lay in a half-completed pile and his gold nib flashed across the page as some livid jewel with a sun breaking at its heart. With what assurance, with what radiance did this slender golden monarch proceed his winding way; and behind him dressed in sombre black trailed his courtiers, his words. The Chamberlain watched in fascination. In whose kingdom moved this king? he wondered. It was of mere paper; and this mere paper lay within the greater Kingdom he himself served. And yet his King did not command it. He who reigned here was a ragged stranger with a ragged beard. Almost as if he had heard the thought, the ragged stranger raised his hand in salutation and looked up.

'Greetings, Friend,' he addressed the Headman. 'You have brought a finely apparelled gentleman to this our ruined Paradise.' And in truth he had to raise his voice in order to be heard above the roar of engines which seemed to encompass the glade at no great distance.

'Chamberlain to His Majesty,' the gentleman in question announced himself, striking the Poet lightly on top of his head with the ebony rod. 'His Majesty commands:

'Your as yet unsubstantiated fame has humbly crept, thanks to His serenest magnanimity, to the portals of the King's ear, which, having deigned to hear, is graciously curious to hear still more. Give me a poem that I may bear it with swiftest steps to Him who, having once delighted, is not slow to reward.' He rapped the Poet's crown again. 'His Majesty commands.'

'Which poem?' asked the Poet. 'They are so many, my dearest children whom even now the nursery cannot contain' – and he indicated the doorway of his little hut through which dim and shadowy piles of paper could be descried almost entirely filling that humble dwelling. 'Which of my children will you take and introduce to the outer world?'

'How do I know which poem?' asked the Chamberlain testily. 'The best, obviously.'

'*Inter pares,*' mused the Poet, 'and with the magnificent exception of the Elegy on which I am currently at work, *primus* is perhaps my sonnet "In Praise of Praise".' He got up, went to the hut, rummaged for a while and returned with a small sheet of paper.

'Read it,' commanded the Chamberlain. 'And it had better be good. It is ultimately for the ears of His Majesty, remember. There are no references in it to Democracy?'

'None,' said the Poet. Then he read in his strange and beautiful voice; and the leaves shivered and the twigs like silver tuning-forks sang in sympathy and the soft ringing of the glade seemed to drown the nearby bellowing of machinery and to abolish its very memory so all became once more just as it always had been. The Headman's eyes filled with tears, so painfully did it remind him of days which were and could not come again, the more so since he had heard this poem many times before and loved its words without quite knowing why. And suddenly he was flooded with a great pity for his Friend.

The Poet ceased; and as from far away the noise of engines gradually returned.

'Take it,' he said at last, and held the paper out. But what was this? The Chamberlain was also weeping. Down his cheeks and down his beard and even down his ebony stick the tears ran, past rubies, onyx and the clearest amethyst, down into the clearing's very dust. His shoulders shook, his lips framed bubbling syllables. He was weeping for he knew not what: for years wasted in foolish office, for the cruelties and the pleasures of his position, for a lifetime spent denying the Beauty that Is. From the very emptiness of his heart the tears sprang; for the Chamberlain was weeping for his Soul.

'Go, my friend,' said the Poet gently. 'Bear my humble offspring to your great and good King, and may it speak to him as it has spoken to you. And now I must complete my Elegy since I feel a strange presentiment and dark forebodings of a waning light.'

So the Headman led the weeping Chamberlain away, who in time recovered, reached the capital and presented himself to his Monarch. 'Sire,' he said, 'I have done as You commanded. I have found this Poet of whom You spake, although only after the greatest difficulties for the way to this, perhaps the remotest, part of Your Kingdom lies defended almost impregnably by the hand of Nature. All manner of rivers, deserts, swamps, mountain ranges—'

'Silence,' ordered the King. 'We care little for your troubles. We gave you a task. Have you brought Us a poem?'

'I have, Sire,' said the Chamberlain, producing it. 'And all that came to your August Ear concerning this Poet is true, and still more than true. He spoke this poem himself, and Nature paused to listen. The very birds were silent and my tears fell as the monsoon rains to hear him.'

'You always were impressionable,' said the King. 'Well, read it anyway.'

So the Chamberlain read; and something he remembered of the Poet's own cadence must have come back with the words, for as he spoke the King stopped fidgeting with his rings and the disdainful glance he cast through the window grew misty so that to his eyes the formal gardens of the palace took on the lineaments of Eden. Even the toiling figures of his subjects became transformed and for a moment unthinkably appeared as noble as himself. When the Chamberlain finished reading there was a long silence.

'I have not heard the like before,' the King said at last, to his Chamberlain's amazement forgoing the Royal *We*. 'I feel I know things now I never knew; yet what they are cannot be said except in the very words you spoke. Truly, a kingdom within whose borders dwells a man like this is rich indeed. You say he lives in a swamp?'

'More of a forest, Sire.'

'A forest? A man of this greatness? It is absurd.'

'Mr Ishugu's men are cutting it down as fast as they can.'

'Quite right, too. We can't have forests. Nasty dank things; they make us look hopelessly primeval and underdeveloped.

Besides, I'm told they harbour guerrillas. No; this Poet shall be brought forthwith to the palace here and housed in the utmost style and comfort for as long as he desires. I shall have a suite of rooms cleared of women immediately. You will return at once and fetch him. Meanwhile the finest engravers in the land shall copy this poem on to a slab of the purest gold and it shall be presented to him on his arrival.'

'Sire, it may be he would not come with me. He is a man of the simplest tastes and perhaps Your generosity will overwhelm him so that he feels unable to appear in Court, clad as he is in rags and beard.'

'Well, who *would* he come with, then?' demanded the King with a slight return to his old peremptory manner.

'He has a friend, it seems; a Headman of the lowest caste. Maybe the Poet would go with him.'

'Very well. Let this Headman bring him. There is no need for you to go at all: you will be better employed here, organising the Reception. Send messengers to the Headman. *Selah.*'

But meanwhile in the clearing time had passed in which the Poet, quite possessed by his creative act, laboured to complete his Elegy before he was engulfed by Progress. His gold nib flew, the pages mounted up. Daily he sent forth the Headman as his scout to keep him informed as to the advancing tide. His friend at his bidding slipped away through jungle paths. But when he came to where the loggers were he stopped and stared with superstitious awe.

Machines like mythic beasts on silver tracks roared and grunted, smashed down trees and tore their hides off. On all sides stretched a barren waste of splintered stumps, barkless trunks in pyramids. The undulating jungle floor which had been for ever hidden and engloomed now lay beneath the blazing eye of day, strangely bare and dull. Something in the Headman's breast stirred in torment at the sight. Yet still more powerfully he felt excitement rise as in his inner mind he saw rolling acres of cassava plant, waving okra, golden maize. Never again need he wend a weary way about the forest tracks in search of food: no longer need he brave the cruel whipthorn to bring his children grubs and pods and acid fungus ears, bark and nut, berry and leaf.

Yet well he knew he would distress his Friend by giving an exact account of this desert's steady advance. So back he went, and the Poet said: 'Tell me, what did you see?'

'Nothing, Friend, but the shaking of leaves, the insects' dance and the lazy shimmer of a summer noon.'

But the Poet, gazing up at him and hearing the nearby snort of powerful exhausts, said gently: 'Headman, you lie. My ears hear more than your eyes see. Go now therefore once again and come and tell me how it goes.'

A second time the Headman sped away. But when he so quickly arrived at the edge of the great wound weeping its sap from uncounted broken stems his heart grew heavy. 'I cannot tell him,' he cried in anguish. 'It is far better he should not know, but write until he fully makes an end.' So back he went, and the Poet said: 'Now, tell me truly: what did you see?'

'The crested lizard on a branch, the spider in its delicate lair, the buttermoth on painted wing.'

This time the Poet laid down his pen. 'I had not thought that all our years of Friendship could be so easily betrayed. It surely is not much to ask a Friend to do. It seems that I was wrong.'

And his face was so sad and stricken that the Headman turned in bitter grief and ran a third time and resolved to bear his witness true. But he now had hardly any distance to go. The topmost branches of the nearest tree were shuddering to the blade. At the edge of the clearing he turned round. At his back an ochre-yellow bulldozer poked its snout through a bush and stopped.

'My Friend, my Friend, my dearest Friend,' he called. 'They're here.'

Across the clearing the Poet looked up, looked down, wrote a word or two, drew a line and laid down his golden nib.

'I know,' he said. 'It is finished.'

Now, when dusk came and the bulldozers fell silent he went alone to sit as usual beside the rivulet. A light breeze sprang up as it always did; but no lemon-censers spilt their fragrance on the air, nor popped any husk of peppernut. A single cicada stropped its legs and then, embarrassed on its own behalf, fell to silence. Even the surface of the stream was iridescent with a film of diesel waste.

'My lovely elverines,' murmured the Poet; but they had fled away downstream and were gone. 'Great and mysterious forest, my fastness and my home,' he whispered. But of the forest only a single line of trees made a thin circle about the clearing. Between their ancient trunks showed an infinity of sky.

So he went to his hut and, composing himself upon his bed of manuscripts, gazed up in the dark to where a solitary firefly drew erratic scribbles in the thatch.

Light my way, firefly, he thought to the tiny insect. Light my way.

And when at dawn the Headman came he found the Poet lifeless with the worn-out firefly dead upon his breast.

Then the grieving Headman's tears fell like rain. An hour he wept and thought about his Friend and, constantly remembering that golden speech to which even the forest had stooped its verdant ears, wept afresh. And as he did there stole from the nearest shadow a young and slender-limbed creature – as it were some newly dispossessed faun of the erstwhile forest – who mourning fell at the dead feet and kissed them and performed loving obsequies. Together they lifted up the body and washed it in the stream, calling upon their deities. Then the Headman took his knife and touched it to his lips and cut from the Poet's body his heart, according to their custom. And they placèd the heart in a box most exquisitely carved in secret over many months, and the sweetest unguents poured therein: most precious gums and balsamums, myrrhincense and liquid nard. They did it about with a rattan thong and buried it deeply at the foot of the beloved *tabitabi* tree.

In silence then they caught up the body and carried it to the hut. And the Headman took some pages from the just-completed Elegy (for in truth the entire manuscript was far too large) and placed them in the dead mouth. 'For', he said, 'is it not professed in our tradition that the words of a man's mouth shall return thereto?' Then he set fire to the hut according to their custom, it being proper for a man's works to perish with him that none might nourish an evil pride. For all things done beneath the heavens are sufficient unto themselves since none shall last, no, for even their smoke is blown away.

So, even as his works, the Poet's body was consumed and became as nothing, and the smoke of it was blown away. There fell upon the clearing a silence as had never been; and the Headman went grieving thence.

In due time the messenger bore the news to the Chamberlain, who told the King how the great Poet was dead, how his works were ashes and his heart lay embalmed beneath the *tabitabi* tree. And the King was exceeding sorrowful.

'Bring from this humble clearing', he commanded, 'that thing which is the most precious in all my Realm and it shall be enshrined in our holiest temple with utmost pomp. *Helas'* (which being interpreted from that tongue means 'It is meet to grieve').

So back the Chamberlain went to that far-off region and found the Headman but lo! the clearing itself the Headman could not find, for it now extended eighty kilometres all about in a waste of stumps and stunted leathery shrubs and the deep ruts made by logging trucks. But after much searching he did come upon a filthy rivulet with close at hand what might have been the site of a long-extinguished fire. And all around were men in metal hats eating sandwiches among parked machinery.

Then, empowered as he was by the King's Command, the Headman – who was soon to be appointed the region's Reafforestation Officer – laid his hand reverently on that most precious thing which long since had been for him a source of hope and pleasure. And to the Royal Presence he despatched, in a Progress aided by a thousand willing hands, an ochre-yellow bulldozer.

Carney Palafox

Something happened to Carney Palafox one evening as he was running for a number 5 bus in London. He was running as fast as only somebody can who despises running and wishes to get it over with as soon as possible. He caught his bus and found a seat upstairs and was so stunned by the insight he had experienced thirty yards ago that he forgot even to pant. Breathing quite normally, this forty-one-year-old scriptwriter suddenly knew he was the greatest athlete who had ever lived. He also knew that he could only ever prove it five times in any specific event; once he had used up those five astonishing victories he would have to remember never to try again since on the sixth occasion he would perform like any other forty-one-year-old scriptwriter who despised sports.

From the moment he got off his bus to walk towards Sadlers Wells and home Carney Palafox was a changed man. His immediate life was utterly clear to him. He knew exactly what he had to do. All he could ponder was how best to go about it so as to make the utmost of his five chances and extract the maximum vengeful pleasure from this astounding windfall. For a start, whom could he tell? It was a ludicrous assertion just to come out with at his time of life, and he knew it simply by listening to an imaginary conversation he might have later that night, maybe while undressing for bed.

'You know, Katie, I sometimes wonder if I couldn't be something of an athlete if I tried' – diffidently stepping out of his

36

underwear and glancing down at his neither fat nor thin physique.

'You know, Carney, I'm thinking of becoming a concert pianist when I grow up.'

No; absurd. Suddenly he had turned into a man with a mission, and men with sudden missions were ill-advised to announce them rather than just get on and fulfil them. *Deeds*. But – and Carney knew as little about sports as a man can to whom it is a matter of pride to have forgotten how many players there are in a cricket team – he had a suspicion that demonstrating you are the world's greatest might be catered for only by a slow and rigid system of entering a heat here, an event there, being picked for a team still later to perform at some sodden track on the outskirts of a city. He suspected there were few short cuts to events at which world records could be set, and with only five chances at each event he could not afford such a slow accumulation of credibility.

Sometimes it could slip his mind that he was under contract to a large and famous television company since he always worked from home and visited the monolithic block of studios and offices as infrequently as possible. However, he now remembered that this television headquarters contained whole suites of studios entirely given over to sports reporting. In particular, he found next day that most of these studios were occupied by the company's star sports attraction, a programme named *Action Replay*. Towards the lunch hour he paid these studios a visit and found a lot of middle-aged men sitting around reading magazines about car racing and horse racing and tennis tournaments. To a man they were wearing rather expensive clothes designed to resemble professional sportswear, things which looked to Carney like mohair track-suits. In addition they all had on running shoes with cleats and stripes and flashes. Their entire wardrobe was covered in brand names and they mostly had moustaches.

'You're Bob Struthers?' Carney asked a man behind a desk which had across the front a large sticker reading 'The Bob Struthers Experience'. He vaguely recognised the name. The man he had asked looked at him over the top of his magazine with genuine amazement and took his feet off the desk.

'Do I look like Bob Struthers?' he enquired.

'I wouldn't know,' said Carney. 'I've never met him as far as I know.'

'Good grief,' muttered the man, glancing round at his colleagues with an expression which was meant to make a conspiracy of their general disbelief and ridicule. They paid no attention since they were still reading their magazines. 'In there,' said the man, indicating a glassed-in sanctum to one side. 'And you are?'

'Carney Palafox.'

'Never heard of you, either.'

'I'm a scriptwriter on *Up Yours!*'

'Well, you've given me a laugh already.'

Once inside the sanctum Carney recognized that the magazine-readers in the other room had all been mere clones of the original who sat before him. His track-suit had the sheen of raw silk, his training shoes had been hand-stitched by Italian craftsmen. His moustache said of itself 'Bay Area leather bar', but the wearer would possibly have been shocked to hear it. This time Carney found the face itself faintly familiar.

'I'm Carney Palafox, I'm a scriptwriter on *Up Yours!* and I need a simple piece of information about sports. Sorry to bother you, but I thought I'd better get it from our top man.'

'Always happy to have the old brain picked,' said Bob Struthers, waving at the sofa. 'Chuck some of those mags on the floor and fire away. What's this – a piece of authentic sporting stuff you're writing into your series?'

'Sort of. . . . It's this. Supposing somebody were completely unknown in the sports world, no connection whatever, but had an amazing talent for – I don't know – let's say the hundred yards. How would he go about setting records and generally getting himself acknowledged as the world's greatest?'

'Well, now, Carney.' The ex-athlete steepled his fingers. 'Let's take it from the top. For starters, do you really mean the hundred yards?'

'Er . . . the hundred metres?'

'What's the world record for the hundred metres?'

'You're asking me? I haven't a clue,' said Carney. 'That's why I'm here.'

'Currently,' went on Bob Struthers with his modulated announcer's voice, very quiet when not being amplified, 'it's nine point nine-three. That's seconds,' he added helpfully.

'Ah. Well, suppose this fellow came along out of the blue and said, "I can do it in eight seconds flat," what would you think?'

'This is all "let's pretend", right? You'd have to think he was off his head. But if he really looked authentic – you know, probably a black American, right height, right weight, thigh muscles out here – I'd still think he was a nut. Maybe he could do it in ten-five on a good day with the wind behind him. But we'd know. If he was anyone at all, he'd have form. Nobody that good appears from nowhere.'

'This one does exactly that.'

'It's a nice idea. Into the office walks this complete unknown whose muscular neck is destined for the weight of Olympic gold. Good stuff.'

'But, playing along with the "let's pretend" for a moment, what's the next step?'

'Well, if he's really just off the streets he joins a club and runs his way to the attention of talent scouts or gets the sort of times and wins which would put him in line for a team selection.'

'Yes, yes, in other words he works his way up. But this guy has neither the time nor the inclination for all that. He can break the world record *right now*, so he doesn't want to waste months joining the Haggleswick Harriers or the Aberdaff AAA.'

Bob Struthers glanced at his watch, a complex affair of overlapping dials and sweep hands, then patted the little high-life pot which his tailored track-suit almost concealed. 'The Bob Struthers inner timing device,' he said, 'which is far more accurate than anything Omega ever made with quartz, tells me it's time for a drink. Join me?'

Without waiting for a reply he reached back in his swivel chair to a shelf of *Wisden*s, opened it and disclosed a small refrigerator stacked with cans. 'Now, this is the stuff,' he said, selecting two and nudging the door shut. He handed Carney a can of No-Calorie Root Beer. 'Do you know I can drink as much of this as I like every day for the rest of my life absolutely free? One more promotional freebie. I could fill my swimming pool with it and they'd be only too happy. "Who but Bob Struthers starts each day with a brisk 100 metres in invigorating No-Calorie Root Beer?" All that good stuff.' His moustache crackled at the opening of the can. Seeing Carney about to speak he held up his free hand. 'Don't worry, I know what you're thinking. But this isn't just a lot of time-wasting bullshit I'm handing you. I'm trying to get across that international sport nowadays has very little to do with packed stands and centre courts. That's the public-spectacle part and it's almost incidental. We're talking about big business, Carney, one of the biggest. Top athletes are bought and traded like wheat futures; the real money is won and lost in boardrooms, not on tracks. Sponsorships, TV deals, promos, franchises, the international games circuit, the betting consortiums, the sportswear manufacturers, the drinks people, the fucking paper-cup makers. . . .'

A note of something or other – passion? mere vehemence? – had crept into the famous voice. In a moment, Carney thought, he'll be asking me to guess which of all the various signed photographs, awards, little silver television cameras on little silver tripods on display around the room had given him the most pride and pleasure, and the answer will undoubtedly be the dented cup over the door, 'Victor Ludorum 1955', which he had won when he was thirteen despite having just recovered from chickenpox.

'. . . the hack writers, the ghosted-autobiography writers, the chat-show hosts, the groupies, the fan-club organisers, the exclusivity-rights lawyers, the city-hall lobbyists bidding to host the Olympics in twenty diddledy-three, the airlines who fly the Olympic teams about, the manufacturers of the nose-hair tweezers used by the pilot of the sodding plane which carried the victorious nation's team back home. . . . You name it, Carney. And every one of those bastards is living and jet-setting and wining and dining and making his fortune on the backs of a few hundred people out there on the tracks and courts and pools, sweating their wretched guts out and praying the latest dope-test techniques are still a year behind what their managers are giving them. Shee . . . *it*!'

'Heavens,' said Carney mildly with what he hoped was an irritating other-worldliness. 'I never thought it was all such a – well, *racket*. So what you're saying is . . . ?'

'What I'm saying' – Bob Struthers brought into his voice a fine edge of patience – 'is that it's next to impossible for someone like your guy to bull his way to the top in one easy move because it does a lot of people out of their cut. Once he's a star, of course, they'll be fighting over his body. But until someone's identifiably a biggie with the prospect of being packaged and sold for real money the industry likes its athletes to be quite conventional and work their way up in time-honoured fashion. Life, Carney,' explained Bob Struthers, 'is a simple knock-out competition and you'd better believe it. You win the eliminator and move on to the qualifying rounds, and then you win and win and win and suddenly it's the quarter finals, then the semifinals and then by the Grace of Whatever it's the bloody Final and you're there. . . . Or not, depending. This isn't hack philosophy, Carney. It's what I see and know, every day, everywhere. Do you know what my proudest possession is in the whole of this room?'

'No?'

'That,' said Bob Struthers, flicking the silver television camera on its silver tripod which stood on the desk before him, 'because it's this year's. And that makes it better than last year's and the year before's.'

'Well,' said Carney, gathering his legs under him into an about-to-leave posture, 'you've been very helpful, Bob. I really appreciate it.'

'Just filling in some of the background for you, Carney; I haven't finished yet. Now, what effect does all this have on the ordinary man in the street who, whenever he turns his TV on, hears and sees nothing but stars – names he knows as well as his own, faces he's more familiar with than those of his own family? I'll tell you. It's made him a *fantasist*. . . . By the way, Carney, this is a pet theory of mine.'

'You certainly seem to like your subject.'

'I love it, Carney, I really love it. Now, it's made him a fantasist because of the nature of publicity itself. My theory is that there are no real stars – very few, at any rate. What there is is star*dom*. It's the top spot in whatever you like – sport, films, er . . . comedy' – he nodded benignly towards his guest – 'and the top spot is occupied by one of a constant stream of winners who come up, get that spotlight of attention full on them for a year or two, then move off into outer darkness. A lot of the people who find themselves briefly at the top are pretty unmemorable, frankly, and this is where your man-in-the-street fantasist comes in. He looks at those stars and he thinks: That bugger's no different from me. Bit better built, nothing a few months of weights and saunas couldn't put right, but that could be *me* being kissed by film actresses and accepting cheques from the Duchess of Doggydo and advertising a lot of rubbish with glucose in it on every high-street hoarding. All I need is the Big Break. He's a fantasist, you see, because he leaves out the hard work bit: the months in the gym, the tons of weights, the push-ups and the lonely miles along the A1 at dawn. He sees instant recognition, immediate fame. The Big Break.'

Bob Struthers reached down and pulled open a desk drawer

from which he grabbed a handful of loose sheets at random. 'There you are,' he said, dropping them on the desk. 'Fantasy. Every day I get them, letters by the sackful.' He picked one up. ' "Dear Bob Struthers, I'm an avid watcher of your programme blah blah. You're not going to believe this but yesterday, 3 July, at the Penge Sports Hall, I was timed at fifty-three point seven seconds for the hundred metres freestyle. I have six witnesses to prove it and the stopwatch was electronic and has since been checked by a certified jeweller blah blah. Could you please ensure that my name is put forward immediately to the England Team selectors for Honolulu next month? It is vital for the success of our country, whose reputation as a sporting nation I'm sure you blah blah. I am sending a copy of this letter by registered mail to Sir Benedict Frowde, Chairman of the Board of British Aquasports Selection Committees. Yours sincerely." Typical.' Bob Struthers let the sheet fall back to his desk. 'The only thing he left out was the "PS I am not a crank. Please take this letter as seriously as it was intended." Most put that in. But you see what I mean? Everybody connected with sports gets letters like that all the time. I just get more of them because I'm so exposed. The Big Break's what everyone's after: you ain't seen nothing till you've tried *me*. Like those women.' And Bob Struthers smiled tiredly to himself, to the letters on his desk, to the silver television trophy. 'Does that answer your question yet, Carney?'

Carney Palafox was still uncertain as to whether Bob Struthers had divined his real purpose in coming, but blushed in any case. Did he have to come for an impromptu interview with a sort of fake-macho has-been to be told he was a middle-aged fantasist? He supposed he did. But searching resignedly to see what had become of the withered little conviction he had brought with him into the room he was considerably surprised to find it intact. There was only one way to settle the matter. *Deeds*.

'Nearly,' he said. 'But I still think for the character I have in mind we're going to have to rule out the slow traditional route and go for this big break thing.'

'I see. OK, what is this guy of yours? A sprinter? Field-eventer? Swimmer?'

'Oh, anything you like.'

'Why didn't you say? I had him fixed in my mind as some sort of sprinter.'

'I sort of did, too. But he doesn't have to be.'

'Try this, then; no problem. Enter him for the London Marathon in November. Actually, it's being run in a week's time. But, anyway, have him carve a minute or two off that. Why do you think all those thousands tag along? It's not just the challenge. How many people do you imagine would take part if there was guaranteed *no* TV coverage?'

'Not so many?'

'Not so many, Carney, is what I was attempting to suggest. It's ideal. TV, a few international marathon names to set the pace for the young hopefuls all after – you've guessed – the Big Break.'

When Carney Palafox unofficially joined upwards of eighteen thousand competitors for the London Marathon a few days later he was still in the grip of his powerful conviction, so much so that he had taken some care with planning his running equipment: a pair of jeans, an old jersey with a hole in the back and a pair of comfortable but beat-up Hush Puppies. His only concession to the occasion was some new laces. Even mixed up at the back of the athletic throng waiting for the off he cut an eccentric figure. It was noble and right that more or less disadvantaged people were responding to this challenge as best they could in a variety of wheelchairs and with an array of prosthetic devices, but they all did so in athletic gear of one sort or another. Indeed, Carney could spot only one other person in street clothes and he was standing about wearing a sandwich board which complained in red capitals about sexual licence. Even the spectators were wearing track-suits, much as elderly men living on houseboats welded to the landing-stage on grimmer reaches of the Thames will affect yachting caps and reefer jackets.

The pack set off, the professionals at the front conspicuous with their practised pace, the eager amateurs behind them yearning to overtake but dissuaded by the thought that if international marathon-runners went at that speed they did so for good reason. Somewhere in the mob Carney Palafox cleared his mind of all but running for an extremely distant bus. At the halfway stage he was lying sixth and had long since been picked up by the television cameras. Those who lined the streets merely took him for another merry-andrew who had tagged on a few hundred yards back to give his friends a laugh, something akin to those maverick riderless horses which always seemed to be waiting for the winner to catch them up in the Grand National; but the television cameras had him firmly on their monitors mile after mile. He was running in a manner so as to give maximum irritation to those taking the proceedings seriously, with a slight frown as if miles away thinking private thoughts which would then produce a brief smile. Once he took a pencil and a piece of folded paper from his pocket and, still running, appeared to make a note of the name of a shop which caught his eye, craning round the farther away he ran until for a few paces he was actually running *backwards* before turning and tucking the paper in his pocket.

With five miles to go he took the lead, glanced at his watch with a puzzled expression, rapped its glass sharply, held it to his ear and with a show of amused resignation doubled his speed. The crowd were beside themselves. Indeed, it had been a privilege for them to see the face of the leading international marathon-runner – a scrawny Japanese with a demon's visage – as this cumbersome figure in jeans and dog-walking shoes appeared at his elbow, gave a cheery nod, shot past and disappeared.

When he reached the line he was nearly four minutes ahead of the Japanese. He stood for a moment surrounded by utter consternation and then, when the second runner still had not appeared, spoke for the first time.

'Well, I think I'd better be off. Train to catch.'

This was picked up by incredulous cameramen, several of whom were still convinced that it was all a stunt, some immense practical joke. But there were plenty who recognised his clothes from way back in the race, and his finishing position at least was beyond doubt.

'You can't go,' said an official. 'There's got to be a proper enquiry about this. In any case there's your prize.'

'Oh, I don't want any prize, thank you,' said Carney. 'I only did it to fill in a bit of time. No, you give it to that oriental gent with the stitch.'

In the middle of the mêlée which greeted the arrival of the Japanese, Carney Palafox somehow disappeared, perfectly inconspicuous in his jeans and sweater. That night he was soaking his slightly blistered feet in the bath, watched by the cat, when the telephone rang.

'God, they've tracked you down,' said Kate. They had been giggling together over newsreel excerpts from the race on television all evening, Kate's initial incredulity now a realisation that somewhere between lunchtime and suppertime a great change had come over her life, and she was in no way responsible. She now brought her middle-aged athlete husband the telephone in his bath.

'Carney?'

'Er, who's that?' he asked cautiously.

'This is Bob Struthers, Carney. Listen, you bastard, you're up to something, aren't you?'

'Yes,' Carney told him.

'Well, I want in on the story. I gave you time the other day and I think you owe me a bit in return. I was covering the International in Antwerp but I got back a couple of hours ago and heard all about it and, listen, I've seen the clips and I think I can work up a theory about how you did it. So we've got to meet.'

'Of course, Bob. Delighted. I could come round tomorrow some time to your studio place. Sort of lunch-ish?'

'Carney,' the voice calmed itself, 'I don't think you quite understand. You've just got away with something which everybody knows is completely impossible. Now, they haven't yet figured out how you managed it, but for sure there're a lot of folks pretty pissed off out here. I mean, you just don't walk away with a marathon dressed like a Chelsea poof in the sixties. Believe me, Carney, you just don't. So when I say we've got to meet I mean right *now*. This very hour.'

'Oh, I couldn't manage that, I'm afraid. I'm slightly weary, if the truth be told, and my feet are a little sore. Besides, at this particular moment I'm in my bath.'

'*Carney!* Listen, will you? God damn it, I can't work out whether you're really that innocent or just playing dumb.'

'I'm just playing dumb, Bob.'

'Nor do I yet know what hook or crook you used to pull today's little stunt, but for the moment, at any rate, you've got your big bloody break. OK? You're a celebrity. Believe me, nobody's talking about anything else. I mean, *you* may be settling down for a quiet evening's Scrabble but out here everybody's busting their guts trying to get a line on you. You'll be all over the front pages tomorrow, I promise you. Probably a good shot of you crossing the finishing line with, for God's sake, your hands in your pockets, and headlines like "Mystery Outsider Makes Laughing-Stock of Marathon". Shut *up*; just listen. Now, by nine tomorrow morning half the country will still be splitting their sides, half will be sharpening their knives and a third half will be trying to sign you up. Now tell me we still haven't got something to discuss this evening.'

'Well, I suppose if you insist.'

'Yes, Carney, I am insisting. I think I'd better come right on over. Where is it again?'

But at that moment the certitude welled up within him. There was a time to play dumb – because it infuriated people – and a time to remember that he had very recently become a man with a mission.

'No, Bob, you're not coming here. If you want to see me tonight, you're going to have to do as I tell you; I'm sorry, but there it is. I'll give you what you say you want – some of my time – but in exchange for what I want.'

'Of course, Carney. I've got you. How much?'

'Not money. No, I don't want money. What I'm insisting on is a short interview with you, videotaped in the studio. That's all. I'm not insisting that it's ever broadcast, just that it's made. I can promise you only that I'll say something which will make you sit up. Between you and me, Bob,' Carney said confidentially, 'I'll take a small bet that some of it at least will go out. Sooner or later.'

The interview he taped that night at the studios did indeed go out – not once but many, many times over the next months. In fact it became famous as source material for a thousand broadcasts in a hundred languages, known simply as 'The Palafox Challenge'. In its unedited entirety the brief interview ran:

BS: Mr Palafox. The sporting world tonight – indeed, the whole world tonight – is still reeling from your extraordinary victory in the London Marathon earlier today. I must admit that in all my years in and around sport I have never seen anything quite like it before.
(*A short silence*)
Mr Palafox?

CP: I'm sorry. I didn't realise you had asked me a question.

BS: Well, I think the question uppermost in all our minds here on *Action Replay* – as, I'm sure, in the minds of all viewers everywhere – is how did you do it?

CP: Oh, I sort of just *ran*, I suppose. It's awfully boring, you

46

know, the marathon. It goes on and on. Actually I was quite thankful to stop.

BS: I can't. . . . You do realise, don't you, that there were world-class runners in the field today? Noriyuki Kume holds the second-fastest time ever for a marathon and yet you beat him by almost four minutes.

CP: Oh, did I?

BS: You know you did. What we want to know is how?

CP: Really?

BS: Yes, really. Holy *bananas*.

CP: If you really want to know, I'll tell you. I just knew I could do it faster than anybody else, that's all.

BS: But that's not all, Mr Palafox. You know as well as I do that *all* athletes tell themselves they can do it faster than anybody else, and they can't all be right. It's called psyching yourself up. That kind of self-confidence is indispensable to all good sports performance, but so are fitness and training. Self-confidence on its own is not enough. I presume you trained quite hard for your victory today?

CP: No.

BS: Put it this way, Mr Palafox: how many marathon distances have you run in the last year?

CP: Only today's. Good lord, that was quite bad enough.

BS: I'm sorry, Mr Palafox, but I don't really – and I'm sure the viewers will find it just as hard to believe. How many marathons have you run in your life, then?

CP: Only today's.

BS: *Shorter*-distance training, then. You must have been running regular stints in practice sessions?

CP: (*After reflective pause*) I ran for a bus recently.

BS: Cut, cut, while we get this fucker sorted.

STUDIO MANAGER: Running, Bob.

BS: Let's get back to your clothes, Mr Palafox. That's surely one of the things which everybody noticed, your almost – if I may say so – deliberate avoidance of traditional sportswear.
(*A short silence*)
Mr Palafox?

CP: I'm awfully sorry, Bob. Was that a question again?

BS: Why did you run today's Marathon in street clothes?

CP: They're comfortable. Anyway, I didn't have any others

47

with me. I imagine all those running shoes and track-suits are rather expensive, and it didn't seem worth spending all that just for two hours' running.

BS: God. Oh, sod it. I'm sure many viewers will find your whole attitude very puzzling. It's almost as if it's a direct challenge of some kind.

CP: It is.

BS: I see. And just what is your challenge?

CP: It's very simple, Bob. I think the whole organised sports business takes itself too seriously by half. I think – I know – that people are far better at sports, at *every*thing, than they are trained down to be. My challenge is this: In any event you care to name – swimming, track, field, I don't care what it is but subject only to my refusing on grounds of boredom – I will undertake to set a new world record.

BS: That's all?

CP: That's all.

BS: And just a small point, Mr Palafox: you are – what – forty?

CP: Forty-one, actually.

BS: OK, the man's a nutter. You can cut now. Somebody go hire a rubber room.

CP: I'm afraid you're going to have to take this seriously, Bob. That was a demonstration today. Set something up. It doesn't have to be public. Just set something up – a camera crew, timekeepers – and I'll prove it to you.

BS: It's crazy. Get me a root beer, somebody.

CP: I'm sure you know best, Bob. But isn't that what your viewers want? Up-to-the-minute sports action? The Bob Struthers Experience?

BS: Listen, Sunshine, I'm a long way from being convinced. There's something phoney going on and I'm going to find out what. World record in anything you care to name, my arse.

CP: Very well, Bob. Your arse is what it'll be if I take this to the BBC.

It took a day or two to arrange, of course, but the television company – two of whose employees were suddenly turning out to be the protagonists in a worldwide news-story – hired a well-appointed sports stadium on a gloomy strip of suburban water-meadow near Twickenham. The grounds belonged to a multinational chemical company whose own fertilisers and herbicides had produced an unnatural springy grass just the wrong shade of emerald. Inside the stadium, however, not a lot of grass had been allowed to intrude. A dull red oval track of international standard lay intimidatingly empty before Carney Palafox early one Thursday morning, its newly marked lanes meeting at infinity.

In the meantime Bob Struthers had been busy. One of his first and shrewdest acts had been to establish that Carney really was a scriptwriter with the company. He had discovered that, far from being a mere writer, he was the deviser of several highly successful comedy series of which *Up Yours!* was only the latest. They all had in common a certain anarchic undertone which many people found unsettling without knowing why, and not a few found downright offensive. Thoughtfully the sportscaster arranged with the Legal Department to see a copy of Carney's contract. Objections were initially raised, but the famous Bob Struthers presence allayed all fears and left a few choice grandstand tickets in its wake. The contract, he found, had an exclusivity clause which bound Carney body and soul to the television company. There was nothing – neither his talent nor even his physical image – which he could legally take to the BBC or anyone else. Bob Struthers's arse was safe.

He remembered this as he escorted Carney out on to the track. The man was obviously a charlatan of sorts, as the morning's demonstrations would no doubt quickly reveal. He was glad it could all be fairly well kept from the public eye. 'Famous Sportscaster Brilliantly Hoaxed' was not a headline he had any intention of reading. Conversely, if by some stroke of the miraculous the man turned out to be what he said he was there was no end to the capital which could be made out of it if handled properly. Certainly enough to pay the hair transplant clinic's bill.

'Now, then, Carney,' he said, 'here we are. You've got what you asked for. See? Cameramen, official timekeepers down there, starter with gun, twenty sober witnesses from *Action Replay* and the old bloke over there who looks like Hitler and I think's the groundsman. OK? I don't mind telling you it's cost the company a fair old sum laying this lot on, so I do hope we're going to get our money's worth. Right, then; it's all yours. Now, what'll it be? Hundred metres for a start?'

'Why not?' said Carney. 'That doesn't seem too far. From

about here down to where those fellows are standing?'

'You've got it.'

'Any old lane?'

'Yes,' said Bob Struthers heavily, 'any old lane. You're really not going to change your clothes?'

'Oh, no, I don't think so. These'll do.' 'These' were the same jeans he had worn for the Marathon, a check shirt with long sleeves and button-down collar and a tweed sports jacket. Instead of Hush Puppies he now wore a battered pair of greyish tennis shoes. 'Besides. . . .'

'. . . you haven't anything else to change into, yes, I know. But I do like the gym shoes. A small step, Carney, but a significant one. OK, everybody. One hundred metres, the gentleman says.' He produced a small radio and spoke into it. Far off down the track a hand waved. The starter loaded his gun. 'Right, Carney, we're ready when you are. Where do you want the blocks?'

'Which blocks are those?'

'These funny old things,' said Bob Struthers kindly, indicating the pair he was holding. 'You crouch down and put your feet against them. It helps you start.'

'Oh. No, no, I don't think I shall want those. No, I'll just stand here until the gun goes off.'

'A standing start, Carney? How wise. What an original touch, too, if I may say so. I don't think anybody's started a sprint from the standing position since about the eighteenth century. So. Here's your line. Cameras running?' He slipped on a pair of headphones. 'It's yours, Starter.'

None of those actually watching, as opposed to peering into viewfinders, could say exactly what happened when the gun went off, but it was truly extraordinary. One moment the middle-aged figure was standing on his line in an archaic, faintly pugilistic stance, for all the world like a motheaten housemaster demonstrating how he had once knocked down an utter cad for calling his sister 'a bit of stuff', and the next he was at full tilt, moving faster than anyone there had ever seen a person move. Carney Palafox was running for a number 5 bus which had got rather a good head start. But he needn't have worried; he caught it in exactly eight and a half seconds. The world record had been shattered, and it was all on tape.

'There's just got to be a trick to it.' Bob Struthers was talking to his colleagues from *Action Replay*. 'I mean, it's totally ludicrous. *Look* at him.'

Down on the track Carney Palafox was diffidently scuffing his gym-shoe toes in the cinders; occasionally he yawned. From the pocket of his sports jacket he took a small notebook and made an entry.

'You saw it, Chief,' said one of the track-suited clones. 'The guy ran from here to there in eight-point-five. Maybe we'd better measure it again. Suppose he slipped down here last night and somehow altered the markings to seventy metres . . . ?' His voice trailed away before the look Bob Struthers gave him.

'I've been looking at tracks all my life, lad,' he said. 'That's a hundred metres all right. But when this is finished I'm going over that film frame by frame. Maybe that'll tell us something. Well, let's see what else Superman can do. Ahoy down there!' he shouted. Carney looked up. 'What's next?'

'I don't know. Have you got any of those round things?'

'Dear God, now what's he on about?' asked Bob Struthers plaintively of his colleagues. He raised his voice again. 'What exactly do you mean, Carney? Discus?'

'No. Cannonballs, like on those porridge packets.'

'You want to do some shot-putting? Why not, indeed? Come on, everybody, it's field-events time.'

The weight of the shot seemed to surprise Carney. 'I say,' he said, 'you wouldn't want to drop this on your toe. Can I use both hands?'

'Yes,' Bob Struthers told him. 'There's a limit to the amount of wind-up area you're allowed, but I don't think there's anything in the rules about how many hands you've got to use. In fact you could probably lie on your back if you wanted to and do it with the soles of your feet. But I should imagine that over the years people have tried all sorts of bizarre ways of throwing this weight as far as they can without mechanical assistance and the present technique which has evolved has been found better than most.'

'Still,' said Carney judiciously, 'I think I'll try it with both hands all the same. It's a bit late for me to start learning new techniques. . . . Which reminds me – I'm going to refuse if you ask me to do pole-vaulting or ski-jumping. I've not the slightest doubt I could do them if I tried, but I might break my neck in the process.'

'We don't want that,' said Bob Struthers.

Eventually, his feet planted firmly apart and holding the shot in both hands between his bent knees, Carney Palafox straightened up as if hydraulically operated. He was aiming to get a number 5 bus which was waiting at a stop a good way off and to his pleasure he did – plumb on the roof. The faces of startled passengers appeared at the upstairs windows like a row of distressed moons.

'That'll dent the bugger,' he said happily.

'Rather more than a dent, Carney. You've actually smashed it to smithereens.'

'What's that?' asked the athlete, returning to earth.

'The world record. Wasn't that what you were after? They're measuring it now, but it looks like a clear two metres, which is just plain ludicrous. Is there *any*thing you can't do?' Bob Struthers asked in a tone of voice which was to become very familiar to Carney Palafox over the next few months. It was a mixture of exasperation and plain awe.

'I'm a lousy cook,' the new world record holder admitted. 'And as a brain surgeon I was lamentable, as I found out during a short stint in Burma.'

And so far still was Bob Struthers from grasping what was happening he found himself asking incredulously, '*You*, Carney? You were a *brain* surgeon? In *Burma*?' before he noticed the back of the sports jacket shaking as if from some Parkinson's tremor. He felt his face burn. 'Third choice, Carney,' he said brusquely. 'Let's get this farce over with.'

'I don't know,' said the champion, bending down and inserting the tip of his ballpoint ruminatively into the split which was opening between upper and sole of one gym shoe. 'You choose.'

Eventually he was handed a javelin. Bob Struthers was evidently learning, because he had predicted to himself that Carney would scorn anything as conventional as a run-up. Instead the radical athlete stood foursquare on the line, grasped the javelin in both hands above his head, bent backwards until the tip almost touched the ground behind him, then hurled it so as to spear a number 5 bus which was moving diagonally away from him like an okapi on the plains of Serengeti. It was a bull's-eye. The spear smashed into the window immediately behind the driver, pierced the bulkhead and transfixed the driver in his seat. There was a distant wail of agony. The bus swerved in a cloud of dust, teetered, then overturned with an immense crash, wheels still spinning. 'Got you!' he said.

'So, gentlemen,' Bob Struthers addressed the stunned witnesses as they packed up their equipment. 'In the last hour and with our own eyes we've seen the utterly impossible happen not once but three times. I thought when I came here this morning we'd at least rumble his trick but I can't honestly see how he can be pulling one. The man's incredible. We have a sporting phenomenon on our hands, no question about it. Cancel the rest of today,' he instructed his PA. 'We've got a press conference to hold.'

And so began a public career which completely dominated the world news for most of next summer. It was a phenomenon which scandalised some, demoralised many, riotously entertained most and riveted everybody. It had the awful hypnotic appeal of watching the lava-flow from a cataclysmic volcano. Day by day on the world's television screens it was viewed from all angles and with absolute fascination as it rolled on, engulfing ancient monuments and living heroes. 'What's Carney goin' to trash today?' was a question which might be heard on a Detroit building site, just as unseasonably early snowfall in Austria was blamed by jocular locals on the 'Karnei Effekt'. In each case there was no doubt what was being referred to.

In its early days, of course, it began with widespread incredulity. The video pictures of Carney Palafox in a sports jacket putting the shot produced international hysterics. The only people not laughing were the athletes and their trainers who had laboured for years to be able to throw the thing two metres less far. General opinion was that it was a hoax: a brilliantly conceived and wonderfully executed leg-pull. But the videos and the recordings and the measurements withstood the closest scrutiny. 'The Carney Tapes' – the record of his first morning's work near Twickenham – achieved a notoriety and a level of bar-room debate on a par with the Nixon Tapes of a generation earlier. Then came the day when he was invited to represent England in a friendly fixture against the East Germans' third team, and his selection made it suddenly clear that somebody somewhere was taking him seriously.

He had consistently refused to be interviewed after the initial 'Palafox Challenge' recorded with Bob Struthers. He seemed to have become semi-fugitive, nomadic, glimpsed here and there but never when not diffidently scratching the back of his head with a preoccupied frown or patting his trouser pockets as if he had come out without his keys and loose change. It was well known he had written a respectful letter to the chairman of the selection committee thanking him for his confidence and saying he would be delighted to appear for the games, although he had one or two conditions to stipulate. The first was that he was not going to take part in any sort of training sessions and the other was that he would wear what he chose. Otherwise he was not taking part. The reply had also been made public: he would be excused the training sessions but 'team clothing' was mandatory under rules which would not in any circumstances be waived. Regretfully, a substitute was found. The interest and consternation can be imagined, then, when Carney Palafox turned up at the games and actually spoke into a microphone which was thrust before him.

'Do you intend to take part, Mr Palafox?' the reporter asked him.

'Yes and no,' replied Carney mysteriously, but would not explain further.

'You are aware that your name has been withdrawn from the England athletics team.'

A short silence fell.

'Mr Palafox?'

'I'm so sorry, I hadn't realised that was a question.'

'*Are* you aware of that?'

'Of course I am, you half-wit. The letter was in plain English and I can read.'

The reporter seemed momentarily taken aback by this reply. It was not often that someone was addressed on camera as a half-wit. Meanwhile Carney Palafox strode away and was lost in the crowd.

He reappeared to general amazement just as the 100 metres finalists were under starter's orders. He positioned himself next to the innermost runner, but off the track. He clearly intended to run up the grass verge, which he did, a pair of black patent-leather ballroom-pumps twinkling on his feet. He passed the level of the finishing line a generous two seconds before the foremost athlete and turned away to write something in a small notebook. His performance was, of course, not officially recognised but it had been witnessed by thousands of spectators, would be by millions of viewers later that evening, and had not gone unnoticed by the unfortunate East German who was awarded the winning medal. A general sense of discomfiture and demoralisation set in, seeming to affect the British athletes as much as their opponents. The games proceeded, but in some peculiar way the heart had gone out of them. It was clear that everyone was on tenterhooks waiting for Carney Palafox's next impromptu performance. Word got around that something unusual was happening and regular radio programmes were interrupted for short bulletins on the games' progress.

Nothing untoward happened for the best part of the day, however, and the spectators had all but lost hope of witnessing another historic intervention by this weird counter-athlete. Then just before the start of the final event, the men's 4 × 400 metres relay, a figure whom everyone had taken for one more of the press corps was noticed assuming the increasingly familiar pugilistic stance on a level with the inside runner. By the time a thousand fingers had pointed and a thousand voices had mouthed his name it was too late to do anything. The starter's gun fired, and Carney was off. This time, in deference to the need for disguise, he was wearing a bright green nylon anorak with the hood up, a complicated-looking camera bouncing on his chest; but there was not a soul present who did not recognise the twinkling black pumps, and a great cheer went up.

Carney kept pace with the lead sprinter, but it was obvious he was not exerting himself overmuch. Now and again he would pull out a lead of several paces and then glance back with a sympathetic shrug and allow himself to be caught up. By the time the first baton changed hands Carney was adjusting his speed to match that of the new leader, a powerful-looking blond German who tore away, stabbing the air with his baton. It was dawning on the spectators that Carney Palafox was planning to run the entire relay race solo *and* win. Every so often marshals would appear in his path on the outer edge of the green central oval, arms outstretched and shouting inaudibly; but each time Carney evaded them with deft footwork and the elusiveness of a rabbit. Just before the last baton change, however, a murmur began growing. The pace was evidently beginning to tell even on Carney Palafox. His twinkling feet were settling somewhat flatter on the turf; his head had begun to roll. As the leading team's last sprinter took over from his exhausted colleague, Carney stopped dead. The cheers mixed relief with disappointment. He produced a handkerchief, mopped his brow, blew his nose, glanced at his watch, shook his head and took off like a bullet. The cries became a roar.

It seemed certain he had overplayed it; the sprinter already had a fifty-metre lead. But to everybody's amazement the gap decreased rapidly. From the stands above the track it was less as though a fast runner were being caught by a faster than that the man in the lead were being somehow *pulled back* by what was on his heels. The weight of contempt which was implicit in every stride Carney took in his dancing shoes appeared to attach itself to the heels in front of him, slowing them down. With eighty metres to go Carney overhauled the man, glancing sideways at him as he did so like an anxious parent on school sports day worried about their child's overdoing it, then shot past. He was far enough ahead at the finish to stop a few feet short and walk the rest, still crossing level with the line a metre or two in front of the winning East German. The crowd were hysterical.

Immediately after the games had ended Carney was mobbed when spotted trying to sneak out of the stadium. In return for the promise of an escorted passage home he condescended to give a short press conference. In a stuffy room behind the royal box he faced some of the world's less distinguished sports correspondents who had been delegated to cover what had been supposed was a minor friendly fixture while the luminaries of the microphone were commenting on more prestigious events elsewhere. As it turned out, and thanks to the serendipity which watches over the careers of the undeserving, these correspondents – who were mostly either rookies working their way up or hacks drinking their way down – found themselves present at one of the more significant sporting interviews of the century.

It began as a bear-garden, a barrage of simultaneous questions which Carney sat out. Sometimes he glanced at his watch, sometimes at his pocket notebook. Once he took off one of the patent-leather pumps and studied the inside thoughtfully. Finally there was a lull. Then spontaneously it started again as each reporter tried to steal a march on his colleagues.

'Mr Palafox, why did you take part in the games today when you had been officially replaced?'

'Mr Palafox, what training have you had as an athlete?'

'Do you have a special diet?'

'Are you on anabolic steroids?'

'Are you a member of a religious sect?'

'Are you really forty-one?'

'Who is your trainer?'

Carney raised a hand. The voices gradually subsided.

'Gentlemen,' he said, and his voice was so quiet they had practically to stop breathing in order to hear him at all, 'let me just give you the odd fact about myself. I will then answer a question or two providing they are sensible and then, I'm afraid, I'll really have to be off; I have a cat to feed.

'As to who I am, quite a lot of you will already have seen my name countless times on television, but only in the credits so it probably won't have registered. As has been rumoured, I am a scriptwriter with the television company whose logo you see on the side of that camera there. If you wish to check further, I am the deviser of a series which I deeply regret is entitled *Up Yours!* currently being shown on, I believe, Wednesday evenings, although I myself have never watched it. I am indeed forty-one years old. I do not smoke, I am not a homosexual, I detest all religions and especially Christianity, I despise the monarchy, I'm strongly against capital punishment and vehemently in favour of putting all pensioners back into useful employment at the earliest opportunity – possibly down the mines since most of the miners seem currently to be busy practising to be pensioners. Oh, and I'm fond of cats but not pathologically so. Does that help any?'

There had been some nervous laughter at these *sotto voce* declarations. The correspondents were clearly unsettled by their interviewee's twin roles as amateur sports phenomenon and professional comic writer: it seemed devilish hard to separate them out.

'Can we quote you on all that, Mr Palafox?' asked a voice. A look of exasperation crossed Carney's face.

'I understood that was the entire purpose of press conferences,' he said. 'Perhaps it would be easier if you went away and just made it all up as usual? Then I could go home.'

'Mr Palafox,' broke in another correspondent, 'I think what a lot of people would like to know is where have you been all this time? Why do you decide now to make your extraordinary talents public?'

'That's a very reasonable question,' said Carney. 'Why, indeed? One of the answers would be that I have only lately had them revealed to me. Don't,' he said quickly, 'don't misinterpret me. Perhaps "revealed" is the wrong word since it smacks of religious lunacy. The Holy Ghost did not pay me a personal visit in my bath one night and whisper to me divine revelations of gold medallions. More accurately, I suppose, I realised what I could do comparatively recently. I can tell you truthfully that it was running for a bus that convinced me, but you probably won't believe it.'

'But now, of course, you'll concentrate on a sporting career?'

'Good heavens, no; indeed, I shan't. I have no interest whatever in sport of any kind, which I suppose is why it took me so long to discover I could do it.'

'You can't be serious, Mr Palafox. We believe you have three world records pending official confirmation and all in different events.'

'I assure you I'm entirely serious.'

'Could you comment on the suggestion that you're in it for the money?'

'Easily. I'm not "in it" and I've neither received nor wish to receive a solitary penny. I do what I do entirely for my own amusement. You may say I'm in it for laughs if you like.'

'Is that why you wear the clothes you wear?'

'Yes.'

'Mr Palafox, one last question, sir: are you aware that in addition to the admiration you have aroused in taking on and beating top athletic performances at the age of forty-er, one, you must also be arousing considerable opposition and resentment by the way in which you have chosen to do it?'

'I am.'

'Would you say it amounted almost to a carefully planned insult aimed at the international sporting fraternity?'

'Strike "almost", as I believe they say in America.'

A clamour of voices among which a reasonable bass was heard to ask: 'Whatever did they do to you to deserve it?'

'Bored me rigid,' said Carney Palafox succinctly, and the press conference was over.

He went back to the life of an itinerant hermit since his modest flat near Sadlers Wells was besieged night and day and Katie was constrained to shut the place and move in with friends, taking the cat with her. She toyed with the idea of beginning piano lessons.

'What for?' asked her friend. 'Did Carney ever practise running?'

'*Carney*? You know Carney, Beth. The very idea. . . .'

'Exactly. So it would be much better just to book the Festival Hall and go right in off the street wearing tennis clothes and play Tchaikovsky like he's never been played before.'

Meanwhile Carney was wearying of dodging reporters. Besides, never having had to live the life of a celebrity, he was rather bad at it, although considerably helped by his all-purpose middle-aged appearance. He looked like Almost Anybody as played by the late Tony Hancock. Still, he often failed to elude the newshounds, and the papers seized on Carneyisms with relish. His views were, as they were fond of saying, 'controversial' and began to be eagerly sought on matters a long way from the sporting field. When asked to express an opinion about an imminent anti-nuclear demonstration which promised to close off much of central London for the day he said although he had no wish to be fried in any global holocaust he thought it highly undignified to winge in public about it. Death was only death, after all, and mass displays of cowardice were unedifying. It was quite unfashionable at the time to call the caring, sharing, Earth-Mother-of-four on a peace demo 'chicken' – not like a few years later – and his remarks led to howls of protest. It was bad enough, they suggested, that anyone as unspeakable as Carney Palafox should ever have emerged to cock a snook at the sporting pleasures of millions but far worse that he should thereby be accorded a public soap-box from which to air his monstrous views about the world in general.

One morning a priest with horn-rimmed spectacles entered the *Action Replay* studios and asked to speak to Bob Struthers.

'I'm afraid Mr Struthers is extremely busy at the moment, Bishop,' said one of the clones. 'Would someone else do?'

'I am not a bishop, my son, merely a minor canon. Rather small beer, I'm afraid. Thank you for your offer, but I fear it must be Mr Struthers. If he will just speak to me for a moment, he will learn something to his immortal soul's advantage.'

Eventually Bob Struthers appeared, a video-cassette in one hand and a preoccupied expression on his face. Track-suit confronted cassock.

'If you've come to tell me you're the world's best pole-vaulter, I shall scream,' he said.

'But I am,' said the priest. He removed the spectacles. 'Father Carney would like an audience.'

'*Carney!*' cried Bob Struthers. 'My God, man, where have you been? Do you realise you're the world's most sought-after person? The phone here never stops ringing. "Who is his agent?" "How can we sign him up?" "Would a million dollars do?" ' He ushered Carney into his sanctum and shut the door. Curious faces pressed towards the glass from all sides.

'The deal I want to make is once more very simple,' said Carney, declining a can of No-Calorie Root Beer.

'Name it. We'll talk it over and then get some lawyers up. This is going to be big.'

'No, it isn't,' Carney corrected him. 'At least, probably not in the way you're hoping. I'm afraid I don't want a manager. But I do need an agent who's in the sporting business and who can fix, er – what are they called nowadays? – *venues*, I think. Dreadful expression.'

'You want to take part in some competitions? As a team member?'

'Dear me, no.'

'Just as well. I don't think it would be easy. You've no idea how ironic it is. You're currently the world's hottest sporting property – or at any rate you're in some insane class of your own – but I doubt anyone would let you into a team. Not only would you presumably refuse to conform in such matters as training, clothing and – dare I say it? – conduct, but I can't imagine you'd find many people willing to compete with you. Or even against you. You make a mockery of it all, Carney, and that people can't forgive. They might at a pinch put it all down to eccentric temperament – genius or something – if you were the world's greatest at one particular thing. Then the only guys you'd really upset would be those directly involved in it. But to be that good at everything and still not give a damn and wear, God help us, tap-dancing shoes while doing it: nobody in the trade is about to overlook that.'

'The expression you see on my face, Bob, is one of pure contrition. But I still feel I have a little way to go yet with my mission – a few more laughs to get. I want to set one or two more records before I get really bored and find something else to do. You can help arrange it just as you did at that dismal stadium the other day.'

Bob Struthers was nodding. 'Sure,' he said, 'we can fix that' – and his brain lobes were thudding with arithmetic. 'Let's see, the TV fees we could charge would be astronomical – we could cover our costs in the first five seconds of bidding. . . . What about spectators?'

'Oh, yes, lots of those. The more the merrier.'

'Great, Carney. Entrance fees. . . . How much will your cut be, do you imagine? A ball-park figure?'

'Nil.'

'You mean *nothing*?'

'I told you before, I don't want money; I'm not doing it for money. I already make quite a decent amount out of my serials, you know.'

'Yes, but no *money*. . . . It's pretty weird. In fact it's the most bizarre thing of all. Limitless talent and you refuse to capitalise on it.'

'I'm laughing, Bob, that's what you don't understand. Deep inside I'm falling about.'

'Well, that's nice,' said Bob Struthers, 'but, OK, if that's what you want. Now for the bad news, Carney. There's going to have to be a *quid pro quo* on your part.'

'I may not like it.'

'Oh, you won't. It's called a medical examination. The plain fact is that a lot of people flatly refuse to believe that someone your age can do what you do without assistance. They suspect either that you're a guinea-pig for a new superdrug or a sort of test-bed for some bionic device.'

'Like the Six Million Dollar Man? Rewired and full of microchips? Servo-motors? That sort of thing?'

'I know, I know, Carney. I think it's crazy, too. But there it is. Without a thorough medical examination . . .'

'. . . carried out before twenty thousand witnesses . . .'

'. . . no record you set will ever be officially recognised. There's a more sinister aspect, too. I had a call from somebody claiming they were working with the Ministry of Defence. Did I know where you were and, if so, would it be OK to ask you to pop down for a chat? All very matey, of course, but need I go on?'

'I'm of potential military value? I get clobbered by the Official Secrets Act? To prevent me from falling into Russian hands I am given a drugged cup of coffee and wake up in a country house in darkest Berkshire where in the course of several agonising weeks implacable army surgeons tear my body and mind apart to find out what makes me different? I like it, Bob, I like it. It's got real potential for a series. I see it all, now. At the end of their experiments they're left with a pile of bones and tissue, the usual human debris, without having learned anything. The silly asses have done what an old proverb from China's Frozen North no doubt says: you don't cook your lead husky.'

'I didn't expect you to take anything I say seriously.' Bob Struthers, on whose words an audience of millions hung weekly, was obviously not used to mockery.

'You're put out, I can tell. Don't worry; I shall know what to do if anybody with an old school tie offers me coffee.'

'Don't say I didn't warn you. Like it or not, Sunshine, you are currently our lead husky. But even huskies get a going-over from the vet before long journeys.'

'I'll think about it,' Carney said.

'Dope tests are perfectly standard practice,' urged the ex-athlete. 'With the sort of publicity you've got there's not a cat in hell's chance they'll allow any record you set without one. In fact, the faster you run or the farther you throw, the more suspicious they'll be.'

'OK, Bob,' said Carney wearily, 'I'll have to concede, I suppose. Set it up, if you would, please. As from next week, though. Until then I'm going to be a bit busy.'

The nature of that 'busyness' did not emerge until early Sunday morning, European time, when the first satellite pictures began arriving of extraordinary goings-on in California. The scene was an Olympic pool on the outskirts of Los Angeles where a major international games was in progress. The actual event was the final of the men's 200 metres freestyle. The swimmers had just left their blocks when a naked man streaked from the competitors' entrance, plunged into a spare lane of the pool in the swimmers' wake and ploughed after them doing a species of crawl. Amusement and head-shaking greeted this piece of light relief until a word began to be heard around the pool, becoming louder and louder as more and more voices took it up: 'Carney!'

At the first turn the naked swimmer was nearly up with the two trailing competitors. The television cameras, torn between capturing a real news event and preserving their viewers' modesty, tried to go into long focus whenever Carney Palafox crossed their viewfinders; but as he began to overhaul the leading swimmers they found him increasingly difficult to censor. Somehow his glistening buttocks rolling in the swirl of chlorinated water exercised a magnetic attraction. In all their glory they crossed a million screens as their owner concentrated on catching an amphibious bus whose image some distance away he had firmly fixed in his mind as it chugged along with its passenger platform awash. On the third length he took the lead and began opening up a prodigious distance between himself and the nearest swimmer, whose rubber cap fell bobbing away behind him like an abandoned fishnet-float. On the third and final turn the cheering became louder still, for it was quickly noticed that Carney had changed his stroke for an inelegant but highly effective back butterfly. Now it was no longer his buttocks which rose and fell mesmerically on a million screens, and station switchboards were jammed long before he touched the end of the pool, scrambled out, slithered like a pale eel through the combined grasp of a stern-faced reception committee and vanished from sight.

His return from America was slightly delayed by the time it took to engage a lawyer and negotiate his television company's going bail for him. He was greeted at Heathrow Airport with scenes reminiscent of the sixties. 'We love you, Carney,' said placards jiggled by bands of teenagers screaming on the terminal roof. It was a declaration not shared by serious-minded people, of which the world suddenly seemed abnormally full.

In the next few weeks Carney Palafox put in a few comparatively sober appearances at prearranged attempts on official world records. They were sober only in that he turned up and did what he said he would. His every appearance was greeted with hysteria by the spectators who jammed the stadiums. It did not escape the notice of professional sportsmen that whenever a Carney Palafox display coincided with a regular event that event drew small crowds consisting mainly of a core of hardline traditional sports enthusiasts who would have nothing to do with this middle-aged wunderkind. He dutifully underwent a battery of medical tests before each occasion. 'Carney Normal Say Doctors,' was one headline. 'Nothing Wrong With Carney – Official,' said another. 'Clean Bill of Physical Health,' said a third, pointedly leaving open to question his mental status.

And so that brief summer Carney Palafox ran, jumped, hurled and on one occasion cycled his way into the record-books. His attire remained idiosyncratic but he was clearly finding increasing difficulty in varying it without having to fall back on ordinary sportswear. On one of his last appearances as a record-setter he amazed the crowd by turning up in a somewhat bulky crimson track-suit with CP in gold embroidered letters on the back. But things were restored to normality when he unzipped it to reveal a full set of lime-green motorcyling leathers in which he then beat his previous record for the 100 metres.

Close observers also noticed that he was clowning less, that he consulted his notebook more often with a frown of worry. There came the day when, after throwing a discus an unprecedented distance he consented absentmindedly to try to better his own 100 metres sprint record once again. His performance was that of a forty-one-year-old scriptwriter. Badly out of breath he crossed the line in seventeen seconds, missing his number 5 bus by miles. Somehow he must have lost count in his short and hectic sprinting career. Never again would he break the world's 100 metres record. The crowd loved it, though. They thought he was fooling.

Meanwhile he was being endlessly begged to appear on television shows in exchange for prodigious sums. The more he turned them down and the more he refused to attend any organised debate of his own phenomenon, the more eagerly he was pestered. The inducements would have corrupted a Gandhi, the sums exceeding many a poor nation's GNP. To all the most prestigious television hosts Carney Palafox said no. To one alone he said yes, and that one had never even asked.

Desmond Lermit hosted a chat show on one of Britain's least-watched channels. He was a benign, fiftyish hangover from the days when the occasional gentleman was still to be glimpsed in a television studio, slightly unsettled like a dodo sensing the approach of beaters. His shows tended to go out late at night and his guests were mainly people in the world of the Arts and more often than not were decayed knights of the theatre. Carney had met him once or twice over the years, running into him at a party here, in a meeting there, for the world of television is still smaller than it likes to imagine. Beneath the courteous exterior he had thought to glimpse a somewhat cynical nihilism akin to his own. Desmond Lermit, however, had not the least idea that he had made this impression, so it came as a complete surprise when Carney Palafox rang him up one morning and asked if he would consider him as a guest on his show some time.

Privately at a loss as to why he should have been chosen while a dozen celebrities in Britain and America had been spurned, Lermit ruthlessly cancelled a forthcoming guest-list which was to have featured the decrepit and much-loved Welsh comedienne Dame Martha Tydfil and substituted the single name of Carney Palafox. The chagrin in the world of entertainment at this windfall for the *Desmond Lermit Half-Hour* was unparalleled. Needless to say, in the event nobody watched anything else. From the opening moments the public found itself privy to what seemed to be a conversation between two people who had just discovered they ought to have been close friends for the last quarter-century and who were making up for lost time. It was a very private coming-together which happened to be eavesdropped by nearly twenty million people. And in its wholly unpredicted manner it turned out to be compulsive viewing.

'Am I right in thinking, Carney,' began Desmond Lermit, 'that you find life as exemplified by modern British civilisation boring?'

'Annihilatingly so.'

'Do you *really*? Oh, so do I. Isn't it ghastly?'

'Dreary beyond belief.'

'It's not so much' – Desmond Lermit recklessly threw social impartiality to the winds – 'not so much the fact that everything has sunk to a general level of proletarian sub-culture, although God knows that's bad enough. . . .'

'Fast food and *Up Yours!*', interjected Carney, nodding.

'. . . but it sometimes seems that every damned thing is so regulated, so organised, so subject to interminable by-laws, restrictions and conventions that the whole tone of life has assumed that of a sort of homogenised sleepwalking.'

'Oh, I like that phrase, I wonder if it means anything?' the erstwhile scriptwriter mused.

'Not a lot, but *I* know what I mean.'

'Me, too, Desmond, only too well. Far be it from me to make too much of the utterly trivial work I've been doing to earn a living, but there was a comedy series I had a hand in a couple of years ago trying to make that precise point.'

'*Gawd 'Elp Us!*? Yes, indeed, I'm sure a lot of viewers like myself still recall it with pleasure. In fact I have here a scene from one of the episodes in which your unemployed young hero Keith is confronted by a warden who reprimands him for straying off the "nature trail" in a Derbyshire theme park, whatever that may be. I've never been quite certain.' He laughed apologetically and pressed a switch on the television monitor.

'Nor me, actually,' came Carney's voice as the picture on the monitor expanded to fill viewers' screens.

After the two-minute excerpt, which left both host and guest smiling, Desmond Lermit resumed.

'All this has been by way of background to what, if I were that sort of person, I might be calling "The Carney Palafox Story". I have deliberately not started with clips from your "Challenge" film, not because they aren't interesting in themselves but because everybody's already seen them *ad nauseam*. We all know what you claimed to set out to do. I'd like to get at a slightly different Carney Palafox, or at least to flesh out the eccentric skeleton we now have, if you don't object?'

'Not at all. Splendid idea.'

'For a start, this sudden ability you admit to having discovered so lately, do you yourself have any idea how it came about?'

'No,' said Carney. 'I've often puzzled over why it should have happened just at this moment. I'm slightly less puzzled about how it happened at all.'

'Might you elaborate?'

'I'll try. I suppose over the years – and quite unconsciously, I might add – I've been formulating the idea that human beings are capable of very much more than they themselves think and infinitely more than they are told. Everybody knows that small children can easily be brought up bi-, tri- or even quadrilingual. There seems no end to what their brains can assimilate. Now look at the educational system of a country like this one – or of any other, come to that. It's lamentable. Children can actually and legally leave school at the age of sixteen functionally illiterate in their own mother tongue. Clearly no one is being educated to even a fraction of their innate abilities and, indeed, the more you stand back and look at the whole social set-up with a properly jaundiced eye the more it seems that it's in nobody's interest that they should be. The whole aim of advanced civilisation, now that the immediate horrors of nature have been more or less held at bay, is to keep people quiet at all costs from cradle to grave. Just that. Nothing else.'

'Yes!' Desmond Lermit was sitting forward in his chair, the rare image on television of unfeigned attentiveness. 'That's it *exactly*. That *is* the Social Contract. In exchange for its total and mindless passivity the public agrees to be entertained for life. More ghastly TV channels, more dreadful sit coms, more awful video-cassettes, more organised sports, more hideous golf-courses, theme parks, computer games. . . .'

'You take my point,' Carney interrupted gently, perhaps lest his host get properly launched into some private Jeremiad. 'Now, it came to me that just as people's brains are not being educated to appreciate much other than organised entertainment nor are their bodies being trained except down to the standards of organised sports. I found myself doubting whether the current levels of physical achievement as measured by world records represented more than a fraction of human bodily potential. It's as simple as that.'

'But how did you liberate your *own* potential?' asked Desmond. 'That's what I want to know.'

'I'm not too sure,' confessed Carney, 'although I can tell you it happened quite suddenly one evening as I was running for a bus. But before that I'd been thinking the traditional shibboleth about endless concentration and single-mindedness being the way to achieve anything was probably completely wrong. Indifference and contempt would be a better start. . . .'

'. . . and a fine maxim for dealing with life,' interrupted his host. Off-camera the Studio Manager buried his face in his hands.

'. . . but what was needed was a way of liberating the mind completely from all thoughts of the effort it takes to do something. I can tell you that, in so far as I think about anything when I'm breaking records, I imagine myself trying to catch an elusive number 5 bus. Five seems to be a significant number for me,' he added, but did not elaborate.

'I think it's brilliant,' said Desmond admiringly. 'I've never heard anything quite like it. But presumably your physical potential could have been expressed in any activity?'

'Oh, yes, of course.'

'Would I be right in thinking that your choosing sport was precisely because you despised it?'

'Perfectly. Actually, I don't despise sport as such; it's merely something people can do if they like. I particularly loathe *organised* sport, the mass international sporting machine, that whole world so beautifully typified by bogus tennis-tantrums. So sports seemed like a sacred cow that it might be quite fun to have a tilt at. The British are so enslaved by their whole social organisation that they've long since forgotten how to say boo to geese, much less moo to sacred cows.'

This made Desmond laugh enough to waste nearly thirty seconds of peak viewing time. 'I think that's a scriptwriter speaking,' he said when he recovered. But then his face fell surprisingly as if an inner sobriety had surfaced unbidden. 'I'm awfully envious, you know,' he said. 'Not of your records, of course; they're rather silly, aren't they?'

'Footling.'

'But I wonder what *I* could do?' mused Desmond Lermit wistfully. 'I'm almost fifty.'

'Oh, anything you like. Motor racing?'

'Much too noisy. And the *company*. . . .'

'Of course. Mountaineering? That's quiet.'

'Not the way I'd do it; I'm terrified of heights. I rather like depths, though, oddly enough. How about deep-sea diving?'

'Perfect. Go to it.'

And so the viewing public was treated to the extraordinary spectacle of a television host planning his own future by using his guest as job consultant. The Studio Manager stood like Lot's wife in headphones.

Desmond Lermit showed a few more clips of Carney Palafox's sporting achievements, then said: 'You surely won't go on with this sports thing now?'

'No. I think I've got as much amusement out of it as there is to get. It's becoming tedious. I'd like to get back to my wife and my cat. No, I'll leave it to the professionals to catch up, although maybe I'll have just one last fling. Do you suppose there's a marathon in the offing? I'll have to ask around and see if anybody knows. I started with one and, although they take an awful time to do, there'd be a certain symmetry to end with one, wouldn't there?'

'*He's completely insufferable*,' said Bob Struthers, who was watching. The wastepaper-basket beside him was full of savagely crushed root-beer cans. 'They *both* are, him and that Lermit queen. As far as I'm concerned, it's goddamned open season on huskies. I wonder what the sod'll turn up to ruin now?'

The answer was a marathon run ten days later in Italy as part of the Rome Games. Carney Palafox was not an official entrant; but a figure dressed as a chef was seen to attach itself to the back of the pack and rapidly work its way to the front. This time he was evidently going for maximum humiliation since within the first kilometre he took the lead and had soon disappeared.

68

Helicopters, gaggles of motorcycles and convoys of press cars with cameras mounted on their roofs kept him on Italian television screens, though, and everybody was prepared to see the fastest-ever marathon. Within sight of the stadium and a clear sixteen minutes ahead the fleeing chef had nearly caught his number 5 bus when a man burst through the cheering crowds lining the road. In front of a dozen cameras Carney Palafox was shot dead on the spot by a disgruntled Turkish miler who then made a dash for it. He was soon outpaced and torn to pieces by devout Carney fans.

And thus ended the more public and the shorter of Carney Palafox's two careers. That summer unquestionably marked an indelible trauma in the collective memory of international sports, and Carney himself would have been the last to be surprised at the conspiratorial way in which the public machine closed ranks and dealt with it. The sporting journals and the *Guinness Book of Records* went on printing their annual lists of new achievements year in, year out, just as they always did. Only in the columns assigned to that particularly memorable year there appeared ten entries right across the range of sporting activities, each marked with one asterisk or two. At the foot of the page the rubric read: '*CP official world record' and '**CP unofficial world record'. It was one way of glossing an *annus mirabilis*. But Carney Palafox's records stood for an awful long time, nine of them outliving his cat and five of them his wife.

Compressor

I

It is a strange moment when, whistling in a bare room, you chance to hit the precise note at which it resonates. For the duration of that note the room becomes live, it rings in sympathy; the very plaster declares its heart. A quarter-tone's deviation up or down and it at once falls silent, you become again a whistler in an empty room. Similarly there can come a moment, maybe only when you are past being quite young, when something happens which makes your lived past vibrate with a kind of accuracy likely to make you say, 'Yes, that's me; that is how I have always been,' but which also might make you much prefer to fall inwardly silent with that shame which is not guilt but years and years of wishing you were not so. Such a moment came, such a note was struck and such a recurrent fault was set trembling into inward audibility when you visited Tagud.

Thanks to Badoy, whose home village it was, Tagud had become a legendary place, a minor Mecca which, once you had heard its name, you were fatally destined to visit. For at Anilao you shared an exile: he from his birthplace, you from yours. And what brought you together in that dull coastal strip with its half-hearted fishing and its weary copra-making? What else but the sea, which, although it scarcely runs in your blood, does run beneath your character like an undertow, tugging and churning and – whenever you are close to it – unsettling

70

the contours of your restless bed.

You did not become conscious of Badoy until several weeks of enforced exile had passed in Anilao. The government project – a feasibility study of the prospects of a dendro-thermal installation to generate electricity for the province with quick-growing timber – had stalled in the way in which such things do in that part of the world. Insinuations had come that the funds set aside for your salary had already bought the cement needed to build a house for the newly wed daughter of the manager of the electricity co-operative. Pending reassurances you stopped work. Many days passed, and in Anilao the days pass slowly. The mornings are blue and tropical; the afternoons are black and tropical, and the rains tramp in from the sea; the sunsets are resplendent until promptly the nights descend like swags of stifling black cloth shot with vast discharges of electricity. Not long, therefore, before your feet took you into the sea as others' take them into the room where the television is. And there you met Badoy.

You are hardly alone in your admiration for people with an elegant physical skill. It is pointless to deny there is always an erotic component, however well disguised, in such admiration since it is impossible to watch any body so closely without seeing your own. One day you were down among the corals in a mask, at least knowing enough so that the corals you sometimes held on to were not those which sting and leave the hands blazed with brown weals. In point of fact you were watching – for as long as each lungful of air lasted – the local species of bird wrasse with its long snout whose exact purpose seems not precisely known. It is a reasonable assumption that it picks its food out of deep crevices which other fish cannot reach; but this, as they say in scientific circles, remains unconfirmed. You had some idea that, as a casual amateur with time on his hands, it would be nice to confirm it one way or the other. They are not easy fish to observe, because unlike other species of small coralline fish they seem to be continually on the move, weaving rapidly from place to place rather than forever circling the same patch (for many species of fish recognise a territorial imperative).

On that particular occasion you had just gone down a fathom or two with freshly held breath when from behind a rock and not more than ten feet away there swam a fat parrot-fish, green and blue and scrunching away at the coral with its powerful

71

beak-teeth. There was a sudden rushing sound, a *pok!* and the fish began flailing wildly. A shadow passed overhead and the parrot-fish rose, still struggling, hauled upwards with a long steel rod spitting it. You rose with it to the sunlight and there was Badoy sparkling and grinning in tiny home-made wooden goggles set with little olives of glass. He passed the struggling fish down along the spear and on to the length of green nylon cord which trailed in the water behind him.

'Did I surprise? But I thought, that's a delicious fish and you are down there without a spear-gun so why waste it?' He refitted the spear into the gun he was holding, a simple wooden stock shaped like a child's toy rifle with powerful heavy-gauge elastic tied to its short bamboo barrel: essentially an underwater catapult. You bobbed your head back beneath the surface. In front of you hung Badoy's legs, one foot wearing a flipper cut from marine plywood and held on by a piece of inner tubing tacked across it, and trailing downwards in the blue water like a thin tail from his spear-gun was the length of nylon which ended with perhaps two kilos of threaded fish, joined now by the still-flapping parrot-fish.

'How long did that take you?'

'Two hours, maybe more. It's not a good day. The water's too clear. Very easy for us to see the fish but very easy for the fish to see you. Also it is daytime. And anyway this is Anilao. Not like Tagud.'

'Tagud?'

'Where I come from. Maybe forty kilometres down the coast.' And Badoy pointed with the tip of his spear (which you now noticed was barbed with a nail bent and hinged ingeniously through a hole) to where the green of the palms disappeared in a succession of hazy headlands into the distance. 'They are real fishermen there. Not like here in Anilao.' He looked sardonically at the beach a few hundred yards away on which a handful of boats was drawn up but which was bare of activity except for the rootings of domestic animals.

'Is that thing very difficult to use?'

'No, not difficult to use. Difficult to *catch* things, yes. Ha, perhaps that is why not many people in Anilao go spear-fishing. They just use nets sometimes or look for small octopus in the rocks at low tide. They are very lazy here. Just drinking.'

Of course you wondered why he was here if he seemed so contemptuous of Anilao and its inhabitants, and of course you were drawn to the only other person in the sea for what seemed like miles in any direction. Above all, you were filled with a great urge to *imitate*, to try spear-fishing perhaps for food (as you would have explained it sensibly to yourself) but more to become accomplished in a new skill, to have some of that nonchalant marine confidence and enter a new world with new companions and rise just as dazzlingly to the surface, teeth glittering with pleasure. But more still – although you did not at the time recognise it – because it promised fear and fresh confrontations with an old bugbear; for your submerged self sniffs out fear like truffles which your daily self shrinks from as poison.

Badoy's elegance underwater was complemented by his ingenious craftsmanship on land. He set about making a second spear-gun using the few tools he could lay hand on, hacking the stock out of a plank of coconut wood with a large knife. The spear was a metre of quarter-inch steel rod in which he gouged holes and slots and raised a jagged tooth at one end to catch wire loops attached to the stretched rubber thongs. And all the time you wondered why he was so eager. Was it because he had nothing to do? Or maybe because he wanted a companion in the water, even a tyro? Or because he was a natural didact anxious to pass on what he knew? A week or two had passed, the spear-gun long since finished and in daily use before you discovered that the much older woman who brooded discreetly in his house was Badoy's wife, evidently formidable enough in some undisclosed manner to insist on their living in her home village rather than in his. Her uncle, recently dead, had left enough money by local standards so that Badoy was not compelled to take regular paid work. What would he do but mooch and fish and, according to gossip, occasionally disappear for annihilating binges in the distant provincial capital?

Frightening as it all was eventually to become, you do remember those early days when you were learning the craft as ones of extreme happiness. Taking the spear-gun and spending three hours in the sea, often twice as long, sometimes with Badoy but more often alone, shooting and missing, stalking and missing, learning the habits of the different species. Exhausting at first: the continual swimming down to fifteen, twenty-five, forty feet in pursuit or merely on reconnaissance, then clawing back up for air, the process repeated for hours until a strange disorientation set in and you became in some sense unsure at any given moment which medium you were in. Learning to

73

manage the long nylon line attached to the rear end of the spear was a slow essay in exasperation. The currents tangled it; the corals snarled it; your legs attracted it and snared themselves in it. One day you said 'Enough' and cut the line off. It happened to be the day you got your first shot at a really decent-sized fish. The spear struck home satisfyingly and the fish made off with it at speed to vanish, heading downwards into the ocean deep.

Badoy merely grinned and unhesitatingly set about making a new one; but it took hours and he cut himself in the process and you felt contrite and sullied by incompetence. Thereafter you learned to use the line, holding the stop-knot on the end lodged between two knuckles until there was enough catch to weight it out of the way in the water.

Soon you began to return trailing small coral fish like paper cutouts on the tail of a kite. Most were familiar aquarium fish: angels, butterflies, Moorish Idols and the like, enough of which fried or toasted constituted a meal. Some days there were none; later there were a few but larger. And all the while Badoy hung around his dark house among the trees, whittling this and filing that or maybe sitting on the step morosely watching the eddies of hens around the pump where the maid did the washing and the sun never pierced the canopies of leaves. Behind him his wife moved sombrely about the house. Your arrival – probably anybody's – would awaken both from their melancholy so that she smiled and Badoy sparkled. But when you left you could feel whatever strange and mutual reproach settle once more and no doubt remain until you next saw them: something which emasculated or unfeminised them into the gloomiest creatures.

Away from his house, though, Badoy was full of energy. Even when alone in the water you felt his presence over your shoulder explaining a diver's worst enemies or making you work the corals harder or pointing out that he always did most of his own impromptu repairs right there in the sea since he had nobody on shore to whom he could bring unravelled rubber bindings or broken wire loops. You were being urged along; steadily, certainly, you were being groomed but you still did not know exactly for what.

'You must come to my village,' Badoy said one day. 'Perhaps at the end of this month or next month we will visit Tagud. You would like to come? The spear-fishing there is very good. But first we must practise night diving.'

'Night diving?'

'It's much better. The fish are asleep there in the corals. You go down and shine your flashlight and there they are. They don't move much. You can put the end of your spear this close' – he held his hands six inches apart – 'and *pum*! Big fish, too; you'll see.'

'Isn't it very – well – dark?'

'We will bring my cousin in a boat and borrow a pressure-lamp. It's not necessary, the lamp, but it makes it more easy for you the first time. Also we will have our flashlights. You have flashlight?'

'Just a cheap Chinese thing. It isn't waterproof, though.'

'Of course. But we will make it.'

Waterproofing torches by means of adding another, slightly larger diameter, lens and encasing it all in a length of motorcycle inner tube was merely one more of Badoy's skills. Two nights later you lowered yourself from a tiny boat into the black waters above what in daytime was a familiar reef. And there it was, pressing in all around you amid the fitful sparks of plankton gingered into momentary luminescence by tiny eddies and swirls. There it was, swimming upwards at you from those pitch depths. Certainly it had been preparing itself in instalments: the first time you saw a moray eel fix you with its blank and white-rimmed eye and bare its ragged teeth at you and at nothing else; the first time a sea-snake came swimming rapidly up in clear water to investigate you alone; the first time you speared but did not kill a stonefish whose poisoned spines could inflict agonising wounds and you were left on a tossing ocean trying to manoeuvre the twisting creature down the spear and back along the nylon line away from your naked feet. Pangs they were when in warm tropic seas a quick cold current ran over your body. But this black gulf which concealed all such things and no doubt many worse made for a fear which did not easily pass.

Then Badoy's torch flashed on and the pressure-lamp outlined his downward-swimming, purposeful body in sad green light like something which could not be followed but which you pursued anyway for your own safety, imagining always, imagining the very worst that could happen: the accident which sent your spear thudding into his body, the bent-nail fluke making it impossible to pull out and which would mean finding transport in the middle of the night (hardly likely in Anilao where the only vehicle was a battered motorcycle) to take a mortally stricken Badoy eighteen miles over atrocious tracks to the only hospital where, if rumour were to be believed, they often performed major surgery by candlelight with the aid only of dozens of ampoules of local anaesthetic since somebody had sold the nitrous oxide on the black market.

But here is Badoy's torch and then Badoy himself, alive and well, flashing his light briefly on the end of your line to see what you have caught and, doing likewise, you discover his own line already weighty with the big reef fish you dream of getting by day. And again you follow him down, but this time the excitement takes over when you flash your own torch unbelievingly into a hole and there not more than two feet away is a good solid half-kilo goatfish, one of the mullet family, its chin barbels twitching in the sudden light. Then your spear pocks through him and you have air enough left in your lungs to sweep him back along spear and line with a now practised gesture, trap your torch between your legs as you reload so as to see where to catch the stretched elastic, regain a lost few feet of depth and move on to the next hole, which contains nothing but a dark red slate-pencil urchin you have never seen by day. And so back up to the surface where the night now seems darker than the sea beneath you except for the single star of the pressure-lamp some way off and the air is almost cold in comparison with the water. You have suddenly shifted elements.

And the excitement never failed even though the fear lurched up before submerging again beneath sheer physical pleasure and interest. You always came back exhausted after three, four and once five hours of working the reefs in darkness but never without some fresh knowledge of the sea and its creatures. Often you returned with handsome fish, many times with cuts and stabs and hydroid burns, various parts of your body embedded with the snapped-off tips of brittle black sea-urchin spines. ('Piss on them, that's the best,' said Badoy the first time. 'It dissolves them.' 'How can I possibly? They're *here*.' 'Forget them. They dissolve anyway in a couple of days.')

The moments of fear were almost always those when you allowed your imagination to intrude. The sudden confrontations with marine hazards were moments of extreme busyness, of co-ordinating spear and breathing; the fright only came later. You have never been phobic about the dark or of being alone, but there were times when both lightless boat and Badoy himself disappeared for upwards of an hour and you were quite alone in a black sea beneath a black sky sometimes not even knowing where the shore was since you were too far out for the breakers to be audible above the local slop of water. Then you felt – not fear, exactly, but a desolation, an abandonment such as prefigured a way of dying which might well turn out to be your very own, unlocatably small between a black space and a black deep. How, then, to explain that this doleful panic could turn, now and again, into the greatest exhilaration and send you plunging recklessly downwards with your torch switched off so that the twinkling of plankton beyond your mask were the stars in a downward firmament traversed by the brilliant comet of your spear-tip? And then, perhaps, far away at an unguessable distance off to one side a brief flash like the dimmest green lightning as Badoy's torch-beam outlined a range of coral like a bank of cloud.

All this time you knew how happy you were by the way the question 'how long can it last?' re-posed itself in a variety of ways. Privately your hope was that the manager of the electricity co-operative had indeed embezzled your salary, maybe in so doing prolonging your stay indefinitely (for it costs next to nothing to live simply in a place like Anilao). But what of Badoy? He frequently referred to his plans for working abroad – in Saudi Arabia, in America, in Australia – anywhere overseas, really, where visa requirements and work-permit laws could be got round, fluffed over or just plain flouted. Did you think his chances of getting a honeymoon visa and then overstaying and going to ground as an illegal immigrant were better in Australia or the US? was one of his ways of starting these conversations.

'But what about your wife, Badoy?'

'She stays here, of course.'

'But surely you'll miss each other badly?' (Was this inquisitiveness or mischief?) 'You may be gone a year. More', you added, thinking of gaol, 'or less', thinking of deportation.

'Three maybe, perhaps five. Of course. But the money. . . . What else can we do? Without work there is no future for me here in Anilao. She will be happy because of the money.'

'But what kind of work could you do in a place like Saudi Arabia?'

'Oh, anything. Construction, labouring, working in the restaurants for other foreigners like me. It doesn't matter.'

'But it may be hundreds of miles from the sea. No more spear-fishing.'

'Alas.'

And finally in a gloomy outburst: 'I don't want to live as a fisherman all my life. I want something better than this place. I want to see the world.'

How uneasy were such conversations, which would recur practically verbatim and with your own lines beginning 'But . . .'. Even more uneasy were they when his wife was present, the looks of hopelessness she shot at him, at you. The atmosphere became heavy with the sense that there was a great inaccuracy somewhere, that you did not understand who was being reproached for what, if anyone were: he for longingly talking of desertion, he for battening inertly off his wife in Anilao, or you for treason in possibly aiding his going. Your own selfishness appalled you, the degree to which you wished to hold another person's life static to make a background against which you could do your plentiful discovering, your peregrinations. Struck then by the image of Badoy's marvellous talents and skills which he ironically so undervalued lying unused or even deteriorating in the blazing heat of an Arabian construction site, you were made sadder still. It became but a small step from raising practical objections concerning the difficulty of legally working abroad to finding yourself entertaining fantasies masquerading as plans to build a large fishing-boat of which Badoy could be the skipper while you – what? – held ropes and jumped over the side, dog-like, to retrieve lost paddles? It was absurd. Yet it was never quite enough to laugh at such plans, because self-mockery, too, has that quality of ringing as if round an empty room. The real self has opportunely just left, closing the door, and can be heard outside in the passage obtusely heading back towards the television room and fantasy.

II

And so in due time your probation ended and you finally reached Tagud. It turned out to be smaller even than Anilao, its greater dependence on the sea reflected by the purposeful way in which the bleached huts had their piles driven into the sand above the high-tide mark and hugged the shore in a straggling line, scorning to spread inland among the sheltering palms. Behind the village rose a mountain whose steep sides were partly forested. A mile offshore was a tiny uninhabited island whose general shape and jungled cap were an aping in miniature of the mountain opposite. In between ran seas whose purples indicated their depth.

'Bad currents,' said Badoy succinctly. 'We will take a lot of rice and water and live on the island. You will like it there; very good corals.'

The first two days there were a continuation of your Anilao spear-fishing but now in paradisal guise. The corals were richer, steeper, the water clearer, the fish grander. Who has never hung above such reefs in the early light of morning, steeped in the bliss of altitude, has missed a vital fraction of the world's beauty. On one side the floor of the sea rises to become the rocks of shore; on the other it falls now shallowly through hillocks of coral – twenty-foot crags like model mountain ranges – now steeply in gorges and vertical cliffs slashed by crevasses into ever-purpler depths of invisibility. On the way down this magnificent descent are ledges of blond sand and creamy patches of coral fragments making irregularly spaced steps on a grand stairway down. Such now is your physical familiarity with what you lovingly see that you appraise each of these steps. 'I could reach that. . . . I might just get down to that one. . . . I'd never make the bluish one, not at my age. Fifteen, sixteen fathoms and then straight back up, all right; but twenty-five fathoms, never.' Yet, even if you will now never be able to get down much beyond a hundred feet without mechanical assistance, how beautiful it is as the light becomes stronger and higher; how bushy and furred those cliffs with multiform varieties of plant, how mysterious the brilliant fish moving isolate or in small flocks at all levels in this fluid mass like birds, how splendid the little sharks eighty feet beneath your soles and flexing like rubber daggers moving haft-foremost. This astounding medium sustains it all; it bears you up, in it you float, entranced by a paradigm of inwardness and depth.

But the fear was not long in returning. You could feel it coming each time you crossed back from the island to Tagud and met Badoy's family and the other fishermen of the community. They radiated a competence so great it immediately annulled your own pride at having acquired a small skill of your own. It soon became clear that this arose not from a disparity in your respective expertness with a spear-gun, superior though theirs was, but from their use of something which was evidently what Badoy had been leading you towards right from the beginning.

The compressor.

'When I come back home here to Tagud,' Badoy said one morning, 'I must seriously catch fish so I can sell them and bring the money to my wife in Anilao. I must work.'

So playtime was declared over; there were livings to be earned. Either you went on dabbling on your own or else you followed Badoy on to the last stage.

'It's exciting,' he urged. 'It's the best. Far better than what we've been doing.'

You felt a pang at this easy devaluation of weeks of pleasure. 'Far better?'

'Not *far* better; that's still very good,' Badoy said encouragingly. 'But you can get bigger catches of bigger fish because you can go so deep and stay down there for hours maybe.'

'How deep?'

'Maybe two hundred and fifty, three hundred and fifty feet sometimes.'

Good God. 'Is it very difficult?'

'Not so. With practice a week or less. We will try later today when the boat comes back.'

Later that day you examined the compressor. The system was simplicity itself. The boat's propeller shaft could be disengaged and a fan-belt slipped over a pulley so that the engine now drove a small air-compressor from which led two thin polythene hoses each hundreds of feet long.

'That's all it is,' said Badoy. 'You control the air-flow by biting with your teeth, and when your mouth aches you squeeze a loop of the tube between your fingers like this. It needs a bit of practice to learn how to regulate it automatically.'

'No valves or anything?'

'No.'

'What about depth-gauges?'

'Do you have one?'

'Of course not.'

'Neither do we. We learn to judge how deep we are from the pressure on the body and the colour of the water. We must also judge how long we have been down. Do you have a diver's watch? No? Did you know if you come up quickly from deep it hurts your joints like rheumatism? There is a man here in Tagud who was very drunk all night and he went down the next

80

morning without sleep and still drunk and I think he comes up too quickly maybe. But he is now, what, paralysed from here. . . . Did you know about this danger?'

Did you know? Good God, had you not heard about the bends when you were at school and since read the elaborate safety-codes for scuba diving? The carefully worked-out pauses for decompression at each depth, to be minutely timed on obligatory chunky watches? The depth-gauges and knives and nose-clips and wet-suits and cylinders and weighted belts and flippers and reduction valves and compasses and underwater flares and so on and so on: the expensive accoutrements of those who quite reasonably wished to take their pleasures safely.

'We will try now,' said Badoy.

'Oh. . . . What happens if the engine fails? It's always running out of fuel.'

'There's a reserve air-tank here.' He pointed to a pitted and rust-corroded cylinder lashed to the side of the boat with nylon line.

'How long will that last?'

'Three minutes maybe?'

'So if you're at two hundred feet you've got *three minutes* to surface?'

'We won't go that deep. This is your first time. Easy practice only.'

'What happens if that fan-belt breaks? It looks pretty frayed to me.'

'Same thing. You will know. For a moment the air stops completely and then it comes again but less, so you will know it is reserve. Now, put the tube around your body twice and loop it over two times only to hold it and bite the end in your teeth.'

With the engine running the compressor sent a huge draught of stink into your mouth, less air than the flavour under pressure of diesel oil and polythene tubing whose walls were infiltrated with colonies of yeasts. You retched.

'Don't worry. Up here the pressure is very great. Later when you have practice you will go down to sixty, seventy feet and the air comes just right. But when you go down to three hundred you must suck it in, the pressure is so few. Very tired, your lungs. Now, ready?'

And because you *weren't* ready you floundered about in the topmost yard of water like a beginner learning to swim. It was hard to remember to do so much at once: clench your teeth to

81

breathe normally, equalise the pressure in your ears, ignore the stink and head down beneath the throbbing wooden hull of the boat. A moment's inattention and the air would burst into your stomach, your mouth open and sea flood into nose and mask; you would flail to the surface, choking and pouring and belching great gouts of diesel stench while the loose end of the tube whipped about in the water hissing and bubbling. And Badoy's colleagues, teenagers mostly, would peer down laughing.

That first session barely lasted ten minutes, but in that time you did get down about thirty feet and stay there for longer than you ever had when you relied on lungs alone, Badoy cavorting round you with his plastic umbilicus in his mouth, trailing bubbles and teasing little fish. Later that night, in the small hours, you went off with them in the boat for spear-fishing; but it wasn't the same for now you were left behind with your lungfuls of air while Badoy and colleague took the compressor's hoses between their teeth and you watched their flashlights going straight down and down and down, becoming green dots of luminescence before winking out behind coral outcrops as the polythene uncoiled on the deck above them. You could not yet join them at such depths, so disconsolately swam towards the black bulk of island to bring you to shallower inshore waters. And so that night you fished alone, spearing a bigger and better catch than ever before but surfacing companionlessly to listen for the faint diesel chug of the compressor out in the dark. Sometimes it moved when the boys on board paddled to keep pace with the long-vanished divers; at other times it disappeared altogether as the noise of the invisible surf nearby drowned out its sound.

Hours later and shivering with exhaustion you found the boat again, bringing with you about four kilos of fish on your line. You should have been overjoyed but you were tetchy, jilted, cold and getting colder still as you sat on deck in the night air while the compressor chugged on and still Badoy didn't return. Then at last the green patches of light growing under the sea and flashing intermittently like electrical storms in tropical clouds seen from high-flying aircraft: the gladiators returning. And here they were, whooping on the surface in the dark, chattering excitedly, swapping stories while their abandoned air-hoses spurted and threshed in the water, then coming in over the side and needing help to pull in their nylon catch-lines with

82

twenty kilos of fish threaded on each: rays, small sharks, groupers, cuttlefish, vast parrot-fish, surgeon fish, a middling octopus, the meat from a giant clam.

So it came to colour your days on the island. Enclosing the mere practice of swimming down and staying at sixty feet without a spear-gun but with your lungs overinflated with oily air, the jaws of that vice: *not to be left out* on the one hand and on the other *the compressor*. And always from somewhere afar off in the mind that ringing of an empty room, that fear which had reverberated for as long as you could bear to remember, reminding you that you were full of the wrong stuff. Sleep, snatched mostly during the days' intense heat, now became obsessionally haunted, shot through with descriptions and apprehensions:

It is just completely terrifying.

Two hundred and fifty feet overhead is brilliant sunshine. The sea is flat calm. Stray half-beaks and flying fish will be breaking the surface almost from sheer light-heartedness, flirting with that nebulous barricade between the two abysses.

But down here the pressure is like dark blue cement, transparent, unset, squeezing in from all sides against mask, hands, ears, genitals. You are in its grasp.

'Of the two kinds of eel the white one – you know, with the black spots? – that's the worst. The black one is bad but it does not attack so often. You must look for the separate lump of coral on the bottom, small like this room and maybe no more than two or three metres high, like an island? They like those for their nests. Sometimes there is the head of the eel sticking out and watching you. If he is about as thick as your leg *here*, he will be about two metres long and very strong. If his head is up like this – like a snake going to bite? – *ay*, he is dangerous. He will keep maybe his last half inside his house; with the rest he will attack. His teeth, they will take everything from your arm-bone, so you must remain to four feet of him and put your spear in the mouth *here*. That is his weakest, but you must be ready for a big fight. He is almost impossible to kill with one shot because the brain is very small and behind the eyes. Sometimes the tip of your spear goes up through the roof of his mouth and destroys the brain – *ay*, very lucky – but his body is stupid and doesn't know he is dead already. If you hit him in the head, he will always pull back into his house and he will take your spear with him. He's very hard to pull out then, and your spear will bend like plastic. But sometimes when we are swimming around we look for a coral like that and we look for a tail sticking out. When we see it we are happy because he is so easy then and we shoot to the tail, *pum!* because when the eel feels it he only wants to get away. He will not attack like that even if he is thick like my stomach *here*. He thinks only of the spear in the tail and leave his house to swim away from the pain. Always he swim away from the pain.'

Away from the pain is straight up, away from this pressing liquid cell: up, up like a frail pink rocket trailing silver platters of diesel air which come wobbling up for half a minute after you first lie on the surface, feeling the sun on your face again, even now hardly believing in the world you have just escaped. But impossible: that exit route is blocked off by knowledge like a concrete lid over your head, knowledge of what happens to your body if you surface like that from an hour at forty fathoms. The images haunt: the agonising fizzing in the joints, perhaps the haemorrhaging in the skull, the crippling, the vegetable future. It is yet another vice (*down unbearable, up impossible*) each of whose jaws is dreadful. There is no room for panic down here. Better to discharge it all while you are asleep so it later lets you concentrate on the only thing that counts: that thin polythene tube wrapped twice around your body, the sighing end clamped between your aching jaws. The compressor.

Down there on the right where the sea-bed shelves steeply towards the violet drop which is the brink of a five-hundred-fathom deep, towards the edge of that monstrous chasm the stink comes sluggishly through the tube. You're now at over three hundred feet, and the compressor can't cope. You drag the air into your lungs as through a miraculous chink in those dark blue walls. Afterwards, when you are on your way back up the shelf keeping a wary eye open for eels hidden in the myriad holes you peer into and slowly decompressing, the air-flow gradually increases. Until the first glimpse far above and some way off: that black lozenge with the twinkling outline which is the keel of the boat, home of the compressor, fount of all nourishment the taking of which makes your jaws ache around its stenching nipple. Right now, though, that mechanical breast is far away, and only from the thinly flowing taste do you know that it is still alive.

And how infinitely further that sunlit western world of safety and back-up systems and fail-safe. The scuba rules, the diving codes, the union regulations. Here they are not worth the drift of plankton and diatoms past the face-plate. Here there is nothing but a polythene tube in the mouth and a home-made catapult, nothing but the actuality of the moment pressing in with stray threads of scald from invisible stinging tendrils which drift through all tropical oceans as if from some single titanic and long-dismantled jellyfish, some toxic Kraken whose fibres still circulate the globe. Much later, if you are lucky (and because day has now magically elided into night) the banter round the driftwood fire, roasting your catch under a starry sky which still seems to draw you upwards hours after you have left the water:

'*Ay*, Badoy, I thought you couldn't manage him so I shot him in the gills here but it only made him madder.' Blurts of laughter.

'And that hammerhead? I guess he was just shy. Big, though, wasn't he?'

The sharks. Some are not at all shy. You are there at a hundred and fifty feet investigating a cavern beneath an overhanging mountain of coral, trying to spot something edible with all the time the knowledge that you yourself may be the most obviously edible thing for fathoms. There *is* something in there, too: a big grouper perhaps, like that monster a week or two ago. It was just such a cave, and you were similarly trying to screw up enough courage to go inside, when a bulk of shadow detached itself and suddenly a gigantic flat eye moved like a dinner plate slowly across the cave mouth followed by a wall of dark red scales with one or two parasites attached. If a pin could snare a wild boar, then maybe a metre of elastic-driven rod filched from the core of an electric power cable might have some effect on a creature that huge, but you were not about to try to see.

And amid such reflections the sense of shadow behind and, turning, you see the shark watching from about twenty feet away. Everything looks bigger underwater and this is a twelve-foot Tiger the size of a submarine. And instantly the word 'requiem' flashes in the brain since the Tiger is one of the requiem family which in turn is one of the worst. The very word makes the liquid blue cement on all sides congeal and press coldly in, squeezing the upper arms involuntarily to your chest, squeezing the mind.

'They don't attack so often, sharks. Usually there is plenty of food for them down there, so they are not always hungry. But he is curious. He wants to know if you are worth attacking. He is attracted to light things, so we wear dark shirts and jogging pants when we dive, but sometimes he sees the soles of the feet in the distance. When he stays like that about twenty feet away, just watching, you must keep like him flat in the water, not upright. Because his mouth is underneath he needs to come at an angle when he attacks, so you must make it difficult for him by lying in the water with your head towards him. Always face him. Always watch his eyes: they look dead but they see everything. You keep your spear-gun pointed at him and you never take your eyes off him. If he moves round, you follow him round too, with the tip of your spear. He doesn't know what it is. He sees your goggles or mask and he sees your spear and he can't make his mind up if they will be dangerous to him if he attacks. Usually sharks just go away when they see you are so ready for them. But if he comes closer still maybe you will soon have to fire your spear. The only place is *here*, in the gills, because the rest of him is too hard and your spear will bounce off. If you hit him in the gills, he will go away; he doesn't like that. Also the end of his nose is sensitive, and he doesn't like to be hit there. If you get him in the gills slightly from behind, it'll go in. You'll lose you spear and your catch, but it is worth it. If you *miss* the gills? *Ay*, ha, I think you must not make a mistake. You are very alone down there.'

Maybe you fire and maybe the shark does go away, but there you still are, a hundred and fifty feet down without a spear and holding a useless length of wood like a child's toy with two impotently dangling strips of rubber, hyperventilating with a plastic hose stuck in your mouth and more or less at the mercy of whatever else turns up. You may have remembered to give three sharp tugs on the hose, and if by some extraordinary fluke someone in the boat was actually holding it at that moment and there was a spare air-line it might just have brought a colleague plunging down to your assistance. But what would he find? A pale figure in a wet cement cell holding a piece of wood. Then the slow, humiliating escorted swim back up the sloping coral shelf, pausing to decompress, waiting down there while your brain is still full of shark and everything inside is screaming at you to go, go, get *up*, get out of it, until at long last your head breaks the surface into the blinding lights and a ring of anxious faces. 'What was it? What was the problem? You have lost your spear.'

'Shark. A massive goddamned shark.' Your voice is squeaky

with air under pressure, your jaw aches so much from clenching the tube that you can't enunciate properly and your teeth no longer meet each other in the way they did, feeling lumpy and displaced to one side as after dentistry.

'Shark? Oh, what kind?'

And you know whatever species you say these boy gladiators in torn cotton will be immensely good-natured and agree it was high time to stop anyway because the compressor's getting low in fuel and we should maybe land and cook some fish. And always you wondered what it would have taken to make them just a little bit worried. Until that day you found out.

III

Well, night it was, to be accurate; for the choking practice-sessions and the worst of the haunted dreams were past and you had graduated to night-diving with the compressor. Much of the fear now could be held down by exhilaration: self-pleasure at doing things automatically so your body could take care of itself leaving your mind freer to speculate, enjoy, and attend to getting a good night's catch. For the fish down there were indeed bigger, though in that speckled darkness as docile as the little painted ones of the shallows when night came.

In point of fact the darker it was the better for spear-fishing, so sometimes you fished in the early part of the evening before the moon rose, coming back to the island at about midnight, the tarpaulin shelter stretched over sticks glinting in the starlight as one person set about making a fire and another began sorting and threading the catch for sale early next morning. At other times, though, the moon would rise as the sun set and you would all have to wait until it disappeared from the sky. On such occasions everybody slept when night fell at seven-thirty; everybody but you, of course, who would achieve an unreal doze at midnight, needing to be shaken awake at one-forty. And at that moment, as reality began to edge in to take the place of whatever dream, the very last thing you wanted was to get up, scramble through black surf into a boat, go out across a black sea beneath a black sky and go down and down with a torch and a spear-gun and a polythene tube in your mouth, the compressor overhead thudding the stink into you so that even next day you could taste it while belching after lunch.

Yet once out there in the dark off Badoy's village, balancing in the narrow boat while by flashes of torchlight masks and goggles are checked, spear-guns sorted, the coils of air-line kicked into more or less neat piles and the engine stopped so the boatman can disconnect the propeller shaft and slip the frayed fan-belt over the compressor's pulley, something changes. Amid those full black waters which so directly oppose the low ebb of your vitality and will the image crosses your mind of what people are doing at that moment in your own birthplace. It is nearly lunchtime there, and those dull shopping malls will be crowded, utterly safe with familiar names and products, utterly reassuring if you could ever suspend spleen and ennui. And the thought comes: what you are really doing is living *against* all that. The world is full of nest-builders and settlers-down but you will never be one of them. For you, only these present wrenches of pain and pure fear and glimpses of magnificent wildness will one day remind you that any of it was real; that it was not all fantasy and television, it was not all insulation; that the reefs beneath are there always. Do you crave a violent end? the mind runs on insistently in the darkness. But the compressor has started and Badoy is already in the water, his line hissing. Maybe; but not now, oh, not now this night. . . .

You should remember every detail of that dive, but you don't. There were just the two of you working an unfamiliar stretch around the seaward side of the island. As you submerged there was a flash of distant lightning which lit the mountain on the mainland, partially obscured by the black bulk of the island in the foreground, then you headed down with Badoy, two abreast, into the dark. The sea-bed here revealed by your glancing torches was different: the same coral varieties but more mountainous and fissured in their formation. There were fewer slopes and inclines, more cliff-faces and crevasses. Badoy worked one side of a ridge, you the other. Often you caught sight of his torchlight although not the beam itself, fitful green lightnings on the far side of crags. The catch increased steadily. It was more difficult terrain but more rewarding. The steep gorges were silvery with hydroids, stinging ferns which waved in the currents; to get into them you had to swim on edge, and the back of the elbow holding the spear-gun was repeatedly wealed. Making your way about became more and more difficult as the drag on your catch-line increased.

Adding a three-kilo grouper made it still harder.

And always the nerves alert, the quick flicker of glance for the least movement, for the white-rimmed eye moving in the eel's lair as a dot among all those undulating forests. The click of unseen crabs, the grunt of a creature disturbed, the directionless drumming on some thoracic air-sac. No longer can you hear the compressor's distant thump, and it seems like half an hour since you last saw Badoy's light or heard the far metallic ring of his spear-point on rock. You are investigating a black diagonal cleft little more than a foot wide. A yard inside and it turns to the right. There is nothing in this pocket other than small white pebbles on its floor, and it is precisely those white pebbles which should be telling you about the thick olive snake embedded among them which you mistake for – what? – the tail of a ray, perhaps. So automatic has become the sighting, the firing, the hauling-in of fresh trophies that you fire without thinking; then the thought, too late, catches up.

The spear is snatched from you so fast that its cocking lug and the first foot of nylon line take skin off your fingers. It lodges at the back of the cleft, quivering as whatever it is tries to drag it round the corner. Then amid the clouds of silt you glimpse what it has struck into and another, darker cloud comes billowing around the corner to engulf you. Octopus. The one creature of which Badoy has spoken with real fear.

'I don't like the feeling on your hand,' he once said after winkling a tiny octopus from its hole with a steel prod at low tide. 'They stick to you.' He lifted up his hand with its dark parasite wrapped around it like a clot of leeches. 'This one is too small; but even a little bit bigger – say, the head the size of half my fist? – and they will bite pieces out of you. That mouth, that beak you remove when you eat them, it's very strong and sharp. The big ones will always try to pull you towards the beak to tear you.'

But even so you are already trying to get hold of the end of the spear, reaching right-handedly into the cleft to rescue that precious weapon, still perhaps not sure of the power and size of the creature you have engaged with and which still lies hidden around the corner. Only when you feel a second tentacle close over your forearm, wrapping it together with the spear and tugging you irresistibly forward, do you realise how truly awful is the mistake you have made and how likely it is to prove fatal. For there is a degree of strength which you know cannot be resisted for long. You know from so many encounters over the months with even insignificant-looking sea-creatures how powerful the small muscle of a clam is, how resistant to dying a little eel. And now you feel your arm being compressed, the skin being dragged forward towards the hand as if it were a long glove being pulled off and simultaneously your right shoulder catching half into the mouth of the cleft, your head desperately averted over it and wedging at an angle against the rock outside so that slowly the mask is being crushed sideways across your face and immediately the water spurts in to fill the face-plate and your nose.

Now, with your head bent back over right shoulder, left cheek ground flat against the coral, everything is dark. By some miracle your left hand still holds the torch, but it is pointing uselessly into the sepia-filled cave. The pulling stops for a moment but does not ease while both creatures take stock of the damage and plan tactics for the immediate future. But you have no tactics and very little future. A grain of reason makes you bring your left hand as far away from the hole as possible and, reaching back behind you, you fire a regular three dots of light in random directions. Your heart-rate is way up and your respiration crazy, panting the rank air out into your skewed mask in the hope that the pressure will empty it of water again but it can only half-empty it: the seal between face and rubber is too weak on one side to stop the in-flood of that liquid black cement.

An age passes; you are locked and entombed, your neck cannot be far from breaking. Then something touches your hand holding the torch. You flail it wildly, trying to shake loose this new tentacle. Badoy's light breaks across your head and he comes round to peer in at your face-plate and, by God, he's *grinning* as if to say: '*Ay*, now you're learning the trade.' And somewhere inside his lair the octopus senses reinforcements have arrived and his pull increases again. Then suddenly your air stops. The tube is pinched between you and the mouth of the hole, perhaps at the rim of your mask, perhaps lower down your body. You wave desperately with the torch, making confused gestures towards your head like someone with an arm amputated at the wrist. Badoy, incredible Badoy, notices straight away amid all else that your bubbles have stopped. He reaches over and pulls your mask right off and the cement crashes into your eyes, nose, mouth, then you feel a stabbing at

90

your lips: another tube gushing diesel stink. You grip it in your teeth and suck and choke and suck and open your eyes. There in front of you is Badoy's face, slightly blurred now that your mask has gone. He hangs there in his little olive-lensed goggles, grinning and grinning until he reaches over and gently pulls the air-hose from your mouth and puts it back in his own for a few breaths. Then he makes a gesture you cannot understand because he, too, is holding his torch in the hand that makes it and it stabs wildly. He thrusts the air-line back in your mouth and disappears behind you. His light vanishes.

Now begins the octopus's attempt to pull its prey bodily into its lair. Its grip no longer feels localised at your arm. Vaguely you know it must have put out another tentacle to grip your body, but it surely cannot pull you in like that: the cleft is too narrow to accommodate you and the tentacle; as long as it goes on trying that way you are going to remain stuffed into the entrance but not drawn in past it. And then that pressure, too, increases unimaginably and you realise that your reasoning did not include the inevitable collapse of your own ribcage. There must be some movement into the hole because your head twists round even further, making crackling sounds. It is now so far round it catches a glimpse of Badoy's torch pointing aimlessly upwards; you wonder why it should be until you sense it is your own, held behind your back in your left hand, now no longer a part of you. So where *is* Badoy, God damn him? Fiddling about somewhere below in the darkness. . . .

Until his light, like a lark descending, strikes from above and there he is again. This time he tears the air-line from your mouth and pants great cavities into the water about you. His spear-gun is gone; in his hand he holds a knife. With this he retreats behind you after first pushing his air-hose back into your mouth. There are sensations of rending from your midriff; light flashes intermittently. Suddenly the appalling grip around your waist eases, your lower half is free to move a little away from the mouth of the hole and swivel to the right to relieve minutely your cracking neck. You are once again held only by the arm, which feels double its length. Badoy appears briefly, sucks air and disappears. This time there are no flashes of light: he is beneath you, wedging himself and his torch into the hole. There are confused feelings of tearing and pain from your arm, and without warning the rock floats away from the side of your head like feathers and a gentle cushion of water takes its place.

Simultaneously there is a great roaring in one ear: Badoy is offering you your now-released air-line and takes back his own. For a moment you both drift, each sucking on your tube as somewhere in the night above the compressor chugs and chugs, blessed engine.

Badoy shines his light back towards the cleft, now ten feet away. A great cloud of ink floats about its mouth and a host of small nocturnal shrimp-like krill, attracted by the light, are prickling at hands and faces like flies on a summer's day. Then he propels you away and upwards in a slow journey that seems to take for ever while pain begins gathering in your right hand and arm, the left side of your head, your neck and nearly everywhere else. The pressure of the air-jet increases as you rise, and you still go on breathing it even after your head breaks the surface, not quite sure that you have left one medium for another. Then you spit it out and it flails and gushes.

'Oy, Badoy! Badoy!' you shout in the darkness into the suddenly cold air. An answering cry comes from close at hand and now you can hear his own hose, discarded and bubbling. 'Where the hell did you get the knife?'

'*Ayy!*' He gives a long exultant whoop. The compressor is close by; it chugs in the invisible boat, rising and falling. There are voices. 'What did you say?'

'The knife. Where did you get it?'

'I went up for it.'

'Jesus!' The implications. 'But I had your air-hose.'

'It wasn't so far. We were only down about seventy feet.'

'But we'd been there a long time. Decompression. . . .'

'No problem. I went up straight and down straight again. You can do that if you're quick.'

'Why didn't we take bloody knives *with* us?' you heard your petulant rhetorical question go out into the night air. 'So *stupid. . . .*'

But what was this world to which you had returned? You still felt yourself travelling up and up into the sky as usual, but this time it was different. Something had changed; for the aftermath of fear is not relief and still less is it reassurance. The exact note had been struck, your whole life was ringing with that undeniable resonance, that messy echo of childhood fear of fear, and hero-worship, and fear of cowardice, and longing for something or other to be over.

You got yourself into the boat, the compressor fell silent, the screw churned. There was not much talk and no banter even from those who had spent the night safely aboard. You slumped, the deck slippery with your blood and the mucus which had come from the octopus and coated everything. In the dark you discovered your arm was burst and a thick muscle now lay exposed; you turned your torch on it in loathing but merely found a foot or so of severed tentacle still stuck there.

'Ah,' said Badoy, 'that was good, bringing a bit of the octopus. Better than none at all. We'll cook it by and by.'

You smiled in the dark at this. 'What was your own catch like before all that?'

'OK. Not bad, not good. Not a very good night for fish. About like you.'

'Damn. Of course, my own catch is still down there.'

'No, it's here. I cut off the nylon before we came up.' He flashed his light on to a jumble of fish bodies in the bilges. He had also brought up your mask.

'You're quite unbelievable.'

You returned to the island where you examined your wounds. Nothing desperate. The round sucker-weals stood out in scarlet over right arm and waist, each pinpricked with livid blood-spots. The side of your face and head was gouged and scratched but it was all superficial. There was a single deep cut on the inside of your forearm where Badoy's knife had sliced through the tentacle. 'Sorry,' said Badoy.

Dawn was coming. The air turned grey. You all packed up and crossed back to Tagud. The story was told and retold, but only because there was nothing else to do with it. There is no way outside the gruff fiction of derring-do to thank someone for saving your life; it is far too complex a matter to merit simple thanks. Must you not have *wanted* to die, just a little bit? Must there not have been that desire tucked down in your unconscious to entomb your conscious as well in those dark gulfs, even as your betrayed body tried to escape them? How else could you have ignored so many danger signals, have been so cavalier? And Badoy, too, had he ever had any real option? What were the psychic rewards for being a hero? Or for failing? How, knowing all this and suspecting still more, could you possibly say anything as banally inappropriate as 'thank you'?

For the rest of that day and, it seemed, for weeks afterwards the stench of the compressor came back up from inside.

On the way back to Anilao, Badoy said once again, and not at all apropos of the incident (which you really believed he had half-forgotten): 'I don't want to be a fisherman all my life. Are there jobs in television in your country? I would like that, I think.'

For a short time you resumed your leisurely life in Anilao, although it took time to muster the courage to go spear-fishing again, particularly at night. As if to urge you through this bad patch Badoy made you an even better spear-gun to replace the other, with a redesigned trigger of whose mechanism he was extremely proud. Then one night he said: 'To be a fisherman you need to be brave.' It was the first time he had ever alluded to questions of fear and courage. You were surprised.

'Of course,' he went on, 'of course you are scared down there. Plenty of people there at Tagud will not go down at night like you, like us. They do not want to use the compressor. We're all scared; it's a bit dangerous sometimes.'

You knew then that right from the beginning it had been a plot. For reasons of his own Badoy had wanted you to feel fear, had needed to set up that howling echo just as much as your submerged self; had led you inexorably to the compressor so you could suck in great draughts of it. The reasons – oh, they were lost in the workings of his psyche maybe; or perhaps they were his direct way of counteracting an impression of impotence he hated giving. For might not a foreigner like yourself so richly endowed with nonchalant mobility, such passports and visas and letters of credit, who moved so fluently in the clear waters above a sullen Third World labour pool – might not such a foreigner be badly in need of a lesson in respect? To make light of two great obsessions of the affluent West, technology and physical security, even as he dreamed of clawing his way into that world – might that not have been Badoy's real elegance, his deadliest accuracy? And if you had not been ruffled by this suggestion of war would you not have allowed a burst of affection for the way it had been declared?

'There's one thing,' you said magnanimously. 'If that night we'd been wearing pukka scuba gear, I'd most likely be dead. You couldn't just have given me your air-hose while you went up to fetch the knife.'

'Perhaps,' he agreed. 'You see? Simple things are best.'

On the other hand, of course, you would almost certainly have been wearing a knife. . . .

You did fish again but it was not the same. Your dreams were full of aggression aimed at Badoy, the lucklessly innocent repository of your fantasies. Nobody is as put out as a jilted fantasist, and the fantasist who thinks to perceive an actuality in what he is doing is the most put out of all. You became tired of his voice, his 'ay!', his wife moving dolefully about their dark house while radiating some tough resolve. You hoped he would soon get a job abroad. One day word reached you that the dendro-thermal project was shelved and with it your feasibility study, but that if you went back to the capital and bullied the right civil servant you could get your accrued salary.

Your leavetaking from Badoy was friendly, offhand, as if in six months or so you might well fetch up back in Anilao and find him still mooching and dreaming of emigration. Then he would dig out your old spear-gun and you would both slip back into the water as if no time had passed. But on the battered once-a-day bus which took you away up the coast you sat on the landward side, ignoring the blue waters creaming over the reefs on your left, staring fixedly into the palm-groves and the forest above them pouring skyward through ravines and gullies to the peaks of the central massif. And what were you thinking? That even if you never did return to that particular place wouldn't the sea always be in waiting? And wouldn't there be other Badoys and other involuntary opportunities to hear that lone whistler with his private note set ringing a bare inner room? For you cannot help yourself.

As even now the distant thud, the compressor's stench rise from inside.

Cheating

The honeymoon was nearly over. That morning the *Mooltan* had emerged unscathed from the Bay of Biscay, and already the gathering overcast and heaping grey-green seas were beginning to throw into brighter and ever more unreal relief the memories of long Mediterranean days, of vivid and pungent ports.

It had been fun, thought Christine, simultaneously catching herself out on the note of wistfulness and mentally giving herself a cross little shake. It *had* been fun, of course; and Paul had been sweet in the way their short (but not indecently brief) engagement had promised: attentive and . . . and, well, *thoughtful*. That was the word, wasn't it, which everyone always used about Paul? There was no escaping it. It was hard not to make comparisons with the other young men with whom she had had somewhat reserved dealings; young men in plus-fours and open cars, young men in Oxford bags, young men in white tennis longs. Some, she admitted, had been attractive to a greater or lesser extent (usually the notorious cads, if she were honest) and all had had that crashing, puppyish nonchalance which – if it were ever capable of being reflective – would have blushingly supposed itself lovable. So if 'thoughtful' described someone who considered consequences rather than perfunctorily observed etiquette, then Paul was undoubtedly thoughtful. The only trouble was the direction that thoughtfulness took.

Christine had of course imagined the honeymoon in considerable detail well before it ever happened and by now, practically within sight of Southampton, she ought according to her predictions to have been feeling a changed person. True, she was no longer a virgin; and nothing in her imaginings had prepared her for the oddity of the experience through which this had come about. It was not that their lovemaking wasn't marvellous – she definitely presumed it was. But the act which above all was supposed to unite two people in each other's sight (unlike the wedding, which had united them in the sight of God) had seemed to make Paul, if not more distant, exactly, then strangely jocular. He called it 'Bonzo' and laughed knowingly before he turned the cabin lights off, at which point she felt her upbringing called upon her to make a proper girlish response such as 'Oh, really, Paul, you are a wicked boy!' but she could only remain silent while listening to her new husband groping his way across the room, barking his shins on unfamiliar nautical obstructions. She must have had other preconceptions, too, since without knowing why she had expected it to last longer. But, although 'Bonzo' was brief, it was quite frequent, so she supposed that was how it was. And then – as at all other times – Paul was solicitous. Was he all right? Was he hurting, pleasing, loving enough for her? Was he all right?

Yet after all that, when maybe the earth had moved for her or there again maybe it was just the swell beneath the *Mooltan*'s forefoot, here at the end of her honey-month she could not in all honesty consider herself changed in any significant way whatever. Well, why should she be? she thought impatiently; her own fantasies had obviously been based on childish suppositions. Paul was untroubled by such foolishness. He was manifestly unchanged.

They had finished their penultimate breakfast aboard; the last night was to be spent berthed in Southampton since the ship would dock too late for convenient train connections to London. They left the dining room and somehow Christine found herself being escorted courteously but firmly via their stateroom to the secluded reading room on the upper deck.

'You can tell we're getting nearer home with your eyes closed can't you, Kitten?' He closed his eyes in illustration before ushering her through the door of the reading room, which smelt of the beeswax and turpentine polish which stewards applied liberally to every wooden surface they could find. 'There's a real edge to that wind. That's why I want you to wrap up well and stay inside today. We don't want chills after all that wonderful sun. Can't risk our baby.'

Now, what did that mean? Christine wondered as she allowed herself to be tucked into a leather armchair like some elderly patient on a health cruise. He sometimes called her 'baby' in joshing recognition of the American films they had watched together (on those occasions when he had said as if impulsively, 'I know, we'll go to the flicks,' but on arriving at the cinema she would discover he had already bought the tickets. Thoughtfulness again). But now might 'baby' mean something more literal?

'You've got your book, haven't you?' he asked. 'You'll be able to get through that comfortably before we have to return it to the ship's library. We might do that at tea-time.'

'I could practically do it now. I'm afraid I've cheated and read the last page already.'

'You bad girl.'

'What are you going to be doing, Paul?'

'Nothing, Kitten; just pottering. Thought I might go and say good-bye to the engine-room. That sort of thing. It's like leaving a familiar old house, isn't it?'

The engine-room had exercised a fascination for Paul right from the start of the voyage. He had asked the Captain on their first night out, who had been happy to introduce him to the Chief Engineer. Rather to Christine's surprise Paul had insisted on taking her as well when the next morning a boy in a white mess-jacket had appeared to conduct him below. The thought crossed her mind that maybe she was expected to find the engine-room so noisy or smelly or otherwise boring that it would give him *carte blanche* in future to spend hours there without her. He had, it was true, passed much of the voyage in visits to the various mechanical innards of the ship, afterwards explaining what it was that he had seen. In point of fact, none of it had struck her as particularly dull in itself or, come to that, particularly un-dull: it was merely machinery doing precisely what she supposed it would. But she was pleased on his behalf because it had obviously given him immense satisfaction, as well as something to do. She had rather liked the engine-room. It was indeed hot, and the noise was so intense it seemed to blot out even itself. She had stood amid a kind of deafened silence on a perforated catwalk gripping the handrail tightly and watching two immense cranks below her, one on each side, alternately rising and falling. Each time they rose their bright steel knuckles brushed against a cloth wick dangling from a brass pot bolted just above their reach. She presumed it was some primitive but effective device to keep the bearings oiled. Once outside, in a different kind of silence, she heard Paul's voice coming as if through layers of felt: 'Did you see the automatic oilers?'

'Those brass pot things with wicks?'

And she had caught something in his eye, a flash of annoyance perhaps, a demand that she let things be his way.

Now she watched him leave the reading room and, through the thick pane of glass next to her, could see him crossing the deck and going down a companionway, tall, boyish, but contriving for all that to look dignified in an elderly way. Perhaps it was his lack of bottom; the back of his trousers seemed empty in a very English manner. She found herself wondering how they would both look in fifty years and was surprised at how easily she should have skimmed over their whole lifetime as if to glimpse the outcome. Not only was that a kind of cheating, it was perfectly ludicrous. What on earth did it matter what they were going to look like, *die* like? They had an entire life ahead of them. Live it to the full, she told herself, but could not quite banish the poignancy of this piece of sententious self-heartening.

She read desultorily for an hour; the ship's library was not well stocked. Restless and feeling guilty for leaving the place in which Paul had installed her, Christine then gathered up her shawl and book and went outside. The sky was still greyer, the bangs of wind still colder and more violent. From far overhead and slightly forward the sound of the exhausts blew back from the funnels. Paul had explained that the ship had recently been converted from coal- to oil-burning, and seemingly this had reduced one of the funnels to redundancy, all the exhausts having been routed through the other. Up here the wind's buffeting carried noise and smuts in gusts: now the exhausts seemed no more than a distant hum, now they leaped out at one with a deep furry blare. Despite the deck-hands' regular sluicings the forward-facing parts of the superstructure were filmed with black deposits, the granules of carbon sticking to the salted paintwork. Seagulls were crying round the rigging, one was perched on the masthead. Their melancholy cries were quite unlike the raucous assertions of identical gulls in Marseilles, Genoa, Piraeus, Jaffa, Alexandria. . . . She heard in them the difference between harbingers and contented inhabitants.

She crossed the deck, pausing uncertainly at the head of the companionway. No, she decided, don't pry, don't pester the poor boy. So she walked on down the deck past the rows of lifeboats to a kind of saloon whose real purpose or title she had never learned. Perhaps it was a still-room or buttery of sorts, if they had such things on board ships. At any rate one could get tea or coffee at almost any time, and she now went in, stepping decisively over the brass strip on the coaming, the door-closer shutting out wind and gulls and yelling exhausts. Inside it was quiet and empty. Behind the small bar a mess-waiter was polishing glasses. She vaguely recognised him.

'Good morning, miss,' he said. 'Turned cold out there now, hasn't it? They say there's some nasty weather off the starboard bow, but no need to worry, it's mainly the Channel that's copping it.'

She smiled at him, not displeased at the 'miss' until a sort of invented dignity caught up, but this only made her smile more. She turned away and sat down at a table by the window.

'What'll it be, miss, to keep out the cold?'

Was it difficult always to be so affable? she wondered. 'A pot of coffee would be lovely.'

'Coming right up.' He began bustling, whistling so quietly it was almost an ostler's hiss.

The peculiar thing about this room, she now remembered on catching sight of it, was the staircase leading up into it from the First Class dining room below so that on occasion it could be used as an annexe. She recalled the last time she had been there: the evening they sailed from Alex when Paul and she had spent so long leaning over the rail watching the mythical coastline of Egypt deepen from rose-and-ochre to shades of invisibility that they had not heard – or perhaps had elected to ignore – the dinner-gong. They had been late; to their surprise the dining room was already full. The Steward was abject in his apologies; since they hadn't appeared he had assumed they had chosen to dine at second sitting and had given their table to *new arrivals*. He stressed these words rather archly, and looking round Christine could see several faces she did not know, very brown with brown hands and pale wrists which gleamed nakedly as cuffs were shot. 'Egyptian Civil Service,' the Steward explained *sotto voce* as if referring to mental patients. 'They normally go from Port Said by their own line. Now it'll be *malesh* and *mafeesh* all the way to Southampton.' Then Paul had apologised for their lateness and said that, though they were both extremely hungry, they would come back for second sitting, whereupon the Steward showed them the staircase leading to the deck above. 'We can't have that, sir; we can't have our guests forced to starve by Johnny-come-latelys' – Christine did think he was rather overdoing it – 'so if you'd care to dine upstairs we would be more than happy to oblige you.'

They had gone upstairs; and much to their amazement that room, too, had begun to fill until at one point halfway through the soup Paul was disconcerted by the sight of passengers in evening dress standing awkwardly at the head of the stairs.

'I say, those poor blighters are in for a long wait.'

'Not more than an hour at the most,' said Christine. 'And they can go and have cocktails in the bar meanwhile.'

'Even so.'

Five minutes passed and then a distinguished-looking couple appeared at their table-side.

'Good evening, sir, madam,' said the man with a grave nod to Christine. 'I am extremely sorry to intrude but I was wondering if by the remotest chance you would consent to share your table? My wife is, well, in a certain condition and . . . but do forgive me – Major Sholto Perceval . . . my wife Humility. Ghastly name, I know, but I can assure you she doesn't live up to it.'

Paul made the introductions; Christine heard herself add: 'We're just married, you know' – a remark clearly addressed to Paul.

'My dear Mrs Fennessy,' said the gallant Major, 'we owe you the profoundest apology. We should neither of us dream of imposing. We spent our own honeymoon not that long ago in Port Said, which is scarcely the most ideal spot, and we know only too well the value of privacy. Permit us to withdraw at once.'

But Paul would not hear of it and Christine found herself going along with his hospitable gestures, summoning waiters to bring napkins and cutlery, reassuring the Percevals that, far from being an intrusion, their presence was all that was needed to complete the evening's pleasure. His thoughtfulness again, of course, although she conceded it might as well have been an undiscriminating desire to be liked. Then she felt mean: how

101

could he possibly have wanted to be liked more by total strangers than by his own new wife? As a matter of fact the evening had then gone off very well: the Percevals were an amusing and well-travelled couple, and by the time it came to leave the table one of those shipboard friendships was well under way and was even now closer than ever. None the less, Christine had permitted herself a small resentment at the alacrity with which Paul had sacrificed their privacy and, once this had taken up residence, she appeared powerless to suppress it completely. It worried her.

A movement beyond the window caught her eye. A long figure in a wind-whipped coat with the collar up was sidling – that was the only word for it – in and out of the davits. He was not so much blurred as darkened somewhat by the smuts on the window, which gave him a shadowed, melancholy air. He stopped outside, his back towards her, leaning on the rail and gazing downwards as if trying to gauge something. My God, it's a suicide, she thought. In a moment that man's going to jump. The whole *mise-en-scène* of emergency suggested itself in a rush: her uncertain cry of 'Man overboard!', the whistles and sirens, the stampede to the rail, the throwing of lifebelts, the shuddering of engines at Full Astern. . . . And in that instant she recognised Paul.

Christine was paralysed. The conviction was so strong she was about to witness a man doing away with himself that she could not relate this in any way to her husband. As the figure at the rail continued to stare down, his hair lashed by the gale into a series of wandering crowns like long grasses on a hillside, the power to think began to return to her. *Why? Why now?* Poor man, was he so very unhappy? To her surprise she found it quite thinkable that he might be, in the same way that she knew she or anybody else might be. Unhappy, yes, but so unhappy as to be driven to that? And why here, as if to taunt her with the spectacle? Then she remembered that he thought she was still sitting patiently far away in the reading room at the other end of the deck and on the other side of the ship, and that even had he glanced round he would still scarcely have seen her through the dingy glass.

She was raising her arm to beat her knuckles on the pane to distract him long enough to reach the door when with an almost furtive gesture he produced from under his coat one, two, three, *four* round objects. And in the moment she recognised them and

102

knew what he was really doing the entire construct in her mind fell apart with an almost audible sense of things tumbling into a long abyss. The objects were, she knew, two-ounce tobacco-tins with screw-on lids and they were full of his used razor blades. On first discovering the tin he was currently filling in the dressing-table drawer she had thought of his habit as being some quaint relic of bachelorhood; perhaps all men did it. Maybe old blades had some kind of value for something she could not guess at. But then she had come upon three more identical tins, all containing heavy clots of higgledy-piggledy blades fused together with rust and long-dried soap and whiskers, and had asked him outright why he had brought them on honeymoon with him.

He had been embarrassed, then breezy, as if he knew it was actually more irrational than the explanation he gave: that he never could bring himself to throw used blades away for fear that the dustmen might cut themselves, or children find them and lacerate themselves, or animals unearth them and suffer terrible injuries. And the more he elaborated his fears the more the razor blades stopped being flimsy pieces of metal which could have been effectively disposed of in thirty seconds with a bit of thought and the more they took on the nature of time-bombs: supremely dangerous by-products of his own masculinity which could at any moment burst out of hiding and slash and maim and kill. To go around casually disseminating such things was, he explained, incredibly thoughtless and *anti-social*. How often had he used that expression! Christine had at first listened gravely, then had been mightily amused without – she hoped – letting it show and lastly had tried rationality. Surely, she said, the problem of what to do with used razor blades was faced daily by millions of men all over Britain, Europe, the world. . . . She could hardly suppose they all hoarded them against a sea-voyage yet she had never in her whole life heard of anybody accidentally injured by coming upon a worn blade as opposed to using one clumsily. For one thing they lay too flat. . . . But she soon recognised this was being too reasonable: he thought she was not giving him enough due for being a responsible social animal. He became defensive, he blustered. Finally he had walked out and spent several hours in the engine-room.

At that moment the mess-waiter appeared with her coffee. As he rested the edge of the tray on Christine's table he glanced up and also saw Paul through the window. He must have noticed her staring, for he said: 'Now what's that queer fellow up to, I wonder?' in a musing, conspiratorial sort of way.

'I thought at first he was going to jump but he isn't, it's all right. He's going to throw something overboard.'

'You sure of that, miss?'

'Perfectly. He's my husband.'

'Oh, I do beg your pardon, madam. I'm sure I meant no offence.'

'None taken. He does look rather furtive, doesn't he? Like some criminal disposing of evidence' – for at that moment Paul, after a quick look to right and left along the deck, began throwing the tins as if reluctant to part with them one by one into the stream of wind roaring alongside the ship.

'You may make light of it, madam, but we've had things happen you wouldn't believe aboard this ship. Some strange objects have gone over the side of the old *Mooltan* in her time, I can tell you; things as are hardly fit for a lady's ears to hear about.'

But Christine, as if already inured to all such terrible details, was not listening. She was counting – *one, two, three, four* – and as each tin vanished she again experienced further stages of that interior crumbling. Just for a moment, just for a half-second when she had recognised Paul and still thought he might be going to jump, she had felt her little nugget of resentment change to . . . what exactly? Relief? A sense of reprieve? But in the next half-second it had changed back again and now, as each tobacco-tin was launched into the void, the nugget grew. And for the second time that morning she could not prevent herself making a temporal leap, that awful elision whereby she slipped to the spent end of her life with a devastating wrench of sadness to see what would become of it. But she found she had known all along; and she gazed at the dark, elderly back of her boy-husband through the window and raised the coffee untastingly to her lips.

The Madonna of Parazuela

One can only see what one observes, and one only observes things which are already in the mind.

Alphonse Bertillon

I

Outside the bullet-pocked walls of the Palace of Governors half a million servings of beans and maize fritters were nearing noontime readiness and the attentions of the population of San Sacramento. Inside the Palace the monthly meeting of the Generals was drawing to a leisurely close. As with most other such meetings not a great deal had been discussed and much of that consisted of hoary topics: how best to deceive the current batch of IMF spies and visiting auditors from the World Bank about the true state of the Parazuelan economy, and what might be done further to undermine the credibility of the three-member delegation from Amnesty International. Now it was time for Any Other Business, which was usually chit-chat while tunics were buttoned, peaked caps found, swagger-sticks sorted out and holsters unfastened preparatory to going outside.

'I suppose we'd better brace ourselves for that ghastly little Jew again,' said General Mendez.

'Which particular one?' asked the Generalissimo.

'That ex-Mossad fellow who lives in Munich. Silverstein? Silberbein? Feigenbaum? The one with the bee in his bonnet about Nazis in hiding. Hadn't you heard, then? I gather someone has written another book saying that Horst Wessel is alive and well and practising medicine in some poverty-stricken barrio here.'

'No, that's not it,' corrected General Ocampo. 'This time it's a reporter who swears he has proof that Hitler's living in Parazuela. It was on the BBC's World Service.'

'*Hitler?* Oh, really, it's too absurd. Whatever will they think of next?' The Generalissimo pocketed the calculator on which he had done some depressing arithmetic during the economic part of the meeting. 'The fellow would have to be a fossil. Wait till I tell old man Schicklgruber on Sunday: I'm lunching over at their ranch. They'll love that. Anyone else got any funnies?'

'Weird report from Tutuban this morning,' said General Edmilson.

'Where?'

'Tutuban. Iguaçu province, apparently; I hadn't heard of it, either. Couple of kids claim to have seen the Virgin Mary.'

'I expect it was Goering in disguise,' said General Preciosa, who was reputed to have had a mean wit in his Military Academy days. Certainly everyone laughed.

'If so, he really fooled the kids. They're convinced it was the Virgin and they've convinced a lot of locals, too. In fact people are starting to go on pilgrimages to Tutuban from other parts of the province, and one or two are already claiming to have been cured of their horrid condition.'

'Credulity, for example?' suggested General Preciosa.

'Don't knock it,' said the Generalissimo. 'Without it this country would be ungovernable, even by us, to say nothing of the rest of Latin America. I just wish someone would discover a way of infecting the Gnomes of Zurich with the virus. And now, gentlemen, shall we adjourn?' With some mutual saluting the meeting broke up.

'But,' said General Preciosa a couple of hours later, 'but but but *but*. . . .' He was a little drunk but not very, having lunched well in a permanently reserved room above San Sacramento's best Viennese restaurant. 'But,' he added thoughtfully.

'But, Fernando . . . ?' prompted General Edmilson.

'But what about *Lourdes*?'

'Oh, dead. Has been for months.'

'What do you mean?'

'Just that. She disappeared in a football stadium. With several hundred others, I believe.'

'What on earth are you gibbering about, Manolo?' asked his friend brusquely.

'That protest singer woman. Maria Lourdes. You surely remember her? Dangerously popular; criminally off-key.'

'Not *her*. The place. You know, Lourdes in France. Kids? Visions? Virgin Marys? Big Moneys?'

'Oh, *that* Lourdes.'

'Exactly. Do buck up, Manny, or I'll have to buy you another tequila. I've had an idea which could do you a lot of good. You are Minister of the Interior, are you not? Well, then, who's our Minister for Tourism?'

'Minister for Tourism? Ah, now, let me see. . . .'

'There isn't one,' General Preciosa cut his friend off in mid-speculation, 'as you very well know. It isn't that Parazuela hasn't got more than its fair share of potential tourist attractions, either.'

'Certainly isn't. There's the Taquarí asphalt lakes, for a start. And the Glass Iguana of Teoxihuatl. Nobody knows how—'

'Oh, do shut up; we had all that in high school, like several hundred other Parazuelans. No, the reason Parazuela is not on the world's tourist itineraries is because for years we were considered far too dangerous for your average American matron, and I agree that forty-one presidents in nineteen years did look bad on paper. But now this country's probably the most stable on the entire continent and we're still being boycotted by those same American matrons because according to their press and despite the imminence of elections we're a fascist Latin junta. Obviously there's never going to be any pleasing them. So write them off; we don't need them, either. But there's a still-untapped source of tourism awaiting an enterprising Minister, were he to drink a little less and play his cards a bit more shrewdly.'

'*Ah*. . . . Ah?'

'Manny! Your *story*. Your own story about these stupid kids out in the sticks in Iguaçu. Can't you see what a gift it is? You could really make it work in your favour. You remember old Raul going on this morning about how it was up to all of us to find ways of raising revenue so we won't have to re-reschedule interest payments on the national debt? Well, then. A really watertight Madonna could be parlayed into quite a steady little source of foreign revenue, don't you think?'

General Edmilson had at last caught up. 'Good God, Nandy, that's bright. Lots of possibilities there. Revenue for the country, revenue for us. . . . What's your cut in all this?'

'Accommodation,' said Fernando Preciosa succinctly. 'I want hotels. All hotels come through me.'

'You got 'em. Er . . . what do you suppose I could have?'

'*Political* power. Kudos. Think about it: as Minister of the Interior it will fall to you to follow up this story and find it genuine. The Minister for Tourism then becomes your appointee. Any developments in tourism which follow from this accrue to you. You'll be quids in with old Raul and you'll have complete control over planning further expansion.'

'That's marvellous, Nandy. . . . I – well, I wouldn't mind a bit of *cash*, too, if you follow me?'

'Use your initiative. Go to Tubitan or whatever it's called and buy the bloody grotto. Get a bit of real estate.'

'Do we know there's a grotto?'

'Of course there's a grotto; there's always a grotto. It'll certainly be one in the eye for the American matrons, won't it? I mean, if Parazuela's good enough for the Queen of Heaven to visit it ought to be OK for some fat harridan from Omaha in purple shorts.'

'That's a point. Yes, we ought certainly to play that up. Seal of approval, sort of thing. Do you know, Nandy, I think you're on to a winner. I'll get someone trustworthy to poke around and get a few hard facts. I only hope it all turns out to be genuine and not some ignorant peasant hoax.'

'There are no such things as fake Madonnas,' said General Preciosa wisely. 'There are only Madonnas.'

'Yes, but I mean it's a good job we're Parazuelans. I can just imagine some jumped-up little Guayadorean dictator inventing the entire thing to make a quick buck.'

'Can you, Manny? Can you really?' said General Preciosa, shaking his head as at the perfidy of the less scrupulous.

Inside three days General Edmilson's spy had reported back to San Sacramento. To the General's relief the story 'checked out', as his informant put it. He had met the children concerned – three little sisters between the ages of seven and twelve – and had convinced himself that whatever may or may not have happened they had not been put up to it by their parents or the local priest. He had interviewed each of them separately and, although they all cried a good deal, they gave identical accounts.

There had definitely been a strange sighting the previous week in Tutuban. Local opinion was, however, divided roughly along lay and religious lines. The common folk all believed it fervently, but the Church in Iguaçu province was decidedly sceptical and would need a lot more convincing before they could accept the event as genuinely miraculous. The trend towards radicalism among the younger clergy had evidently forced their superiors to sharpen their wits. The Madonna's physical appearance was, among some of the older clergy, one sticking-point.

'She was black, you see,' said the spy.

'*Black?* You can't have a black Madonna,' said the General. 'They're blondes or brunettes. Everybody knows that. Long blue robes and a sad smile and a sort of haze of light around them. At least, so I've always thought.'

'The children insisted she was black. Apparently there are precedents, sir.'

'Not', said the General firmly, 'in Parazuela.'

'Also she wore spectacles.'

'Oh, great. That's terrific. Everybody else gets the original version but poor old Parazuela draws some damn great buck Madonna in shades.'

'One or two priests are beginning to think this is a point in her favour,' the spy explained. 'They say that if the kids had really invented it all they would have made her conform to the traditional image. To have deliberately made her black and spectacled would have been creative originality way beyond their capabilities. I must say I think it's quite a convincing point myself.'

'Well . . . ,' said the General dubiously. 'Well . . . I suppose if that's the story we'll have to live with it. What else?'

'My impression is that, sceptical or not, the Church is going to have to take it seriously. There are already reports of miraculous cures attributed to her.'

'Are there indeed? That's good. What sort of cures, I wonder?'

'Fairly minor stuff so far, I believe. Warts and sprains. But it's early days yet and, after all, the halt and the lame are probably going to take a long time actually *getting* to Tutuban. When they do things will become a bit more organised. It only needs one per cent of them able to throw away their sticks and walk home for real pilgrimages to start in earnest.'

'*Bus company*,' murmured the General to himself.

'I beg your pardon, sir?'

'Nothing, nothing. I'm sorry, just thinking aloud. Go on.'

'That's about it. I'm afraid I don't know very much about these things so I have no idea what happens next. I don't imagine the Church will ever come out completely in favour of something like this because they've been made to look pretty silly in the past. Some sort of noncommittal tolerance is probably the best we can hope for. On the other hand, certain priests there are seeing it as evidence of renewed spiritual interest on the part of some of their flock and will be happy to use it as a way of reaching those they feel had begun to get out of touch, if you see what I mean?'

'No,' said General Edmilson.

'No,' admitted the spy, 'neither do I. I'm simply repeating what an Irish Dominican father told me. Oh, and there was one other odd thing about Our Lady of Tutuban which the children all swore to. She was holding a beautiful casket and as the children watched she gently threw handfuls of greyish dust towards them. She looked very sad and raised her hand to bless them before she disappeared.'

'There,' exclaimed the General, 'that's more like it. I knew she had to look sad and do some blessing. I've never heard of the dust before, though.'

'It got one of the old priests very excited. Apparently there's a precedent for that, too, somewhere in Italy in the sixteenth century. It was interpreted then as the dried tears of the Mater Dolorosa. This old fellow thinks it puts the whole thing beyond doubt as there's no way these illiterate kids or their family could ever have heard that story before. It was officially discredited at the Council of Navarre in 1887 and has been suppressed ever since on the grounds that Our Lady's tears would have been far too pure to have left a precipitate other than salt. Certainly nothing greyish.'

'There you see the inexorable march of secular man,' said the General. 'The faith of centuries judiciously gives way to high-school chemistry.'

'You're probably right, sir,' the spy agreed. 'As a matter of fact, there is no high school yet in Tutuban.'

'There you are, then.'

II

Mexico City,
11 June 1985

Dear Ruthie,

It feels like about a hundred years since waving goodbye to
you from a train window in Rio, but my little squeaky
calculator tells me it's only eleven days. I've had the weirdest
things happen in that time, so it's all a bit dream-like and I
shall wake up soon and find I'm still a Volunteer and you and
Ed and I'll maybe get a little high and drift on down to São
Felipe and go on a *favela*-hunt like we always do Tuesdays.
Boy, did we ever find some! I really believe we found places
even the city council doesn't know exist still less Holy Bob
Krummmmm!

Well, I haven't woken up yet and it's still Mexico City
outside and I'm still sitting on the balcony of this place
belonging to some Volunteer I've never even met because
she's off in Baja or someplace and the Peace Corps Office here
gave me the keys! Can you believe? It's full of her tacky
cassettes and books. *Small Business Management in the Develop-
ing World*, yeccch. I fly out tomorrow morning and I've got a
feeling that Galveston's going to seem real tame after Brazil,
but Life has now got to Begin In Earnest, careers have got to
be carved out, a husband lined up and all that shit I think I'm
no longer cut out for. But enough of that and on to the weirds.

Well, you remember I was going to go through Parazuela
and drop by Handsome Jack out in the boonies and give him a
heart-attack and poor old Poyson? The problems took a day
and a half to arrive, which is the time it takes the train from
Rio to reach Taquarí on the Parazuelan border after crossing
what's got to be the biggest stretch of unwanted real estate in
the world, all cactuses (cacti?) and giant ant-hills. The train
stops at the border, and if you want to go on you have to get
out and walk a hundred yards and change into another
because of course it's Parazuela and they built their railroad
three inches narrower than everyone else in South America.
So after a long wait and me putting off going to the john (if
only I'd known the john was enough to put you off going: a
cupboard with a crusty hole in the floor) we set off and

111

travelled maybe all of a mile before stopping again. In a million years you couldn't guess why. The answer was *tar* – you know, like we have on roads back home? – but in Parazuela they've got it in damn great lakes and they turn out to be *tidal* for one month in every fifty years and wouldn't you know Sage Maclean chooses that one month to hit Parazuela. This tar – and I'm not kidding – had suddenly flooded in great black smoking gloops over the track and was pouring slowly like treacle over the embankment and out across the fields. So everybody got out carrying their luggage and *walked*! a huge detour right round the fields coughing in the sulphury fumes. I was really pissed off for about a hundred yards and then I started laughing and I just couldn't stop, specially when this little kid came trotting alongside offering to row us across in an asbestos boat for a dollar fifty. Well, I just collapsed. I never did see the boat incidentally and I expect he made it up except of course we *were* in Parazuela and you never quite know. Finally we came out on the far side and climbed into three old Greyhound buses hitched together and mounted on railway wheels, and they chugged us along nicely to San Sacramento, the capital.

I was pretty bushed after the journey as you can imagine specially since I've left out a lot, for example the Customs at the border going through every one of my bags for about an hour – shook them all out over a table and then examined the luggage itself, I suppose for coke hidden in the handles, etc. They were pretty fazed by poor old Poyson in my jewellery-box. They sniffed him while I deliberately held off saying what it was until one of them stuck in a wet finger and tasted him as I knew they would eventually, they don't believe a word you say. I explained then it was a pet pooch belonging to a Peace Corps Volunteer working in Parazuela and which had died in exile in Rio but they didn't believe that, either, and I can't say I blame them! Anyway I thought I was wonderfully patient, and my whole face was aching from my easygoing co-operative smile. Oh, and they didn't like my passport photo, either, because they'd shot me in contact lenses before I had that conjunctivitis in Brazil and had to go back to glasses. So one way and another I was feeling pretty much Looney Tunes by the time we reached San S.

Anyway, get to the point, Sage. Next day I found the Peace Corps Office and discovered how to get to Handsome Jack's and my heart began to fail a bit when I heard it was this two-day trip by bus and river but I reminded myself of how hunky he was and looked at his picture again and sort of felt my resolution coming back. Then off to the airline office to learn if I wanted to get to Caracas I'd have to go at the end of the week in 5 days' time or wait another week after that. So I booked the earlier flight to keep to my schedule and thought, OK, time enough for one torrid day with Handsome and who knew anyway? he might have some secret way of getting me back to San S. in less than 2 days – you know, wangle me on to an Air Force flight like FAB in Brazil.

I won't bore you with the journey – it was just like anyone's used to anywhere in South America: buses with crazed drivers and green-tinted windows crossing endless non-country and stopping in the middle of nowhere for leather steaks and manioc flour or, of course, corn fritters and beans beans beans. The sleepless night with the Latin advances from the seat next to me, the dawn arrival at a riverside quay, the rotting steamer going slowly up-river while avoiding some of the sand-bars. By the time we hit Tutuban it was of course night and the Office was closed and I checked into the usual dump where you just step into the shower and cover yourself in real good smelly lather when the fucking water stops. I was so tired I just sat in the shower and cried, but it made the soapsuds run in my eyes and sting so I had to get out and there was just enough water in the drinking jug to wash the worst off my face. Then the electricity went off, too, and I just thought to hell with the lot of them and lay down on the bed, suds and all, and fell asleep and when I woke it was morning and the suds had dried into a sticky coating which itched like hell. But the water was back on so I got it all off me but it left sort of a rash all over – great, I thought, really looking my best – and I set off in a filthy mood and covered in that freesia lotion of yours – for which bless you because it did stop me scratching in public, more or less.

Well, Handsome Jack's got this really neat bungalow on the edge of town with hills covered in banana plants behind it, you know *quiet* compared to Rua Caxias. And I was admiring it at the same time as trying to kick the door down and get my clammy hands on him when this Indian lady appears from a hut nearby and says that Señor Brunner is away for three days at some project he's got, only it took a bit of time to work out because she obviously wanted to explain in Guaraní or something and Parazuelan Spanish isn't Brazilian Portuguese and I didn't want to believe her anyway. I guess I puzzled her, too, because I was wearing the famous Togo toga to be cool (and hide the rash!) and I guess she didn't realise I was a gringo or whatever they are in Parazuela because gringos have got to be peroxide blondes in Dior safari-suits with paunchy husbands trotting along carrying the home movie camera. They sure as hell can't be African Queens.

So, dear, dear Ruthie, back to the Hotel Bristol to put on a brave face and drag around Tutuban seeing the sights, which can be done in 5 minutes. Boring Spanish-style church with graven image on the roof, beggars on the steps, people selling religious cards and herbal medicines. Town square with statue of General Santos Velasquez y Something on a horse waving a muzzle-loader in the air, the Don Miguel Baixos Memorial Library (burned out), the local government offices (closed) and the market stretching down to the river which is by far the most interesting thing in town. Lots of indios from up-country selling slabs of compressed leaves (?coca but didn't risk chewing any, though, they might have been donkey-poultices) also pretty blankets very rough and cheap which were tempting but I couldn't face humping any more stuff around. I bought some batteries for the radio to see if I could get VOA but luckily I noticed in time they were all fizzy round the ends and took them back and they gave me some more, but you could see they weren't absolutely delighted. Screw them. So I went back to the hotel again and fell asleep and then woke and thought, right, Sage Maclean, you don't come all this way to turn round and meekly go away again with your tail between your legs without at least telling Handsome Jack what he's missed. So I wrote him a letter and was just going off to deliver it when I remembered Poyson still sitting there in my jewellery-box and I got real sad suddenly. I mean he was a great dog even if he never did get much less scruffy than when Jack walked in with him that day in Rio. Do you remember how he came in and stood there holding the dog in his arms and saying, 'Hi, I've just found this little fellow outside about to get *all et up* by a hound the size of a mule, no kidding, so I've rescued him and I guess he's kinda neat,' all this in his best laid-back strong silent manner and then without changing his voice, 'Oh God,' as he discovered it was pissing all down his shirt. (I think there ought to be a question mark at the end of that sentence but I can't get worked up enough to put one.) But it was quite witty and unexpected when Jack thought up his name. 'Nothing soft and cutesie. Anything with pus in one eye which pisses on your shirt has got to be an anti-Snoopy. *Poyson*; that's an anagram. And now I'm going off to boil him in Drāno.' And I guess it really was that moment as much as any other I first thought of Jack as handsome, which by golly he *was*, wasn't he? (Maybe still is but now I'll have to wait until the end of his contract to find out.) But we did all have some great times together, didn't we, Ruthie? And how poor old Poyson howled and howled when the eight months were up and Jack went back to Parazuela and I guess now I've seen the place I know it was best he didn't take him. He'd probably have been turned into pie at the Customs. And anyway the poor animal only spoke Portuguese and English.

I've gone off again, haven't I? But it's still Mexico City here and I've nothing better to do (no offence, it's actually very therapeutic getting everything down on paper to you of all people). Anyhow, I thought I couldn't leave Poyson in the care of an unknown Indian lady and I couldn't explain about cremation, etc., so I reopened my letter to Jack and added a PS to tell him what I was going to do and went off to stuff it under his door, grabbing the radio for company, I guess, but perhaps I did have some crazy idea of sitting on his stoop for a bit, which was as close as I was ever going to get to him, damn him, and a whole lot better than stuck in a hotel room. So back I went and I *did* sit on the stoop, corny as it was, and found the cassette in the radio was yours! still there from when I was packing my last night in Rio; those Bach cantatas, I'm afraid, and I know it's about your favourite and I've got it right here and I'll mail it tomorrow with this letter without fail, promise, promise. Anyhow, I put that on not too loud, although there wasn't anybody else around thinking I was maybe some insane trespasser. But after a while the sun was going down and the mosquitoes came out in clouds and I saw that Jack had screens up on all the windows and doors – obviously a bad place and as it's Parazuela probably malarial into the bargain. I don't know if you can stomach the next bit, Ruthie, as it's to be honest *sentimental* and I can just hear you laugh scornfully saying '*Sage*, sentimental? Sage *Maclean*? Ms Spit-in-your-eye herself?' But I guess it was all to do with Jack not being there after all that and my feeling inadequate when faced with reality after stupidly having looked forward to it too much for my own good. You know? There I was, unannounced and unmet, covered in a rash which still itched like crazy and all I had to give the absent man was his own dead dog when what I wanted to give him was. . . . Well let's not go into *that*.

Anyhow, I took the radio and climbed up the little hill behind his house and went through some bananas and things and came out on a grassy patch overlooking the roof down below (which had a flat bit on which he'd left a lounger and bottles of sun lotion – so he *is* vain after all! The strong and occasionally silent Jack is aware of his Bodddy!). Now comes the sentimental part – brace yourself, Ruthie – I scattered poor old Poyson to the four winds hoping he'd drift down to Jack's roof and become incorporated with his master's next tanning session but there wasn't even *one* wind and the pooch, unhelpful to the last, bless him, fell all over my feet and I was about to brush him off when I noticed these kids watching me. Well, I can tell you I was embarrassed all to hell to have been witnessed scattering the remains of a Brazilian mongrel to the sound of 'Also hat Gott die Welt geliebt'. I gave them a sort of grave salute and faded back into the bananas and switched off the cassette and made it back down to the road without being seen but feeling like a real idiot. And so my long-awaited visit to Handsome Jack Brunner was abortive and ended in farce! Just my luck. But I'll bet you laugh all the same.

I got back to San S. in time to catch my plane and I wasn't sad to see the last of Parazuela – that is, until I landed in Caracas which is *the pits*!! although I saw Ellen and Paul who're doing fine and send their love. And now here I am in MC with writer's cramp and promise to write you again if anything of interest happens to me between here and Galveston. I'm not betting on it.

Love to João, Sadie and anyone else worthy of it. But most of all to you.

SAGE

116

III

A letter from Fr Ignatius O'Malley, Order of St Dominic, Parish of Pampola and Tutuban, to the Chaplain to the Bishop of Iguaçu, Parazuela, dated 16 June 1985. (Original in Spanish.)

Dear Father Xavier,

Word has reached me via the good offices of Brother Aristeo that your Bishop has requested you should write a report about the Tutuban Affair so that he can, in turn, inform Cardinal Celso in San Sacramento. I shall do my best, of course, but have no experience in such matters and anyway you know me – I'm bound to be too outspoken or undiplomatic so you'll have to censor this as you see fit. Treat it, therefore, I beg you, merely as notes towards a report rather than as anything more final.

I refer to it as 'the Tutuban Affair' because with the best will I cannot dignify it with a title such as would lend it the least respectability. It is from all viewpoints lamentable. Briefly the facts are as follows:

(1) On 5 June this year three children of this parish (Nimfa, Rosario and Milagros Irubú) were on the hillside behind Calle Sta Isabel picking medicinal herbs at approximately 6.00 p.m. It cannot have been much later since the sun set at 6.22 on that particular evening and herb-picking in the dark is probably beyond the capabilities even of these favoured children (censor that). They allege that Our Lady suddenly appeared to them and blessed them. After perhaps ten seconds this apparition vanished.

(2) The children ran home and told their mother, specifying that the alleged apparition had been of a young black woman wearing spectacles and a long white robe. She was accompanied by 'heavenly music' and in her left hand held a beautiful casket from which she took and scattered a greyish dust with her right. Her demeanour was 'sad', and when she saw the children she smiled sweetly and lifted her hand in blessing before fading from their sight.

(3) The mother immediately summoned Fr Ayma of this parish, who on hearing the children's account induced them to take him to the exact spot, which he then blessed,

117

together with them, possibly to be on the safe side (excise that).

(4) News travels fast in rural areas, as I need scarcely remind you. By the next evening at the same time a crowd of some 150 parishioners was waiting on the hillside for a possible reappearance, which, however, was not vouchsafed them.

(5) Within a week pilgrims had begun arriving in Tutuban from as far away as Coatiara. In the meantime sermons had been preached in every church in town urging people to be cautious before accepting any rumour as well founded, the more so if that rumour purported to be of something miraculous. This warning, to judge from the ever-growing crowds besieging the home of the three children and the site of the alleged apparition, fell on preternaturally deaf ears.

(6) On 9 June a man named Gustavo Mittelwalder arrived in Tutuban on the personal authority of the Minister of the Interior, Gral. Edmilson, in order to discover the facts of the case. I spoke to him at some length and told him all I have summarised so far. He appeared quite satisfied and left.

(7) Three days later I received a visit from an American Peace Corps Volunteer named Jack Brunner who lives in the parish and has been working here for some time. Mr Brunner had just returned from a trip up-river to Meycauara where there is a tilapia-breeding scheme (a species of fish, I gather). His return had been delayed by transportation problems. On his arrival he found his house besieged, for he lives on the Calle Sta Isabel in a rented bungalow at the foot of the Miraculous Mountain itself (your blue pencil, please). On enquiring he soon learned how the quiet house he had left a week ago had in the meantime been transformed into a centre of pilgrim-age. But the reason he came to me (we are quite well acquainted and have discovered a mutual friend in Dublin) was because he had found a letter left at his house in his absence by another Peace Corps Volunteer whom he had known in Rio de Janeiro and who had just passed through Tutuban on the off-chance of seeing him on her way home to America.

(8) I append a photocopy of this letter left by Sage Maclean

for Mr Brunner which he has most kindly allowed me to send you as documentary evidence. You will, Fr Xavier, be unsurprised to learn that the lady in question is black, bespectacled and has a penchant for wearing long African-style robes. You will also be amused to read the all-too-plausible explanation of the 'grey dust'. Indeed, all that remains unexplained is the children's 'heavenly music' – presumably pure imagination on their part – and the abject credulousness of their elders, who should know better.

(9) I immediately notified Sr Mittelwalder – who had meanwhile returned to San Sacramento – of this turn of events, enclosing a second photocopy of the letter.

(10) The next day, 14 June, a parishioner, Sra Marajacú, who is a near neighbour of Mr Brunner's, claimed that she had also 'seen' Our Lady on 5 June, but earlier in the day than the children. She told me she had not come forward before in case she was thought a liar who had invented it to cash in on the Irubú children's fame. She was indeed timid and confused, poor woman, but did add a detail. She made no mention of any 'precious casket' or 'heavenly music' but did say the apparition 'smelled sweeter than the sweetest flower'. Indeed, it was this intense fragrance she remembered most clearly. She also claimed the vision had spoken to her but, unfortunately for Mankind, was quite unable to remember a word. (Axe that.)

(11) Yesterday, the fifteenth, Sr Mittelwalder returned to Tutuban by military helicopter, landing close to the site of the 'apparition'. His manner was considerably changed, being altogether more brusque, even menacing. He at once demanded the original of Mr Brunner's letter. I told him truthfully that I did not have it. And then, because there was something in the man's behaviour I could not trust, I confess to having told an untruth. I said I had made only the one photocopy I had sent him whereas in point of fact Mr Brunner (who considers the whole thing a vast joke) had told me to make as many copies as I liked in order to expose the whole misunderstanding as soon as possible. (He finds the crowds which perpetually beleaguer his house extremely trying and says they stop him from sunbathing on the roof! I admit to finding him a highly sympathetic young man.) However, seeing no real

need beyond one other copy to send to you I made only the two. Between ourselves I think it important that as the secular authorities already have a copy so also should the ecclesiastical authorities, especially since a matter like this is far more our business than the military's (you had better eat this when you have finished with it). Altogether I was disturbed by Sr Mittelwalder's tone, which had become positively threatening. I was told later in the day that Mr Brunner accompanied him in the helicopter when it took off for, presumably, San Sacramento. I'm not sure I like the sound of that.

I think, dear Father, that concludes the chain of events up to yesterday. As you can see by the date, I'm getting this down on paper while still fresh in my mind because, to be honest, I have a hundred more urgent spiritual matters to attend to and do not wish to waste time later having to rack my already unreliable memory. To summarise the entire thing, then, there is a completely rational – not to say banal – explanation for the 'mysterious apparition' of Our Lady at Tutuban ten days ago. She was in fact a visiting Peace Corps Volunteer who, by the merest accident of circumstances compounded by a regrettable superstitiousness, innocently induced three ignorant peasant children to believe she was of heavenly origin whereas she is, I gather, from Texas. No fraud was ever remotely intended, and I write at this length – and enclose Miss Maclean's letter – so that your Bishop or even Cardinal Celso himself can issue the clearest possible statement and bring this episode to a swift close. Its prolongation can surely serve nobody's interests. Indeed, I cannot imagine why the military authorities have not acted so far to quash the story: they are not generally slow in suppressing local newspapers and so on. Yet in the present instance there must be dozens of people in Tutuban who saw Miss Maclean during her visit – not least the staff of her hotel – but there has been not one mention in the *Noticias de Tutuban*. Strange and sinister times we live in, indeed. Meanwhile there are pressing human needs here in Tutuban as in every barrio of the entire country and we should not allow ourselves to be side-tracked for a moment from ministering to them.

I greet you fraternally in Xto and entrust this letter to Brother Aristeo, who is returning almost immediately to Iguaçu.

IGNATIUS O'MALLEY, OSD

IV

A memorandum dictated by Ambassador Philip Kleinman later used as the basis of his report to the State Department with particular reference to the official enquiry into the death of Jack S. Brunner, a serving Peace Corps Volunteer in Parazuela:

The first I heard of this sorry business was when I was informed at eight-fifteen this morning comma June 17 that the police in Barrio Yagros comma a suburb of San Sacramento comma were holding the body of an unidentified Caucasian male believed to be a US citizen which had been found an hour earlier in an alley stop I immediately despatched John Socco er give him his full title etc. to make a preliminary identification but by the time he had arrived in Barrio Yagros the police at the precinct there claimed to have quote just found close quote an American passport in another alley approximately three blocks over from where the body was allegedly discovered stop and, Gloria, leave allegedly in, will you? er The passport was US passport number etc. dated etc. in the name of Jack initial S Brunner and from it and having inspected the body John Socco was able to make a clear preliminary identification of Mr Brunner stop, no, comma whose injuries appeared to be a single stab wound in the left lower back stop better make that injury singular At first sight, no, new para.

At first sight Mr Brunner seems to be one more victim of the brutal robberies which are endemic in this city for the pockets were cut out of his pants but there is increasing evidence to suggest he had very recently been in police custody if not under actual detention by the military without comma of course comma this Embassy having been notified stop If confirmed this would put a new angle into the whole caboodle stop can you massage that last phrase please? You know, give it the Gloria treatment er The reasons for this suspicion are as follows colon

(1) Mr Brunner was reported being escorted into a military helicopter in Tutuban comma Iguaçu province three days ago on whatever date it was stop Our informant was an Irish priest working in a parish there named O'Murphy I think but better check that stop He mentioned it in a phone

121

conversation with a priest in San Sacramento a day or so after Mr Brunner was flown out of Tutuban because he claimed that quote on reflection there was something not quite right about it since Mr Brunner had no luggage with him and had not yet returned close quote Since then we have made every effort to reach Father O'Murphy to confirm this but without success since nobody in Tutuban knows where he is stop It begins to look as though he too has quote disappeared close quote stop

(2) On learning of his allegation comma however comma strenuous representations were made yesterday from this office to General Tuig at National Integrated Police HQ and to General Mendez at Camp Gutierrez Command HQ and both denied absolutely that Mr Brunner comma or indeed any other foreign national comma was in their custody stop

(3) Approximately two hours ago I received a personal summons to visit urgently the Minister of the Interior General Edmilson from whose office I have just returned stop He expressed regret at Mr Brunner's death and informed me bluntly he had proof that Mr Brunner had been involved with an antigovernment rebel movement and was in close contact with guerrilla forces in the remote Meycauara district upriver from Tutuban where the Peace Corps Director here and the RAPCD in Iguaçu tell me Mr Brunner had personally instituted a successful fish hyphen farming project stop Needless to say I denied this allegation in the strongest possible terms and demanded substantive proof stop General Edmilson offered none whatever but claimed it was quote on its way close quote and added that there was a further suspicion that Mr Brunner had been involved in the narcotics trade stop At this point I asked the General if Mr Brunner had not also been suspected of theft comma arson comma and counter-feiting thousand hyphen peso bills and could he still assure me that in view of these suspicions and allegations Mr Brunner had never been in official custody stop I added that I now had the gravest doubts about the circumstances surrounding his death and that the US did not take lying down the murder of its innocent young Volunteers stop To support his drug hyphen running theory the General made an extraordinary circumstantial allegation based on a letter he claimed was in his possession from another Volunteer

122

he declined to identify who had seemingly come from Rio de Janeiro bringing drugs with her stop In this same letter comma the General alleged comma this quote courier unquote had written that she had come quote to scatter poison unquote comma a phrase I found opaque but which the General informed me was Brazilian underground slang for drug trafficking stop I wish it to be on record that I did not then believe a word of this nonsense and nor do I now stop New para, Gloria, please

At this time we are awaiting the autopsy report so there is not much more to add except some private speculations which comma since they come from someone who has had close dealings with Parazuela for almost seven years comma may retrospectively prove pertinent stop Good stuff, eh, Gloria? I regret to say that in the light of experience I have the gravest doubts that we ever shall learn the true reason for the unfortunate Mr Brunner's death stop It may be that he was indeed the victim of casual street violence and certainly he was found in an area of the city notorious for such crimes stop It is an area full of bars comma brothels comma and night hyphen clubs which might well be thought to have offered strong temptations to a young single man having to spend months on end in a remote country region with almost no er facilities for relaxation stop new para

However comma there are aspects of this case which lead me to suspect that Mr Brunner was deliberately killed with the sanction comma if not on the direct orders comma of high hyphen ranking military or police personnel stop If this is so comma the truth will probably never be known stop Even in democracies such things have occasionally happened and have proved enormously difficult to establish semicolon in a country like Parazuela under the present regime they are well hyphen nigh impossible to prove stop At all events the poor boy is dead and the reasons already given for his death by the police here will undoubtedly be the ones which it will be the US Government's melancholy duty to pass on to his parents stop There is absolutely no need to cause distress by advancing alternative theories which might fuel speculation about conspiracies which can never be unravelled stop new para

At this point I would like to state unequivocally and not for the first time that I do not consider Parazuela a fit country for the services of young Volunteers stop God knows the people on the ground could benefit from their presence comma but er in my opinion it is not fair to send such young comma inexperienced and highly motivated people out at large in a country which cannot offer even minimum standards of lawful protection and is wholly without the traditions and infrastructure which could support a democratic way of life stop I would now most earnestly recommend the closing down of Peace Corps operations in Parazuela stop new para

There is one further and quite probably unconnected aspect to Mr Brunner's death but which is at the very least a strange coincidence stop There are reports of a new religious cult centred on a plot of land immediately adjacent to Mr Brunner's house in Tutuban stop It is claimed that some local children saw the Virgin Mary there a fortnight or so ago stop It seems to me eminently possible that Mr Brunner maybe put some fervent believer's nose out of joint by complaining or scoffing colon he was only 24 and it should be noted that he was unafraid on all application forms and official declarations to give his religious status as quote atheist unquote stop The religious er sensitivities of the Parazuelans are considerable and deep hyphen running comma whether they are Catholic or charismatic or just plain superstitious stop It seems to me that youngsters coming from a culture which is to say the least often pretty sceptical about such things ought to be better briefed about how easy it can be for them unwittingly to give offence stop new para Sorry, Gloria, it's getting a bit long, I know, but I've hit a vein. Don't worry, we're nearly through. New para or did I say that?

If there does turn out to be a quote religious angle unquote to this unhappy affair we can rest assured that the Parazuelan Church hierarchy will experience little reluctance in siding with the military and supporting whatever line is chosen by the Generalissimo providing it is not too outrageously compromising stop Church links with the Government comma especially at the level of Cardinal Celso comma are extremely ramified as I believe I made clear in my Confidential Report entitled whatever and dated whenever stop Since that report was written links have been still further strengthened by the founding of the caps Gloria PFCTP colon the Christian Family comma Tradition comma and Property Party stop new para

A private footnote colon it would in my view be a miracle if against this background we as foreigners in Parazuela can ever unravel the truth in all this but I have just been assured by the Embassy Chaplain comma a man whose tongue is never knowingly in his cheek comma that the age of miracles is not yet past stop That's it, Gloria. Print it. And, oh, I'll liberate some embassy wine for our dinner tonight: I'm sure as dammit not drinking that Barrio Plonk again.

V

Transcript of extracts from a Global Probe *television documentary entitled* Sister Pia: Saint, Hoaxer or Dupe? *transmitted worldwide on 5 June 2025:*

PRESENTER: Parazuela. A hillside outside the bustling provincial town of Tutuban.

On this very spot exactly forty years ago three little sisters had an experience which lasted a mere ten seconds but whose echoes simply won't die down even today.

For what those little girls claimed was that on the evening of 5 June 1985 they saw a vision of the Virgin Mary, who was the mother of Jesus Christ the prophet.

Almost from that moment Tutuban . . . Parazuela . . . even the Christian world itself was sharply divided between those who believed in the vision and those who could not.

And almost from that moment the miracles – as many claimed they were – began.

Within a week of that fateful evening this place had become the destination of the first of countless thousands of pilgrims who began flocking here to worship and seek cures. Pilgrims who, to this day, still flock in undiminished numbers. For let us make no mistake: Tutuban is today the centre of a vast pilgrimage industry.

It is Latin America's answer to Lourdes in France.

It is perhaps too easy to look at these hotels . . . at

these restaurants . . . souvenir shops . . . fleets of buses at the bus station and rows of aircraft at the airport . . . in short at all the evident signs of prosperity glittering among the poverty like gold in a rotten tooth.

Too easy to look at it all and think only of the enormous wealth which has undoubtedly been generated in four decades largely on the word of three illiterate Indian children. We should look also at these hostels for the pilgrims . . . at Tutuban's impressive hospital with one of the most advanced psycho-surgery units in Latin America . . . and at the pilgrims themselves.

Often poor, many have walked to Tutuban from hundreds of kilometres away.

We should look, too, at these literally hundreds of thousands of testimonials of miraculous cures, many attested by independent medical opinion, and at these countless votive notes of thanks to the Virgin for spiritual and physical help. . . .

You will never convince Ms Josefina Kaspar that she was the victim of some cynical racket.

This is how she looked eleven years ago when, as thirteen-year-old Josefina Suarez, she made the pilgrimage to Tutuban. Paralysed from the chest down in a street accident at the age of five she was pushed in her wheelchair across the Andes from her home town of Santiago by her father, himself a sufferer from a heart condition. . . .

So. Big business or a uniquely miraculous source of help?

Well, maybe somewhere in between.

It is a familiar story: at Lourdes . . . at Fatima . . . at Guadelupe. But there is something about the Madonna of Parazuela which makes her different from the others.

A unique mystery surrounds her.

Indeed, from the very first a key question-mark hung over her. Let us go back forty years to that evening.

This imposing shrine which can seat three thousand

pilgrims was not here then, of course.

In those days this was a simple bare hillside.

It was here that Milagros, Nimfa and Rosario Irubú were picking flowers when they had their vision.

Every effort was made to fault their story but despite countless separate questionings it stood up in every detail.

And this great picture hanging above the Grotto itself was painted under the children's direction so as to be an exact likeness of the vision they claimed to have seen.

A dark-skinned lady wearing old-fashioned spectacles, some sort of twentieth-century version of today's moon-shift, and holding a jewelled box.

In close-up here we can see the box is full of a grey powder and there is a pinch of this between the lady's two fingers. We shall be coming back to this detail later.

An unusual vision, perhaps.

Certainly unexpected in that it did not conform to any Catholic images which the children would have been familiar with.

And ever since that day there have been rumours.

These rumours have said that this picture, far from representing a supernatural manifestation, is the portrait of a real person whom the children saw and merely mistook for the Virgin Mary. If this could ever be proved it would have shattering consequences.

And from this first mystery a second one hangs.

Why didn't the investigators of the Church make more effort at the time to determine the true facts?

And might this failure have something to do with the military government of the day?

A good question.

To understand the labyrinthine relationship between Church and State in Parazuela forty years ago we will need a brief explanation of the nature of Parazuelan politics then.

Today's social-democratic administration is an incredible twenty-seven governments removed from that military dictatorship in power in 1985.

In those days the Roman Catholic Church was still a very powerful institution in terms of influencing the way ordinary people thought.

But the secular power of the military was even greater in terms of the everyday control of life in Parazuela.

Throughout the 1970s Church and State had been squaring off for a fight . . . and by 1985 State had won.

The military could never have abolished the Church in Parazuela and nor would it have wanted to.

It merely needed to ensure the support of the more important of the Church's leaders.

Such as Cardinal Celso, Archbishop of San Sacramento and effectively the head of the Church in Parazuela.

A man whose weakness for rubber sex made him uniquely vulnerable to blackmail.

Among officers in the Government who were directly involved, Generals Manolo Edmilson and Fernando Preciosa played a key role in. . . .

Global Probe has managed to reconstruct some of the major events that fateful June of so long ago and, against the background of the leading dramatis personae we have just been introduced to, can now present a diary which is probably as close to what really happened as anyone can ever get.

One problem, of course, is that nearly all the people directly involved are dead.

But *Global Probe* investigators have finally managed to trace a lady living in Australasia who may have the key to the entire mystery.

She is Ms Ruth Tressell and her claim is a startling one.

According to her, the story begins in Rio de Janeiro where she was a community service volunteer from 1984 to 1986.

One of the other volunteers at the time, and a close friend of hers, was a certain American girl named Sage Maclean, who, in mid-1985. . . .

Why did Ruth not come forward at the time despite suspicions aroused by the first letter she had received from Sage Maclean and then the international press coverage of the story?

More important, why did neither she nor Sage Maclean come forward later, after extensive correspondence between them in, respectively, Rio and Texas?

RUTH
TRESSELL: Look, you've got to remember we were practically kids then and the whole thing struck us initially as too crazy.

I really forget the sequence of events now but I do remember Sage and I were badly shaken by the news of Jack Brunner's death, and as there didn't seem to be any connection between the two stories the more personally urgent one took precedence.

Then not long after she got back to the States poor Sage learned that she was pretty sick and that she might not make it, you know?

I think they gave her up to a year to live, but she didn't last that long.

I swear it was Brazil that killed her; just one bout of hepatitis too many, they said.

That, too, tended to push the whole Tutuban Virgin story on to the sidelines as far as we all were concerned.

After Sage did die I remember looking around and thinking, well, there's really only you left of the old gang, Ruthie, and look what happened to everyone else.

And, besides, have you ever tried standing up in public suspiciously late in the day to pour cold water on a religious story that plenty of respectable people were accepting and which by then was becoming an industry?

Me, a single girl, going on national TV to talk about conspiracy theories and in effect calling three kids liars who by then were practically little saints?

No way.

I'd lost two good friends and I was sick of the whole thing. And, God, you know those drug allegations about Jack Brunner? Some of that shit stuck and it was absolute lies from start to finish.

I don't know where that story came from.

Jack was never into that and in that respect he . . .
he was Mr Clean. I think it was that which really
broke up his family.

But I'm glad it's all coming out now.

We none of us live for ever and I'm happy not to
have to . . . well, die with the story untold.

PRESENTER: More and more the evidence seems to be indicating
that there was a massive cover-up by the military
government of the day, aided and abetted by senior
Church officials.

Three people could perhaps have cleared up the
mystery once and for all but two are known to be
dead and the third presumed to be.

Jack S. Brunner. Murdered on the night of 16 June
1985.

Sage Maclean. Died January 1986 of a liver disease
almost certainly contracted during her service in
Brazil.

Foul play is not suspected.

And the Irish priest, Father Ignatius O'Malley.
Disappeared on that same 16 June aged forty-four.
Never seen again.

Foul play very strongly suspected.

So we have to rely on the cover-up theory to explain
certain otherwise inexplicable things.

First, how was it that nobody else came forward to
suggest that Sage Maclean had been mistaken for
the Madonna?

She must have been seen by dozens of people both
in San Sacramento and Tutuban during her short
visit.

Only the military had the sort of power which could
have prevented their voices being heard.

And, secondly, why a cover-up at all?

What was in it for the military government to have
an American girl mistaken for the Virgin Mary?

It is only a theory, but many people nowadays,
Global Probe among them, think it was a shrewd
piece of psychology on the part of the Generals.

130

A sudden interest in a non-political, supernatural event gripping the imagination of the common people of Parazuela could divert their attention away from their very real grievances and make them that much more docile.

Dr Zeke Chaffee is Professor of Humanist Psychology at MIT. . . .

Our story almost ends there.

Almost, but not quite.

For there *is* one other survivor of those fateful events, perhaps in her way the most important of all.

This is the Convent of Our Lady of Perpetual Help, Tutuban.

And this nun quietly embroidering in the peace of its secluded garden, far removed from the hubbub of pilgrimage for which she was directly responsible, is Sister Pia, born Nimfa Irubú.

For she is the last of the three sisters who saw the vision still alive.

She has never left this convent since the day she entered its doors at the age of twelve.

Still only fifty-two, she looks a good deal older.

For even the reclusive world of the nun is not untouched by controversy.

Sister Pia is by far the most famous nun in Parazuela, probably in the whole of Latin America.

But this very fame, unsought though it may be, has inevitably brought with it the rumours, the gossip, the doubts.

It is an open secret that even some other members of her Sisterhood privately question her popular status as the Convent's visionary and bitterly resent her celebrity.

In terms of fame she easily outranks her own Mother Superior, whose position she has never coveted.

The rumours persist that she was the innocent victim of her own youthfulness and gullibility.

But Sister Pia herself has never had a moment's doubt.

131

She remains supremely convinced that on that evening forty years ago she and her two little sisters were granted a glimpse of heaven on earth.

And the Madonna she saw – unconventional in appearance though she might have been – lives on in Sister Pia's memory as a person more real and more vivid than those who have surrounded her ever since.

She has seen photographs of Sage Maclean but has always maintained that the young volunteer looked nothing like the person – or vision – she originally saw.

Today Sister Pia devotes her time to prayer and embroidery.

She declined to speak to a *Global Probe* investigator since all verbal contact is forbidden to her Order, although they talk freely among themselves.

However, in a reply to written questions we submitted through her Mother Superior she stated that she is perfectly well aware of the rumours concerning the validity of her claims.

She insists that all such reports casting doubt on her vision of Our Lady were originally manufactured by the corrupt military regime of the day in their unceasing and often brutal campaign against the spiritual values of the Church.

Viewers of this documentary may well feel by now that such a view is at best simplistic. . . .

The question has sometimes been asked: 'Is Sister Pia a saint?'

It is something she herself has always emphatically denied.

The Roman Catholic Church certainly doesn't recognise her as one since she has not yet even been beatified, itself a necessary first step for full canon- isation, or sainthood.

Nowadays the Church's rules governing beatifica- tion are so strict as to make becoming a modern saint virtually impossible.

Indeed, Cardinal Nutzbaum of New York recently remarked that if Jesus Christ himself were to reappear on earth he might not even qualify.

So once again we ask the question:
Sister Pia: Saint? Hoaxer? Or Dupe?
Global Probe believes it has put forward enough facts
for open-minded viewers to be able to form their
own judgement.
But perhaps in all fairness the last word should go
to Sister Pia herself, expressed in the earthy
imagery of her own Indian origins:
'The proof of the boat-making is in the floating,' she
says.
'Are there or are there not miracles here in
Tutuban?
'Do not the incurably sick take up their beds and
walk?
'Do not the lame run, the afflicted smile again?
'Have not a million hearts been filled these last forty
years with that supreme happiness which is the
special gift of Our Lady of Tears?'

ENDS

The Hidden Life

When you are 'something in the City' – and more especially when you are some*one* – you become sad as you get older. Very likely people everywhere become sadder, but I wouldn't know about them; I can only speak for myself and for certain of my close contemporaries. We are a select few among that great army which used to be mocked as 'the pinstripe brigade' whose regular commutings were the butt of every *Punch* humourist who, because he worked from home in a polo-necked sweater and didn't have to shave every morning, flattered himself that he was somehow less trammelled by the conventions of society. I should like to say, *en passant*, that some of the most conventionally minded people I have ever met have been professional satirists.

I have often wondered why we become sad, but of course we never discuss it. Everything is conveyed by looks, by glances, by an eyebrow scrupulously raised across a table, by an acknowledged *coup d'œil* from the other side of a railway carriage. I believe it has partly to do with the irony of our position. Here we are, the most conventional of social animals (if the humourists are to be believed), simultaneously being bulwarks, repositories of confidence, sustainers of traditional values as well as (if our company propaganda is to be believed) thrusting, innovative and forward-looking. I cannot think of a description in which I recognise less of myself and my few friends than in that piece of executive blarney; it alone would be grounds for melancholy. But there are plenty of other grounds, too, most of which in combination form a thousandfold treason. Treason here, betrayal there. For how can any of us pretend that what we think of and love as England and English values are nowadays comprehended to the least degree either by the work we do or – to put it bluntly – by the new class we have to do it with? Something has been let slip for ever; some quality is irretrievably gone, and it has to do with the heart.

Ah, you think we're grieving fuddy-duddies, we of the 7:42 from Sevenoaks? But, good heavens, we know about deficit financing and I don't believe a single one of us cares a hoot despite having been brought up with that firm admonishment ringing in our ears: *Neither a borrower nor a lender be*. We also, believe it or not, know about computers. I myself use a desk-top micro every working day, and very boring it is, too, but I can *use* it perfectly fluently. The other morning one of the junior partners – a bright youngster, incidentally, an agreeable but to me uninteresting representative of the new breed – let on that when he went home at night he and all three of his children played computer games together. And this stopped me in my tracks because it suddenly crystallised what had changed. It was that for this young man life had become seamless. All day long in the City he sat at his desk and used a computer and then in the evening he returned to Beckenham or Petts Wood and went on using a computer.

Why not? you ask. Why ever not? No reason, of course; I and my friends can only fall silent. There is no *reason* why not, except that of desire. When we were younger one of the piquant pleasures of life was the great gulf fixed between work and play. Going to work in the City every day was absolutely unreal, for all that there were occasional episodes of pleasure and pain. (In this respect it was very much like school.) Eight hours of formal unreality earned you an immediate holiday in the shape of twelve hours of informal reality. Once back home and out of the suit and into some comfortable old cords or tweeds all lingering thoughts of the office and the recent swift passage through suburbia dissolved in the open fields and woods. A walk with the dog along the river-bank to watch I don't know what, the black gyres of mayflies above the crinkling water, the moorhens come and go in the rushes, the cows switching their tassels in the evening light while from way beyond the woods the parish bells drone faintly in waves as if beneath the setting sun a great door were being opened and closed. That was real, no doubt about it; that was the England of my childhood where one could still – if one listened very attentively – hear the piper at the gates of dawn.

But now? Well, not only has suburbia spread like a cancer across the face of southern England, making it almost impossible to see an honest field with an honest cow in it much inside an hour's travelling time, but that blissful idea of the two lives – the *hidden* life – has gone as well. Nowadays I gather that most of my younger colleagues take work home with them for the evening and even for the weekends, and in consequence their faces look as featureless as the screens into which they gaze all their working lives: mere blank surfaces across which flit the endless columns of glowing figures, adding up and multiplying and adding up to nothing.

For when I described the work we do in the City as unreal I was being entirely accurate. All that rhetoric about harsh realities and fingers on the world's commercial pulse betrays a communal fantasy of extraordinary proportions. What on earth are we to think when serious, clean-shaven young men in suits are described as 'eager to meet fresh challenges'? Why, that they are figments trapped somewhere between Arthurian legend and Evensong, sharpening up their attacking slogans before spearheading an assault on traditional product strongholds while always striving for the highest prize. And now not even the money we deal in is real. How well I know the fictions of 'creative accountancy'; how familiar the hypnosis of those flickering electronic figures. Not a banknote to be seen anywhere! How chimerical the wealth which translates into Rolls-Royces and military hardware! I am glad now to be nearing retirement. I shall not be sorry to leave this Disneyland which, for all that it is a filigree world of ever-dissolving castles and turrets, leaves on the air a taint which is solider far than itself.

This must be so, and it must be starting to contaminate me since the other night – I'm not sure if I should tell this because it may be yet another betrayal – I had a dream, an appalling dream as it happens although there were no monsters or anything conventional of that sort. Its dreadfulness resided entirely in an atmosphere which was of terror and melancholy. Not easy to imagine, I grant you; but easier perhaps if I say that the terror was more a panic not unlike those at school which kept one awake thinking of the imminence of an examination, incredulity

136

mixed with self-upbraiding for having let things get to this point, while the melancholy (which would not have been possible then) came from knowing that in a million years one could not have done any differently. Anyway, the dream was of an unidentifiable voice and what it said was: 'Imagine that at the instant of death you were told, *Well, Tom old boy, that's it. Very short and never again. What do you remember of it? What's the first – and last – image in your brain, the legacy of it all?* So, what is it?'

Of course I knew what I wanted to say. I wanted to offer up a memory of a special place by the river, or how the sun looks on a moving cornfield, or rooks roosting up in elms, one of those ordinary moments which leave one without thought or speech. I wanted to offer up my poor boy Adrian before he became ravaged by his last attack, bouncing round the paddock on Minefield in the sunlight, as lost in timeless pleasure as any other twelve-year-old on his new pony. But nothing would come. I could not form a single image. Everything gave way before a clear view and I was forced to speak the truth.

'A corridor, that's what I see. There's a water-cooler halfway along. I . . . I don't know where I am, an office, a hotel, a government department, a hospital. Everything's beige. The floor's beige, the walls are beige, I'm walking along behind three men in beige suits and with beige hair. Even their aftershave smells beige. And there are beige sorts of office sounds coming from behind the doors we pass. The corridor is without end.'

'Is it like anywhere you recognise?' the voice asked recedingly.

'Yes, it is exactly like anywhere,' I heard myself say. 'It's like everywhere in particular.' And then I woke up weeping and weeping, although I know how silly it sounds especially after so banal and null a conversation. But, as I said, it was the atmosphere far more than the words; that and the blank enigmatic backs of the three men.

Well, it's hardly news that we shall all be swept away. Yet the unspoken sadness I share with my friends in the City, what we read in each other's eyes, is something more than that knowledge alone. It concerns, I think, a loss of more than mere self. Certainly the closer the great erasing broom approaches each of us the more it seems to me I should do my remaining year or two in the City with great good humour and an absent mind, for inside I am immortally nine or ten and buried in summer grass among orange tips and clouded yellows and red

137

admirals. I may say it is becoming easier all the time: not only do the years of practice help but so does sheer age itself. We senior partners do not spend much of each week in the office, and if one no longer has to commute daily one can afford to live in ever remoter shires.

Of course we live nowhere near Sevenoaks – that was a satirical example. As a matter of fact we live in another direction entirely and a good deal further from the City. An odd thing is how close-knit we are, geographically speaking, and this without our ever having planned it. Some mysterious gravity has drawn us together in this region – and draws us still, as I discovered this morning. I had woken in the river-bank and was watching the stately skid of water, its dimplings reflected on the low ceiling. I cannot tell you the happiness of eating toast and marmalade while watching a grebe, its feathers aflame in the early sunlight, pass the window on a level with your eyes, its feet working busily across the glass. I walked over to look at it more closely and the movement must have caught its eye, for it stopped abruptly and jerked its head round. What must it have thought, expecting to see muddy river-bank and finding instead a sheet of glass through which it could see into a large room with a man standing considerably below the river-bed and eating toast and marmalade? Off it sailed, not completely startled, into the morning brightness, and I went up the steps to join it. Despite the most ingenious (not to say costly) lighting, insulation and damp-proofing my river-bank den which is so cosy at night or in overcast weather becomes slightly gloomy and chill when the sun is shining outside. So up I went and emerged in the bushes which conceal the entrance.

In the distance across two fields I could see the kitchen corner of the house where Mrs Simmonds the housekeeper was no doubt eating her own breakfast, and nearby the paddock where so often over the years I have seen a boy on his pony in the long evening light, for he rides there still. But what took my attention was the sudden coming to life of a chainsaw from the corner of Rokesy Wood nearest my little estate, and I remembered having heard sounds of activity there for some days now, sounds which reminded me that I was reputed to have a new neighbour but which had not been enough to overcome my natural uninquisitiveness. But a chainsaw was a different matter: who knew what monstrous damage might be casually inflicted by a new

138

owner chastising his woods for becoming so overgrown? As it turned out, though, I need not have worried.

I crossed in the skiff and moored up under the great willow, conscious that I was now in enemy territory, then walked up the tufted meadow strung with webs still glittering with dew to the nearest corner of the wood. With schoolboy stealth I crept from tree to tree under cover of the saw's awful howling and moaning which now had a muffled quality. From behind a stout beech I could watch the scene of operations from within a matter of yards. There was a massive oak I had often admired, not particularly tall but bulbous with age and, alas, with scarcely a sprig of green left as evidence of the thready seasonal beat of its thousand-year-old heart. At its base it could not have been much less than ten feet in diameter and there, almost at ground level, someone had cut a neat narrow hole. In this opening was visible a pair of legs as the sawyer inside carved away with his bellowing blade. After a bit the noise stopped abruptly; there came a muffled exclamation and the man emerged stoopingly, spitting, his hair sprinkled with white chips. By then I, too, had broken cover and he caught sight of me with a start as I stepped forward.

'Forgive the intrusion,' I said, 'but I'm your neighbour, Tom. I heard you at work and thought I'd come over and introduce myself. Magnificent tree, that.'

'Isn't it? Name's Colin. You must think me an appalling vandal, taking this stinking machine' – he kicked the stopped saw, which was gurgling to itself like a kettle on a hob – 'to a grand old oak. But I'm sure you've noticed the poor thing's practically dead and I wanted to get at it before it rots. In fact the heartwood's virtually dry already. Come and see.'

Inside was a freshly hewn cell still barely large enough for one man to crouch in. It smelled deliciously of autumn in there. A thousand years of England enfolded me in a redolent cocoon; I was incorporated into its heart.

'It's coming along,' I said. 'You're Wol, of course.'

'Of course.'

We had recognised each other instantly – the eyes as usual – and I could feel the surge of pleasure which comes from knowing one's world is not after all going to be intruded upon by an outsider. Colin was one of us. 'Who are you with? Or are you retired?'

'Durrant Anderson. No, I've got a few more years in harness. You?'

139

'Mence Gibb. But let's not think about all that. When you've done your stint come over for a beer or something. Go straight down to the river and give me a shout from the willows. I'll hear and fetch you across.'

'About an hour, I should think,' said Colin, picking up the chainsaw. 'That's about as much as I can stand, what with the noise and the smell. Still, it's sweet work.'

'Of course it is. A lifetime aim.'

'Exactly that.'

I was all ready for him when I heard his hail from across the river. I whisked him over in the skiff and was pleased and surprised he did not spot the sheet of glass let into the river-bank, although it is true that since it extends below the surface and is somewhat browed with grasses (plus the fact that I took elaborate pains to set it unobtrusively) a casual observer might easily miss it. But when I ushered him into the clump of whitethorn to the little entrance he understood at once.

'Ratty!' he exclaimed with pleasure. He went down. 'Oh, it's perfect.'

And, though I say it myself, it *is* perfect. One descends the steps and there beneath the river-bank is a snuggery with twin chintz-covered armchairs drawn up before the grate, shelves full of books and objects, the waxed table gleaming in the reflected light of the river. Nothing very valuable, you understand – at least, not in market-place terms – but comfortable and well worn. The slipping river held back by glass and forming the fourth wall would alone be enough to show that one was embedded in England, but even in winter with the curtains to and the firelight twinkling merrily on china and glasses of port one would scarcely be in doubt. Perhaps only in that single corner of the room devoted to Adrian may there be a sense of melancholy but definitely not of gloom. Beneath several pictures of him from babyhood almost to the month of his death are certain keepsakes most emphatically not laid out as if in a hallowed museum but merely left as if tidied away for his return at evening: a pair of scuffed Clark's sandals with rose-window air-holes cut in the toes, an old Aertex shirt, a grey sun-bonnet, a cricket bat. Here, at least for as long as I myself survive, he will always be, galloping endlessly across the vivid meadows on Minefield while poor Frances wrings her hands with maternal impotence. 'Tom, Tom,' I hear her say, 'it *cannot* be safe to let him out on that pony without a hat.' Poor Fran, how her worries echo vainly across all those years.

Meanwhile Colin was repeating how perfect it was. I poured him a glass of beer and we stood by the window watching the water boatmen scud in the dazzle.

'I feel at home here,' he said. 'I'm glad I came.

'You're among friends now,' I told him. 'We've quite a community in these parts; we must get a little party up and introduce you. Durrant Anderson, did you say? I wonder if there's anyone here you'd know already. Sir Arthur Cramphorn of Schwolb's?'

'Certainly I've met him, although I don't know him at all well.'

'He's a bit staid but as loyal a friend as you could hope to meet. He's Badger: owns Yesterham Hall but lives in what he calls his sett about a mile from here. Who else have we got? Oh, of course, there's Little Grey Rabbit. That's Caroline Parry-Savage.'

'Not with HPD?'

'Yes, do you know her?'

'Absolutely. I was over at Harkness Pithers & Drew not six weeks ago for a meeting. She's senior investment analyst there now, as I recall.'

'The very same.' We raised our glasses.

'I'll tell you what,' said Colin, 'if you can muster the people I'll throw a house-warming for us all when I've finished my hidey-hole. How's that?'

'Won't it be a bit cramped?'

'Oh dear, I suppose it will. Funny, I never thought. One's so used to seeing Wol in his parlour with dressers and grandfather clocks and what not it's hard to remember that, well, one's *scale* is a bit different now.'

'Never mind. We'll pay you a visit and then we can all come back here. My experience tells me we might need a bit of floor-space. Little Grey Rabbit's apt to bounce a bit when she gets some cowslip wine down her. But you know how rabbits are.'

In point of fact it took almost a month to fix up the party, owing to Badger's gout, by which time Wol had finished his nest. One day the sounds of hammering from the hanging woods across the river ceased and the next I skiffed across and made my way up towards his tree. I did it quietly in order that I might withdraw without being noticed, for that particular moment when at last one can return unhindered to a private

141

reality is very precious and cannot be shared. And so it was that, standing in the lee of the beech, I could see the front door of the oak was shut. How beautifully he had made it, I thought in admiration. Colin had clearly been to immense pains to cut it as true as possible, for the curved outer section he had removed and hinged now closed so snugly into its massive frame that one needed to look twice in order to see it. Searching for windows I found still more cause for admiration. Instead of merely hacking rectangles he had made apertures at points where there had been the involuted scars of long-vanished boughs, retaining their original irregular ovoid or circular outlines. They had been glazed, but one at least could be opened, for framed in the topmost window I caught a glimpse of Wol's face, fixed in a silent broodingness, staring out of his eyrie into the light-patterned trunks and glades with which he had surrounded himself. It was not a moment for intrusion; I turned and crept away down the hill to my own river-bank.

So there we are: another one of us has found his way unerringly here to this enchanted place. Tonight is the night of the party, and if previous occasions are anything to go by it will be merry and bonhomous. For, necessary as our private isolations sometimes are among the rivers and fields and woods, we are very much at our best in each other's company. Then those silent messages sent flashing across the fairyland of Cheapside, Poultry and Cannon Street find at last their proper expression in the only true reality which is companionship. And then what tales are told far into the night! What strange rites and goings-on there are among the night creatures of these distant shires! It is as if long-lost nurseries came alive again, and I know that even the solitary brooder in his oak-tree will tonight spread his wings underground with us. So happily, sadly, swiftly the time will pass until suddenly the stars are paler in the sky and the dawn wind springs up and it is time to say goodbye. As the river gurgles and the drowsy farewells of the parting guests die away along their separate paths through field and thicket, the strengthening light is enough to reveal the marks crushed into the dew by our feet, little animal prints which will remain in the dabbled grass until the sun rises to bake them away!

Monkey Tricks

Not so long after dawn Jhonny and Siyo were sitting by the stream watching the preparations rather than overseeing them, Jhonny more intent on his feelings of quiet satisfaction and his friend slightly stupefied by the day's getting under way, still loggy after the previous evening's drinking. The stream at this point meandered uncertainly about in its bed as if without a downpour somewhere behind it in the forests of the interior it had no idea how best to flow in the overlarge space it found itself in. It gurgled around the boulders where the women came to spank the dirt out of the laundry and pooled beneath the eroded bank of the bend opposite. In this wallow under the low earth cliff threaded with exposed roots a buffalo lay with its chin resting on the water. Various insects skittered around its muzzle, their feet making swift dimples on the surface. For a long minute a small pink and black bird perched on the end of one of its horns.

'My head aches,' said Siyo.

'You were drunk last night. Rum and beer. There weren't really enough snacks, were there? It's very bad for you, drinking without eating. Plenty of food today, though.'

'*And* drink. That's the best thing about birthdays. If they're properly organised, you can forget it means one year nearer the grave.'

'Hush,' said Jhonny automatically. 'I prefer to think of my eldest son as twenty-one rather than . . . well, he's twenty-one.

143

He's not really any *older* yet.'

'Of course not. But Boyet's certainly turned into a fine young man. And that's taken time,' he added somewhat to himself.

The heat was rising with the sun. Behind them Jhonny's dog Tiger lay on a bench, wheezing. His feet were tied, likewise his muzzle. Blood from his expertly cut neck was being caught in a plastic basin. A circle of onlookers, mostly children, watched his waning arterial spurts with interest. A little way off between two closely growing palms a couple of young men had built an unlit fire of dried fronds. Jhonny half-turned, cast an appraising glance over the scene and, satisfied that matters were properly in hand, turned back to where a large and brilliant butterfly with transparent hind wings was drifting about the buffalo's head.

'I hope he comes after all this,' said Jhonny presently.

'Of course he will. Didn't he send a telegram? Where else would he go on his twenty-first birthday?'

'The launch might not sail.'

'The sea's flat calm; I looked from the hill this morning.'

'It might have broken,' persisted Jhonny. 'It often does. I was talking to an engineer the other day who'd just made the trip and he'd looked into the engine-room. He says the motor's over twenty years old.' He picked up a couple of longish sticks from the ground, examined them, threw one into the stream, unsheathed his knife with which he peeled the remaining stick before whittling one end into a blunt taper.

'You're beginning to sound as if you don't want Boyet to come,' said Siyo.

'And you?'

'Oh, Jhonny, you know that's untrue. Apart from anything else he's my godson, isn't he? How could you say such a thing?'

'Joke only,' Jhonny said. 'Joke only.' But already it seemed a ruffle had passed over the day which was so beautifully dawning. On this subject he managed to abolish most of his own thoughts while retaining a dully sensitive recognition that people were ambivalent about Boyet and always had been. He was not like his siblings – some bright, a couple frankly dumb, but all of them equable, biddable, sunny even. But from the outset Boyet had evinced a certain querulousness, a pettishness in addition to being so *argumentative*. No one denied him his brains – or much else, for that matter – but he had always acted as if people *were* constantly denying him things which were his as of right. The slight unease his father felt when thinking about him was caused partly by a fear of the scenes Boyet had always been good at making and partly by a lingering doubt as to whether he really had perhaps denied the boy something even though he couldn't imagine what it might reasonably be. Was Boyet not at this moment attending the country's oldest and best university? And had not the entire family gone without in order that they might afford the tuition fees?

He turned back to the activity behind him, freshly peeled stick gleaming in his hand like a wand. Tiger's bonds had been cut and the dog now lay limply on the bench, eyes half-closed and with one of his thigh muscles twitching. He looked as he often had asleep and dreaming in the sun. The young men took a back leg apiece and carried the drained carcase to where the fire was laid. They tied a leg to each tree so that the dog's head hung to within a foot of the brushwood. A red and pink drool of blood, mucus and serum descended slowly from the tip of his black nose. One of his legs was still twitching, and the drool swung a little as it lengthened. A match was put to the fire and flames leaped up, engulfing Tiger's head. There was a violent spasm of the hind legs.

'Dead now,' said one of the young men. Tiger's fur flared to a crisp. As soon as it had all been burned off they cut the dog down and carried it to the river. The brief flames had seared the flesh enough to stiffen the limbs, which now stuck out aggressively in black prongs. They dumped the body in the water at the feet of Jhonny and Siyo and began scraping away at the frizzle with their knives. With surprising ease a bright white and bald Tiger began to emerge from the case of char which crumbled away and was whirled off downstream, taking with it a pungent fume of smithies.

'Quite fat,' observed Siyo. 'That's a decent young dog you've got there. He'll be juicy, all right.'

'He certainly ate enough rice over the last month,' said Jhonny. 'You should have heard the wife complaining; said it ought to go to the pigs instead. But it's not every day your eldest son has his twenty-first, is it? And, besides, the animal was greedy. He was always stealing food.'

When Tiger's body was clean his head was cut off and skinned and placed on a rock in the stream. His eyes bulged out at what was being done to the rest of him, grey tongue protruding through a snarl. It delighted the children who with twigs investigated the gristly holes leading into the skull and through which, not half an hour earlier, he had heard the summons to attend his own demise. Had they been so inclined, everybody present could have formed an accurate mental picture of Tiger trotting round the corner of Jhonny's house after beginning this day, like any other, with a brisk chase through the undergrowth of the dozier chickens, the tips of his ears flapping. Until that moment he had been incorrigible, and quite a lot of trussing had gone on before he realised this was not a game.

Meanwhile his paunch had been opened and his entrails were being sorted in the stream. There was practically nothing other than the gall-bladder (carefully separated in its greenish pouch from its nest in the liver) which could not be eaten by someone or something. Even the pigs would eat the contents of his bowel given the chance, but Jhonny had moved to squat ankle-deep in the water and was gathering up the yellow and white mass. He took a length of it, expressed Tiger's last supper into the stream and inserted the tapered stick he had been whittling into one end. When it lodged he went on pushing gently so that the end of the intestine began turning inwards. Easing it with his other hand, he rolled the length inside out, washed it carefully and deftly peeled off the now outermost membrane which he discarded. On the bank the large aluminium washing-bowl of Tiger's constituent parts began filling up.

By the time the rinsed and jointed carcase had joined them Jhonny was again apprehensive about Boyet's non-appearance.

'Stop worrying,' Siyo told him. 'Have a glass of beer or something. The damned dog isn't even cooked yet.'

'So what? Since when did all the food have to be prepared before one's own son returns home? This isn't a wedding.'

'All right,' said Siyo pacifically and then, hoping for distraction, asked: 'Have you done the chickens?'

'*No.*' It was so gruff as to be a kind of expletive, then 'No,' he said again in a different tone as thought overtook mood, 'no, that's a point, I haven't. We'd better do those. Two'll be enough, don't you think? Or three. Better make it three, be on the safe side.'

The chickens proved difficult to catch. Normally there were at least a couple scratching round the earth floor of the kitchen which could be cornered between the firewood and the low bamboo palisade beneath the fire-pots. Today there was not a hen in the house, probably the result of that damned dog chivvying them around; another good reason for eating the beast, Jhonny thought crossly as he set about looking for some light cord. He searched a shelf up under the roof which held among other things two defunct batteries, a carton of 'Beatles Hair Pomade' containing fish-hooks, a green plastic bottle of rubbing alcohol and some nylon thread for repairing nets. He found the cord tucked into the roof between bamboo and thatch and made a running knot in one end. He laid this noose, about half a yard in diameter, on the ground outside the house and lightly disguised its outline with a few pebbles and bits of stick. Then he scattered some rice around it but mainly inside it, took up the end of the rope and retreated into the house, squinting through a chink in the thatched wall. The house was full of women cutting up vegetables. Above the general hubbub he called to Siyo: 'Could you just check on the water? There's probably enough but it may need hotting up again.'

'Do you remember Dong's son coming back after his graduation?' one of the women was saying. 'Now, that was a party.'

Somehow this depressed Jhonny. He did indeed remember: the boy had done it in style, arriving in a crimson jeep full of rowdy friends and hospitality girls with stereo cassette music and two whole cases of whisky. That was how it should be done, apparently; fattish young men with chunky fraternity rings throwing up over the banana seedlings. Everybody in the village had said what a memorable occasion that had been, not least because there had been enough whisky for everyone to get drunk, the children included. That had been quite funny, it was true, with a great boiling-pan full of Coca-Cola and whisky into which they had gone on dipping their glasses. As the day wore on the house and yard had become littered with the bodies of sleeping kids who simply lay where they fell until various raucous mothers dragged them together and laid them all out in a long line, their heads resting on a mushy banana-bole. How people had laughed! And how deathly quiet the village had been next day, except for the cursing whenever a dog barked or a cock crew. . . . He jerked the rope and snared a flapping chicken by one leg, sending its companions running off in alarm. Well, this wasn't going to be like that party. It was just a twenty-first, anyway, not a graduation. But he couldn't deny that on the strength of his son's rare visits over the last three years it was difficult to see him in a crimson jeep with hospitality girls. Jhonny shook his head as he bound the squawking bird's

147

feet with a stray piece of sisal. There was something wrong, but he couldn't figure out what.

It took twenty minutes and more rice than he cared to think about to get all three chickens lying side by side on the kitchen table. Jhonny looked them over critically: not fat, maybe, but by no means scrawny. In the market they'd fetch. . . . He suppressed this line of speculation. What did it matter what they were worth? This was family; one did not begrudge family. Still, a farmer was permitted to look at such things neutrally, a *tenant* farmer even more so. Having looked at these things neutrally he left them there to be dealt with and went back outside. He found that Siyo had brought over his own big wok and had lit a fire. The water in the wok seethed lightly and feathers of steam blew off it into the morning sunshine.

'It never stops, though, does it?' said Jhonny with sudden force. 'Raising and killing, raising and killing. We work our hands sore and then blow it all in one great stuffing session. It doesn't make sense.'

Siyo was quite accustomed to his friend's sudden gusts of philosophising. 'I agree,' he said.

'It certainly makes no sense raising and killing even before you know for certain that your damned guest's going to arrive.'

'He'll come. Anyway, Jhonny, he's not your damned guest: he's your own son.'

'One of them.'

'The one you've done everything for.'

'Perhaps that's it,' said Jhonny darkly. 'You can always be sure, can't you? Nothing's ever going to be as you expect it, nothing ever turns out predictably. Now, I never gave Boyet the chance to go to college thinking he was somehow at the end of it going to come back here and take over from me when I get too stiff and tired to plough paddies and make copra and go to the forest for bamboo and plant rice and make beer and look after buffaloes and pigs and goats and chickens *and* keep our bastard shark landowner happy. In any case he was always useless at the ordinary sort of things like that, wasn't he? Not like his brothers. I don't believe he ever learned to climb a palm-tree. I can never remember seeing him up one.'

'But he was brilliant at school.'

'Oh, yes, he was *brilliant*; at any rate all his teachers said so. Correct me if I'm wrong, but it wasn't unreasonable to expect that he would go off and get his degree or diploma or whatever it is and start a business so that he could make lots of money for the family so we could all live a little more comfortably as we get older. That's what sons do when they get on. The ones without diplomas go and work abroad doing the sort of things you and I do every day but paid fifty times more; the ones with diplomas make money with their brains and pay back their families that way. Simple, huh? So why isn't Boyet like that?'

'Give him a chance, Jhonny; the kid's not even *got* his degree thing yet. I thought you said he had another year to go.'

'Yes. But I've got a brain; there's something telling me that when he does get it that's the last we shall ever see of him.'

'Jhonny!' Siyo was genuinely shocked at his friend's blackness, which seemed suddenly to have risen up from the bodies of the slain and engulfed him.

'It's true,' said the father. Through the doorway into the kitchen the early sunlight fell on a cameo inside. On the table stood his two youngest daughters, five and seven, each holding a leg and a wing apiece while his wife began sawing away at the neck of the chicken through a bald patch she had plucked. Since the knife was blunt she twisted the bird's head back until there was a U-bend in the neck at which point the blade sliced easily in. Blood began pulsing into the enamel bowl she held, as rich in the light as melted rubies, until it became a dribble, then a drip. What might have been a final crow (it had the right rhythm) produced a froth of pink bubbles at the gash. The little girls began shaking the legs energetically, still pinioning the wings at the joints to prevent the spasmic flapping. When they thought there was no blood left to shake down they dropped the bird on the table and picked up the next with squeaks of excited pleasure.

'You could try sharpening the knife,' Jhonny called in to his wife.

'True.'

One of his children handed out the killed bird to Jhonny, who dipped its head experimentally into the wok of boiling water. Its wings moved convulsively, the tip of one of them catching the surface and spattering both men with scalding drops.

'Ow!' they cried and laughed. 'Dead now,' Jhonny added as he let the rest of the chicken sink into the water for a moment before pulling it out and setting to with the plucking. The feathers came out very easily by the handful.

'I know I'm right, Siyo,' he persisted, but now in a quiet, resigned sort of voice. 'You think I say terrible things, but I don't. I'm just describing things which are terrible. You see the difference?'

'Not really. But, then, I've still got a hangover.' Siyo's slight attempt at humour fell like the sodden feathers beneath his friend's hands.

'I say that Boyet won't come back. Oh, today he might; he probably will. Why else send a telegram? They're expensive. But how often has he come home in the last three years? Three times? Four times? How many other sons away at college have you ever heard of doing that? Arentin's boy, Nomer, for example. Comes home every vacation for weeks and always once every semester. Goes fishing with his old friends, mends his father's nets, makes crab traps. *Reads* a lot in between, but of course he has to. What I mean is, he acts normally. When he comes back he does the same things he always did, the things any of us do.' He laid the stiff bird on the ground, its naked waxy flesh dotted with tiny beads of yellow oil leached out by the boiling water and now flared by the sun into fragments of topaz. A child came running out of the house, scooped up the bird and dumped a still-flapping body in its place.

'Perhaps Boyet's bored doing that.'

'Bored.' Jhonny looked carefully at his friend before plunging the fresh chicken entirely into the wok with a decisive thrust. Again the wings went, but this time only weakly, sending wavelets over the rim and hissing into the embers. '*Bored*. Well, I'm so sorry we can't entertain him to his new standards. I agree if you're used to television and refrigerators and . . . and' – Jhonny struggled to imagine some exotic luxury – 'electric typewriting machines and films and night-clubs and hospitality girls, then, yes, I agree, it's not the same thing living in a wooden house with earth floors and kerosene-lamps made out of peanut-butter jars.'

'*Jhonny!*' Siyo slapped the ground on which he was squatting. He was actually as much upset by his friend's implied lack of respect for education in general as he was by his unfatherly bitterness. Some things were beyond questioning. 'That's enough. You're just working yourself into one of your moods because Boyet's a bit late. Poor boy, the ferry probably broke. What sort of a welcome will he get when he does arrive?'

'Not a bad one,' said his father. 'Quite a blow-out, in fact.'

'That's not what I meant, and you know it.'

'I know something else, Siyo old friend. He despises

us. It's as simple as that.'

'Don't be ridiculous.'

'He does, you know.' Jhonny's voice had taken on a faint surprise as if he were listening to his own mouth talk and hearing it say things he hadn't quite thought of yet. 'Me. Rubie. You, too. All of us. Not hate, of course. But to despise people is even worse. It's all those books. . . . You remember the few times he's condescended to return home to see if his family were still more or less alive? You remember his conversation – if you can call it that? Lecturing us about phil . . . phil . . . philoposopy or something and what was that other thing? About money?'

'Macroeconomic theory,' said Siyo, whose memory was notoriously excellent when he was drunk even though as in this case his understanding was nil.

'That's it. My God, how he bored *us*. We all sat there for hour after hour being lectured. He wouldn't let Laki sing his songs and he wouldn't allow the children to sleep. . . . How could you possibly remember what it was called?' he asked his friend with sudden admiration. 'You were wonderful; you saved the day.'

'Did I?' asked Siyo, pleased.

'You know you did; enough people told you next morning. You just sat in the corner drinking rum in complete silence for an hour or two before suddenly toppling over like a dead ox, out cold, and letting off this gigantic fart. God, how we all laughed. Boyet didn't, though; not a bit. He was sitting there with a sort of disdainful smile as if to say "Yes. That's the peasantry for you." He never did have much sense of humour, the little bugger, especially about himself, but I don't know how anybody could have kept a straight face. There he was, droning on about books, books, books, and everybody's in a doze or wanting to pee and suddenly there's dear old Siyo, flat on his face with a great *Prrrrrrrt!*'

Both men were now laughing reminiscently and it was the *moment juste* for the absent Boyet suddenly to arrive. But he didn't, and they went on scalding and plucking, each giving private guffaws as the memory struck them afresh.

He didn't arrive and he didn't arrive and by eleven-thirty so many other people had turned up and so many of those were already slightly tipsy it was obvious that in some undeclared way the proceedings had started without the guest of honour. After a certain point in his own hesitancy had been reached

Jhonny himself began drinking with the other men, sitting at a small table outside while the women kept them supplied with bowls of snacks. By then Tiger had been transmogrified with all sorts of culinary skill into roast Tiger, boiled Tiger, Tiger stew and Tiger done in coconut milk, very rich and creamy. Tiger's intestines had been cooked and glazed and were now served on slivers of bamboo to the drinkers. Everyone complimented Jhonny on his late puppy. 'Good dog,' they observed. 'Good dog.'

Jhonny's mood had changed once more. He beamed with pleasure, he became expansive, he became drunk. As if by some general agreement Boyet was not mentioned, so that when he came his arrival would bring all the pleasure of a genuine surprise. Inside the house the women stirred pots, tippled and made lewd jokes. Outside the house the men made lewd jokes, tippled and just plain stirred. Now and again a wife or a grandmother would come out and sit with them and the gossiping would merrily take a turn for the worse. In between and all around ran the children. Laki arrived bringing his battered bamboo guitar; Sanso wandered off looking for a wild lime-bush for leaves with which to accompany him; Kedo brought his banjo made of a turtle-shell covered with dogskin. The palm beer which had arrived fresh in thick bamboo containers still sweet and mild became stronger and more acrid. On the table was a large Nescafé jar of it fermenting rapidly, the currents set up by bacterial action bringing to the surface dead palm-flowers and insects before carrying them back down to the bottom in a continuous seethe.

The songs started, all the old favourites. People joined in or talked over them or fell into light stupor, eating mechanically and tossing inedible fragments to scavenging pigs and chickens and to the dogs who happily crunched away on the bones of their recent playmate. Groups went into the house in relays to eat because there was no table big enough to hold everybody at a single sitting. Huge heaps of rice were consumed and still more came. At two o'clock Jhonny got to his feet and stretched his tough old arms.

'Feeling good,' he said. Clearly it was a sign, for several people looked up at the swaying paterfamilias.

'Go on,' Siyo urged him. 'Do you good.'

'Yes, go on, go on,' the chorus was taken up. 'Do it now or you'll be too drunk.' 'It's ages since you last did it.'

152

'Bet you can't.' 'Too old.'

'Bugger off, the lot of you,' said Jhonny good-naturedly and crossed to the nearest palm-tree, a venerable sixty-foot giant which must have been well over half a century old and thus nearing the end of its productive life. Chairs were pushed back and children gathered round the bulbous roots. Without more ado Jhonny did a handstand against the base of the tree, turned round so that his nose appeared to be sniffing the bark and, gripping with the sides of his horny feet, began to climb upside down.

It was a famous trick. Many youngsters proud of their strength had tried, but only Jhonny could do it: forty-year-old Jhonny, apparently burned up with endless work and drink and cigarettes, turned out – upside down at least – to be nothing of the sort. And now the strain on his immense arms could be seen; gasps of effort floated down to the onlookers as the inside edges of his soles groped for the staggered slots long ago cut into the trunk to aid the regular ascent of more conventional climbers. The backs of his polished legs bulged and writhed. A forgotten box of matches fell out of the pocket of his shorts and bounced off the head of a child. Everyone laughed and, seeing that Jhonny had nearly reached the crown, began encouraging him: 'Only a metre and a half, Jhon-boy; go on, lad, you're there.' For everybody knew the extreme effort, how the agony in the back and arms was only half over for him: the descent was just as bad with arms quaking with fatigue, the head-first fall of sixty feet down the curving trunk ever more likely. His wife turned away. She hated his doing it while at the same time feeling a pride which made her eyes prickle, especially when a bit drunk as she now was. There was nobody else who could do it. People had heard of only one other man able to do it and he had lived ten miles away and died twenty years ago. She risked a quick glance. Her husband was halfway down now, and she knew that once more he was going to finish safely, drink or no drink, forty years old or not.

When Jhonny's hands reached the roots the waiting onlookers gave a great cheer and lifted him bodily off the trunk, turning him up the right way. His eyes were closed, his face was black, his legs were gone, so they carried him to the house and laid him in the shade and stood over him until he had stopped panting and opened his eyes.

'*Ahh*,' he sighed, half-lost for faintness. 'That calls for a drink.'

This was the sign for another great cheer and a general rush to offer glasses, bottles, containers of drink. Jhonny seized the Nescafé jar and gulped down its contents, dead bees and all.

'Unbelievable.' 'The man's ageless.' 'It's not quite human.'

The pride, the affection, the *solidarity* engendered by Jhonny's feat, which had brought alcoholic tears to the eyes of many more than his wife, if the truth be told, had so concentrated their attention that the presence of a bystander had gone unnoticed. Standing somewhat apart in brilliant white trousers and holding an attaché case, he was watching with cool gaze.

'Father up to his monkey tricks again,' he said. An awful silence fell.

'Ah,' said Jhonny again, sitting up now and wiping his mouth on his stained T-shirt. 'Boyet. Good of you to come, son.'

'I fear too late to catch the whole of your performance,' said Boyet. 'I'm sorry about that. The stupid boat broke down, can you believe it?' He looked round at the faces he'd known since infancy, at Laki with his guitar and Kedo with his turtle-banjo and the whole familiar, endlessly repeating pattern of relentless parochialism. 'I had to stand in the sun on deck for two whole hours while those idiots did their usual trick of trying to repair a prehistoric engine with hammers and string. Bodging; absolutely typical. It really is high time people in this country got their act together. Anyway, I'm sorry to be late,' he said again, as if to offset any gracelessness his rufflement might have caused. 'Now I am here I can see I'd better change.'

He went into the house, keeping his shoes on, his mother following him with the gleaming attaché case.

' "Monkey-tricks",' Siyo heard Jhonny mutter.

'Joke only,' he told his friend earnestly, but the phrase undermined everything. Nobody else was paying any attention, however, being busy with expressing pleasure at the son of the house's sudden return and the confirmatory power of his father's prowess.

'Happy birthday!' they shouted towards the house. 'Drink, Jhonny; relax now. Everything's OK. You've earned it.'

Kedo began strumming on the banjo, someone took up a song, and Sanso held his leaf edge-on to his bottom lip and began a piercing, wavering accompaniment. The high, doleful whistle cut through the din with its reassuring familiarity, reminding everyone of countless evenings' home-made conviviality in countless huts dotted among the coconut-groves, the sound so perfectly redolent of palm beer turned sour with its own vinegar, with raising and killing, with the sharpness of tears falling impotently on thin and wiry forearms grasping a variety of crude everyday implements. People began to be very drunk indeed, Jhonny most of all, swallowing great draughts of anything he could lay his hands on with a kind of single-minded recklessness. The morning's sunlight had given way to cloud; a light rain fell, driving everybody into the house, cramming it so full that they were jammed thigh to thigh on the bamboo floor, their sandals in a great jumbled heap down below in the mud at the foot of the steps. Boyet was off in one of the cubicles; his voice could be heard rising above the woven partition, protesting to his mother and sisters. It went on and on.

Suddenly Jhonny stood unsteadily up and reached down the plastic bottle of rubbing alcohol from the shelf. In a strange and clear voice he said: 'I can climb any palm. I can drink any drink.' He sat down again.

'Don't be silly, Jhon,' said Siyo, weaving his head blurrily. 'Can't drink rubbing alcohol. Wrong sort of alcohol. Got menth . . . menthol in it. It'll make you sick.'

'Nah, not Jhonny it wouldn't,' said someone.

'No,' said Jhonny, 'not me.' Without hesitation he unscrewed the cap and drank the contents. Then he put the bottle down, looked at it for a moment, closed his eyes and jerked both knees violently into his chest. He made a weird sound, 'Idzizz . . . sizz . . . sizz,' before falling backwards and hitting his head on the door-jamb.

'Whad I tell you?' Siyo asked him rhetorically. 'Serves you right. By God you'll have a headache tomorrow.'

But Jhonny was not sick; he was stone dead.

That night Siyo, utterly sober, wept and wept and would not be stopped.

'We're all to blame,' said his wife. 'He was too drunk to know what he was doing.'

'*That isn't the point, woman*,' said Siyo in a miserable, quiet scream. 'The point is he *must* have known, *I* must have known. For God's sake, we'd been out fishing often enough for me to know he kept his poison in that bottle. You don't just forget you've put cyanide and *tubli* root into a rubbing-alcohol bottle, do you?'

'You might quite easily when you're as drunk as he was. One

155

bottle of rubbing alcohol looks much like any other; they're common enough. I expect what he thought was, "Aha, rubbing alcohol. I'll drink that – that'll amaze them," because he was still high, he was still on top of it all after his climb, wasn't he? Go on, Siyo, wasn't he?'

But Siyo wouldn't be consoled, and it was many days before his attacks of crying stopped and many months before he could pass an entire day without that hollow ache of loss, and he never again in his life went fishing illegally with poison.

As for poor Boyet, he acted the part of head of the family with perfect decorum for as long as was needed over the period of the obsequies. Then one morning he sat on the river-bank opposite the wallow with his godfather, awkwardly, at times aggressively, telling Siyo things about himself which were profoundly shocking. For Jhonny had been right: there was something wrong, Boyet was not like the other sons with whom he had always been so unfavourably compared; there never would be hospitality girls in crimson jeeps. Siyo, whose own grief had now made him better able to sense it in others, was shocked far less by what the boy confessed to than by his isolate misery. That inveterate difference which he had always felt would drive him out of his village and which had made him repudiate it together with his family, his origins, his very intellect: he hated it all and in so doing hated what he had become.

Shortly afterwards he left, seemingly for good. They expected to see him at least for the death anniversary, his own birthday, but Boyet never came. Siyo often longed to send him a letter telling him funny village news, that his family were well, that he was loved, that he understood. But, alas, he was unable to write and he could not bring himself to lay bare to some gossipy amanuensis confidences stumblingly expressed.

So that was that. And ever afterwards his eyes would fill with tears when passing that spot on the river-bank, as at the least mention of his friend Jhonny and the terrible accident.

Vanishment

Leaving her mother to rest back at the hotel she wandered out into the blinding sunlight once again. Eventually, because she did not want more coffee or more ice-cream, she went into a church and sat down. One could do that in Italy with the excuse that one wished to look at something: there was generally a minor painting, a flaking fresco, an altarpiece. In this particular church there was nothing, however; just gloom and stale incense and soft cooing overhead.

How vivacious her mother must have been then! Still was, for that matter, nearly eighty and amused by so much. So many memories, so many people. She had come here all those years ago in her mid-twenties with Dorothy, the famous Dorothy. A composite image here came to Janet's inward eye of faces from the pictures in her mother's photograph-album, a document she had thought was as utterly familiar as anything else she had grown up with. Yet now the album with its images was retreating strangely and acquiring a deeper unknowableness. There had been a moment that morning in the Piazza delle Tre Marie when she had recognised absolutely the fountain in the middle with its circular cobbled surround. She had shut her eyes and the photograph became vivid near the bottom of a right-hand page of her mother – snapped presumably by Dorothy – perched on that thick iron railing, her fingers on the crown of the stanchion maintaining her balance, smiling right out of the picture with a spout of water coming from the top of her head.

'The fountain!' Janet had exclaimed.

'Oh, pretty. I like the little lion.'

'But you *must* remember it. You were here before with Dorothy.'

'Was I? Well, I dare say we were, but it was a long time ago. Also, it's not the most distinguished piazza, is it?'

'But, Mumbo, it's all in your album at home. Look at this railing, up at the end here. Now put your hand on it. Go on. . . . *There*. Exactly fifty-three years ago you sat on that precise bit of iron and smiled.'

'I doubt if I should do so again; it looks uncommonly sharp to me. I always wondered why when they have a rail that is square they should set it on edge like a diamond so only a bird could enjoy perching on it.'

How was it, Janet wondered, that she herself should be more touched and made more aghast by the passage of time than her mother? Were the old so used to seeing places and thinking of themselves there in younger days they were no longer affected? How did one acquire resistance to making the obvious equation: that girl in the photograph equals this old woman here, now probably half a head shorter? They were not the same person; of course they were the same person. But the upshot of it all was that a certain kind of validity which she had always ascribed to her mother's photograph-album was now thrown into doubt. If the places, why not the faces, too? Girls with bobbed hair and the look of having been good sports; heavy black bicycles, thick wood raquets, boxy cars with running-boards. And smiling through those missed years when Janet did not exist the face of her future mother's especial friend Dorothy. 'D in Verona', 'D in Lowry's Morris', 'D coaching St C's hockey XI', and later on 'D convalescing'. None, though, of D's funeral.

'Oh, she was such *fun*,' her mother would say from as far back as Janet could remember. 'We had such lovely times. We used to laugh so much we would choke. She was one of those special people; I think everybody loved Dorothy.'

When she was quite little these words used to fill Janet with a deep pity for her mother as if Dorothy's death had left her for ever friendless; and she would cry on her mother's behalf and at her own inability to comfort and protect her. Later the formula 'everybody loved Dorothy' would induce a less sympathetic feeling amounting almost to a grudge. It was unjust. How could she help comparing herself to this unknown friend? How could

158

she not ransack her mind for a single schoolmate of her own who might conceivably say such things about her in twenty, forty, sixty years? She would sit with her chin on her knees, long grey woollen stockings concertina'd round her ankles like any boy's, wondering why her white shins were so pronounced and bruised and shiny. How *did* one acquire friends, anyway? The people with friends like Dorothy seemed always to have had them, like blonde hair or athletic ability, never to have acquired them suddenly. Also there was about those kinds of friendship a suggestion of a golden age which had existed before her own creation: sunnier times which lay somewhere between the demise of the dinosaur and the institution of compulsory games at school. Then it had come to her how absolutely peculiar it was for one's own mother to have existed at all before one was born, more still that she could carry forward memories into modern times of extreme happiness with someone who – as far as one's own chronology was concerned – had only ever lived on this earth as a chemically imaged shadow on squares of glossy, dog-eared paper.

There was a thud behind her as the church door closed, then slow footsteps along a far aisle. Janet being Janet had not sat somewhere up the nave but off to one side in the shadow of a pillar; any visitor would at once believe themselves alone. Soon came a murmur from a distant confessional. Other lives in progress, she thought, whereas hers. . . . A billow of familiar irritation and anxiety swelled upwards from her viscera, crushing her lungs a little. The dreary stagnation, the awful sense of irredeemable time slipping always. Forty-five in September and nothing to show for it but the unmistakable signs of ageing. No husband, no lover, the same librarian's job in the same Oxford college for twenty years. True, there had been affairs – especially Teresa, always and forever Teresa – and, true, there had been holidays abroad, the odd experiences and minor adventures which were inescapable for anybody not actually screwed into an iron lung. She had been caught in an avalanche and had been trapped on a rotting medieval roof of oolite shingles for half an hour by a fire in her college and she had once had a series of ever-more-menacing and crudely drawn notes pushed under her Egyptian hotel door followed by the blade of a knife *through* the door. But now they had happened (and she had long since felt self-disgust at dining out on them) they were finished, over, past and done with. It was as if they had happened to somebody else entirely, leaving no apparent residue in her own life. So now it was perfectly possible for that intestinal billow to lurch up and make her unable to stop the thought: 'I haven't lived. And soon I'll be dead.' But what would it take to stop it? What inconceivably transfiguring affair, experience, belatedly discovered talent or whatever?

At moments when she was better defended against the billows – most of the time, actually – she could be realistic, even cynical about herself. She did it, as any other sane and observant person did, by looking at those about her and absolutely failing to detect much difference in their own lives, still less anything very enviable. Even the ones with families agonised and were secretly miserable, although they all worked hard to maintain that outward grimace of pleasure, that inward censorship so they could later say with such self-pleased worldliness, 'Oh, we had our ups and downs, didn't we, William?' or 'Of course kids are a real pest much of the time but just occasionally' – pause for effect – 'one of them says or does something that makes it all worth it a million times over.' And, well, yes, it *filled the time*. But other than that they had not lived in Bokhara, either, nor had an affair with an entire string quartet, nor been in an aeroplane which was hijacked. They paid mortgages and school bills and phone bills and once in a while one of them would publish the book she or he had been working on for nigh on fifteen years: *Coleridge's Thought and the German Philosophical Tradition* or *Kinship Systems among the 'Utuwâ*.

What, then, was it which produced the sudden bursts of upset and restlessness? *What is it, Catullus? Why do you not make haste to die?* Janet stared up at the ceiling, which, her eyes having adjusted to the dimness, she could now see had been nastily restored with a vault of bright blue plaster. Her gaze wandered downwards to the wall across from where she sat. There was a marble plaque surmounted by a plaster wreath containing a portrait of the head and shoulders of a young man wearing some sort of military jacket. Peering closer she could see the picture was actually a photograph which had somehow been glazed on to the surface of an oval porcelain tablet. The process had resulted in an excellent cameo likeness, very sharp, but in sepia tones like a daguerrotype. The text beneath read:

IN RESPECTFUL AND EVER-CHERISHED
MEMORY OF LIEUTENANT FRANCO
CIAPPI, INTREPID AND DEDICATED
ITALIAN AVIATOR, WHO THROUGH A
SUDDEN FRENZY OF NATURE YIELDED
CONTROL OF HIS MACHINE INTO THE
HANDS OF GOD, CRASHING WITH
TERRIBLE FORCE INTO THE ROOF OF
THIS CHURCH JANUARY 12TH 1932,
AGED 23.
HIS GRIEVING COMRADES AND BEREFT
PARENTS, HIS BROTHERS AND SISTER
ALL WEEP FOR HIM, THOUGH IN THE
SURE FAITH THAT HE WILL RISE AGAIN.

She got up and crossed over to look more closely at the
picture. It was a wonderfully handsome and sensitive face,
luxuriant hair (surely it had been a glossy black?) brushed
straight back, in all very much resembling the pianist Dinu
Lipatti. Now, there, she thought, was a way to go. What to
everybody else had been merely a sharp squall sending them
scurrying across the slippery cobbles into warm cafés and shops
had been, a thousand feet above, a fatal frenzy of nature for the
lost boy in his Fiat or Caproni. It was right: it didn't much matter
how you lived as long as you died well, and young Franco,
buffeted and blind in his rain-streaked goggles, had died with
splendid drama. She wondered if he had come right through the
ceiling, whether the nave she sat in had been littered with
masonry and pieces of alloy and fabric, filled with the stench of
burned castor oil and aviation spirit, the perhaps headless body
in its flying jacket bundled into a corner near the battered engine
which ticked as it cooled. Or had it stuck in the roof so that only
the bent propeller and cowling protruded through a ragged hole
above the altar, hot streams of glycol and blood and hydraulic
fluid pattering among pyx and plate?

161

The crash in its various forms and possibilities had now become completely vivid to her. If she walked round the church and really looked closely, might she not find other evidence for that event of January 1932? A chipped flagstone, perhaps. Or maybe if the dirt between the flagstones could be analysed there would still be traces of burned oil or haemoglobin. And then it struck her: 1932 was the very year her mother and Dorothy had been here in this city. True, they had come a bit later, in summer. But now the photograph Janet could so clearly visualise in her mother's album took on new interest. Mumbo had sat on that fountain railing five months after young Franco had done his death-dive a few hundred yards away. Merely a coincidence, of course, without the least significance. Still, the mind turned it over.

She stood there with her mouth open seeing and not looking at the plaque while pigeons cooed and the muttering in the confessional went on and on as if some penitent were pouring out their whole life-story. She had the conviction that she herself would never form part of anybody else's history. That was what old photographs did so mercilessly: they reminded you of other people's continuities. 'We had such lovely times. . . . We used to laugh so much.' But you had to have somebody to show them to. It wasn't enough just to go around snapping pictures. Janet knew plenty of people who took photographs, but in general she could swear that, once they had come back from the developer's and had been pored over with amusement, they were practically never looked at again. Had it not been clear only that morning that her mother had no idea she'd ever been to that piazza before, still less been photographed there? When had she last looked at her own album? Come to that, when had she last taken a photograph? All her hoarded pictures seemed immensely old, many of them still pushed into the wallets of long-defunct chemists now marked with the rust of pins and staples. What, then, had it all been for?

'Darling Janet, what you need is a camera.' Mumbo had said it time and time again. 'They're such *fun*.' And time and time again her daughter had refused as if she knew that what and where she had been were more likely to return to mock her than to console. It was as if she had always known that nobody would ever show pictures of her to their children: Janet the good sport (why, she wondered, did cars no longer have running-boards for good sports to put one foot up on?); Janet who was such a dear . . . you couldn't help laughing when Janet was around. . . . Oh, but you could, actually; you could very easily help it because she was sharp and angular-minded and serious all at once and could deflate you with the same bleakness with which she could deflate herself. Permanently deflated, that's what she was, and when she came into contact with the world it seemed inexorably to follow suit. And it was not what people liked at all, she knew, but neither could she help it. She just saw things discomfortingly.

'*Signora scusi.*' She turned to the quiet voice behind her. An elderly priest with thick grey hair brushed straight back and wearing a black cassock greenish with age stood there watching her. Funds, thought Janet. He's soliciting for the poor of the parish, the upkeep of the organ, for himself. 'Forgive me, signora,' he continued in his soft Tuscan accent, 'but I could not help noticing your attention. You have been looking at this memorial for ten minutes or more. I hope you will not think me impertinent if I ask you what there is about it which so holds your interest?'

'Really I was daydreaming,' she admitted, smiling. 'Did I look stupid? I have my mouth open when I daydream; I've often been told.'

'Of course not, signora, no, no.'

'I thought so. . . . But, yes, I was interested in the plaque. It's an incomplete story as it stands, but it's unusual to find oneself on a spot where someone once died so dramatically.'

'*Certo.* Are you perhaps a writer?'

'I'm a librarian.'

'Ah. It must be wonderful always to be surrounded by the wisdom of the past.'

'Not a bit. You'll doubtless think me mad if I say that sometimes when there is so much evidence of where and who one *wasn't* it makes it that much more difficult to discover where and who one *is.*'

This made the priest look at her quite sharply. 'May I ask, is this your first time in our city? Not in Italy, of course; you speak the language too well.'

She explained that she was accompanying her elderly mother on a sort of nostalgic grand tour before she became 'too decrepit to travel, like an Egyptian king' – Mumbo's expression, not her own.

'How interesting,' the priest said. 'I was born only ten miles away and I've never left the area, but it must be an experience to return to distant places one knew fifty years before. I've seen everything here evolve gradually so I can scarcely remember how it used to be. Except this church.'

'Before the aeroplane crash?'

'Exactly. I see you've put two and two together. Did you see the postcards?'

'No?'

The priest led her to the main door. Just inside was the sort of table she habitually ignored with its freight of prayer-sheets, notices, collection boxes, magazines about the work of missions in Uganda. There was also a pile of sepia-tinted postcards.

'This is how it was,' he said, handing her one. The interior of a Renaissance church, its features oddly shaped and shadowed by the floodlights which must have been used so as to bring out the chancel ceiling which, as far as she could tell, had been magnificently painted.

'Fra Benedetto della Croce,' explained the priest. 'One of the two best ceilings in this part of Tuscany. It was utterly destroyed.'

Janet had the unstoppable thought: *brilliant boy*.

'Poor Franco. Had he known what he had done he would have been devastated. An exquisite treasure of the Tuscan *quattrocento*.'

'You sound as if you knew him.'

'He was my brother,' said the priest simply. 'His action that day has shaped all my days since. There is a shame in the story which is not written quite plainly there on the wall. Come' – he took Janet's arm – 'let us sit down for a minute. There seems to be nobody else since that unhappy woman wishing to confess their sins to me, so let me do a little confession of my own. I hope I don't presume, signora?'

Without waiting for a reply he led her back to her original seat by the memorial tablet and she sat down again, although not without thinking very briefly of her mother and wondering if she were asleep.

'I expect you noticed, signora, that the word "glorious" does not occur in the text? But it is asking too much from a foreigner, even one so perfect in our language. These memorials are often written in a kind of code from which much may be deduced by one who knows. Now, if the word "glorious" had appeared in Franco's inscription, it would be commonly inferred that he had died on active service if not actually in combat. But his memory, we are told, is to be respected merely.'

'The shame you mentioned?'

'Precisely. The truth is that, far from being on active service, poor Franco had actually *stolen* the plane.'

Splendid boy. 'Stolen?'

'More or less. He was a pilot all right and in the air force, but he had been grounded as a punishment for some misdemeanour. . . . I'm sorry to say it was insubordination.'

She glanced sideways at the priest and surprised a fond smile of recollection somewhat at variance with his words. *More and more splendid.*

'It was a terrible January day. Right from the Alps – Milan, Bologna, Florence, even as far south as Perugia there were blizzards. So what does Franco do? Naturally, he decides it is exactly today he must go and see his girlfriend near Siena. There is a military airfield near to her at Campobasso so he will take a plane, hop across, spend the afternoon with her and hop back again. Hopping, you see, although it is a hundred and twenty-eight kilometres to Campobasso and the same back. Open cockpit, zero visibility, instrument-flying and dead-reckoning.'

'And youth,' said Janet.

'That above all. A flask of coffee but five litres of hot blood. *Dio benedetto.* So he takes the aircraft and tells the ground crew to fill the tanks but not to warm up the engine since of course he doesn't wish to alert anyone in authority. The ground crews. . . . Well, in those days the pilots were like knights, you know, so dashing and glamorous; they only had to put one boot in a stirrup and the flight engineers would fall over themselves to fettle up their chargers. So there they are at Pratosammartino, the officers, standing around in the flight operations room drinking their coffee and staring out of the windows at the snow when suddenly across the airfield comes this sound of an aero-engine starting. Nobody pays much attention: engineers taking advantage of the weather to do some servicing. Then it grows and grows. It can't be. . . . Everybody in the room is at the window now. . . . It *is.* Some crazy lunatic is taking off and no one can even see him the snow flurries are so thick. He roars overhead; he is gone. The squadron leader rushes to the telephone and cranks the handle furiously. But he's off and away, my elder brother Franco. A complete lunatic but with great charm. People adored him.'

The priest was still smiling fondly, then shook his head at Janet's question: 'Did he make Campobasso?'

'No. He was right on course, right on course. But they think the altimeter was wrong; perhaps it hadn't been reset. He became confused, maybe he came down a little to see if he could spot a landmark. . . .' Unconsciously the priest glanced up at the roof. 'They said later it was inexplicable how he could have hit this church. There are so many higher buildings all around it: the dome on the Basilica, for example, or the towers of San Sebastiano or the Palazzo Tradescanti itself. But, no' – was there a note of pride? – 'Franco had to destroy himself and Fra Benedetto's masterpiece; it was destined that he should. So he did. The whole ceiling, the entire roof came down.' The arm in its sheened black made a descending gesture. 'Franco was killed at once. They found his body in the organ loft. By the grace of God there was nobody in the church at the time, but an old sacristan died of a heart-attack when he heard the news. I was seventeen at the time and already studying for the priesthood. Can you imagine what it was to be the younger brother of a boy whose youthful prank had gone so disastrously wrong? All Italy had heard of him by the next morning; think of it. The jokes of semi-admiration from my own peers: "How irresponsible, how *Italian*. . . . How beautiful was she, this girlfriend? I bet she was worth some boring old painting, anyway. And you already stuck in the *seminario*, Marco. Did Franco have all the balls in the family?" All that was bearable. But the weighty regret of their elders, the artistic world, official opinion, that was truly terrible. And in a way it still is, although it's now just part of history. At the time the newspapers were full of phrases like "tragic and irreparable loss to our cultural heritage and to the world of art". Nowadays if you read guidebooks or art books there is usually a single reference to Fra Benedetto's masterpiece "The Raising of Lazarus" as "destroyed". There are plenty of old photographs of it, of course; copies and sketches and colour reproductions. But the original is gone, just like poor Franco there.'

Janet could hardly take her eyes from the young man's cameo face. How innocent it was; how ironic that in dying he should have become a famous iconoclast.

'I felt the shame very much. I was confused, crushed beneath it, our family's shame. There was even for a while a new verb, "*ciappiare*", which meant to destroy something of far greater value than yourself. For three years this church stood in semi-ruins, open to the sky while they haggled over whose responsibility it was and how it should be restored. So what could I do but beg my superiors to let me take it over, to make it my life's work to repair the damage, to do something to make amends? And so I have.'

'No more guilt?'

'None,' said the priest. 'It was all more than half a century ago, you must remember. Franco to me is a few childhood memories and that photograph on the wall. I have no connection, either, with the teenager I was in those days. "My life's work" as I called it then did not have the same meaning as my life's work does today, with most of it behind me. Nowadays this church just feels to me like the place I have always worked in.'

'It's beautiful,' Janet said untruthfully.

'Isn't it? There was no point trying to restore the original roof or re-creating the painting, so I decided on this. It's simple, that vault. It's clean and blue like the sky. In fact to me it's a better memorial than that plaque on the wall. Besides, I couldn't raise enough money for anything more elaborate. This was almost all done with donations, you know. Nowadays, of course, it would have been restored as a perfect replica; no sum too great to lavish on a Renaissance church with a priceless ceiling. But this was then. . . .'

Behind them the door opened and an elderly man came in holding his hat across his chest. The priest turned in the pew and called out:

'Sandro! I shan't be more than a minute. How's the foot?'

'I must go anyway,' said Janet, slipping the strap of her bag over one shoulder. 'I can't thank you enough for your time. You've made my day, quite possibly my entire holiday, too.'

'Not at all, signora. Sometimes I think it is good to make the past come alive for a bit even though it's dead and gone. Today's what matters, isn't it? But it's better there should be a little *resonance*.'

'Just one thing. Do you always tell visitors the story?' *Are you still dining out on it? Doesn't it disgust you?*

'*Dio buono*, no. Not only is there not the time but it would be too boring. Do you know what it is after all these years, signora? It's a *fable*. Good day to you.'

He said no more but squeezing her forearm hurried away to attend the old man with the hat. On her way out of the church

Janet made a decent contribution to a collecting-box and kept the postcard; out of the corner of one eye she saw that the priest did not turn round. What had he meant, a fable? Surely not an elaborate fancy concocted in order to screw more money out of visitors (an atheist herself, she had that inherited Anglican suspicion about Catholics and money)? Then just inside the door she caught sight of a notice handwritten in once-white paint on a little black board stating that the priest in charge was Father Marco Ciappi. That much, at least, was true.

'Fabulous' was how she quite truthfully described her afternoon when her mother asked. 'What about yours, Mumbo?'

'Dear, I slept and *slept*. I'd no notion I was so tired. I had such a sad dream; it must have been that fountain this morning which set me off. I dreamed about Dorothy, of course – it must be the first time in goodness knows how many years. I knew it was her but I couldn't remember her face, and this voice kept saying "unless you get the right face she will *be paid by vanishment*" – those were the words, *"be paid by vanishment"*. It was horrid. I was desperately trying face after face to put on the shoulders of this shadowy figure, but none of them was right. And then she was somehow *put away* – I can't describe it better than that – and the fountain, Italy, us, it was all scrumpled up.'

'I think a pot of tea,' suggested Janet. 'Then we'll go out and see how wonderfully un-scrumpled Italy is.'

'More than I'm feeling, I should imagine.'

Janet laughed and bounced down on to the bed beside her, putting an arm around the thin old shoulders, conscious of their formidable toughness.

'Darling Mumbo,' she said.

Cat & Kitten

Knobby hands on lap Mr Raffish sat and watched the student –
assuredly a student? – throughout the overture with intentness.
The boy sat out (that had to be the phrase) Mendelssohn's 'The
Fair Melusine' and, if the older man were right, it was
nervousness rather than impatience with which he switched his
gaze repeatedly from the auditorium's ceiling to floor and
stretched and stretched his fingers. The overture ended and
stage-hands began opening the great Steinway which had stood
like a gloss coffin beside the conductor's podium. Now the boy
was definitely nervous. He had brought out the score of the
concerto and had it in readiness on his knees: not a pocket score
but a soloist's with the orchestral parts reduced for an
accompanying pianist. He took out a white handkerchief, wiped
his hands, glanced about him. The seats immediately on either
side were empty, it being a thinnish night given the popularity
of the programme and the soloist; probably it was on account of
the unseasonably warm weather keeping those Londoners in
the parks whom rain might otherwise have driven indoors in
search of culture. As Mr Raffish watched the student their eyes
met briefly, but when the boy broke contact it was surely not
through shyness; the watcher understood this nervousness had
another cause, a preoccupation to an unnatural degree.

The conductor returned followed by the pianist, dapper in
tails. As the audience gradually fell silent the student sat in
unbreathing anticipation, watching the conductor's back and

the soloist settling himself. Was he or wasn't he? Mr Raffish wondered again. No stalking of a sexual prey could ever be so delicious as this inspirational guessing game.

The opening *tutti* began. On the platform the pianist, a celebrated Viennese, sat staring at the keys. Among the audience the student unconsciously adopted the same pose, looking not at the open score on his knees but at the edge of the seat-back in front of him. Then as the *tutti* drew to its close both soloist and student glanced up at the conductor at nearly the same moment. Raffish, himself affected by this little drama, watched the boy at the soloist's entry as with mouth half-open, eyes fixed, he began to shake his head with a frown of disagreement. Good, thought the older man. Excellent, in fact. As the movement proceeded he relaxed his vigilance, half-concentrating on the music which was so painfully rooted in him, half-amused to see the boy as involved as if he were himself playing. Which in some sense he was, Raffish knew. The boy's concentration had a certain latitude to it such as one reserved for things so familiar there was scant need to follow every note – which one could have written out from memory, anyhow. Moments of pleasure made the student nod and bounce his thick brown hair; passages he disliked brought back the frown, one of impatience rather than censure as if to say, *Yes, I understand exactly why you're doing it that way, it's simply dull, let's not have to sit through it.*

Mr Raffish rose stiffly when the boy left his seat at the interval, score tucked under one arm, and was little surprised to see him leave the concert-hall entirely and walk away across the dark promenades. He hurried to catch him up, a short, awkward figure moving without fluency and urgent none the less. 'Excuse me!' The boy looked round. 'I say!' Both figures came into a douche of light shed by a street-lamp fitted with an imitation Edwardian globe.

'Golly,' said Mr Raffish, breathless, 'I say, you walk too fast for a poor old gent like me.'

The boy said nothing but waited, hair shining in the lamplight, the pale green of his score leached of its colour and glaring beneath his arm. He noticed his pursuer had a suggestion of foreignness about him, though of accent or gesture he might not immediately have said.

'Perhaps you saw me in there?' went on the older man, not turning back to the concert-hall. 'I noticed you, however, indeed

170

I did. "Aha," I thought, *"there'*s one if I'm not very mistaken. That one I must speak to." So here I am.'

'One what?' asked the student. 'Oh, let me guess. A shy, lonely young man. . . .'

'. . . having difficulty coming to terms with an aberrant sexuality? Oh, bravo!' said Mr Raffish admiringly. 'You're quick; we're going to get on, I can see that. Let me reassure you here and now that your sexuality – no matter how aberrant or prosaic – is something I have no interest in. None whatever. I don't suppose it's much more interesting than your digestive system. No. I'm fascinated by something completely different. Now, let me guess. You're a student? Of music?'

The boy touched his score reflexively. 'You wouldn't have to be Sherlock Holmes to know that.'

'Indeed not, but bear with me further. . . . A pianist, and a good one. Good enough for a career. If only.'

'If only what?' The boy was suddenly anxious to hear. A certain pettishness of manner left him. His halo tilted as he leaned towards the shorter man.

'Aha. Just that. *If only*. Now, you see, I'm not mistaken: I do know something about you. It's your secret, isn't it? But first forgive me, my dear fellow, how rude of me. Anthony Raffish.' He extended his knobby hand.

'I'm Zeb. That's short for Zebedee' – and it seemed to be a well-worn apologia. 'My parents are from the sixties.'

'My dear,' said Anthony Raffish, 'mine were from Poland. I was christened Antonin Raffawicz. We are both victims of circumstances beyond our control, or would be were it not for the wonderful British institution of Deed Poll. Zebedee what, though, I wonder?'

'Hoyle.' The young man shifted his balance awkwardly, and the lamplight cast a certain distinction across the planes of his face.

'Zeb Hoyle. Zebedee Hoyle.' Anthony Raffish tried the names, head on one side for a moment. 'No,' he said regretfully. 'There's no music there, is there? We'll have to do better than that. Now, then. You're not going to tell me you've got something important to do right this moment, because I wouldn't quite believe you and, besides, we're going to talk about your career and there's nothing more important than that, is there? Not just at present' – and he glanced shrewdly up into the boy's face.

171

'My career? But I. . . .'

'Don't prevaricate, my dear, we're too intelligent to have to go through all that. Yes, your career. Or, rather, its lack. You're eaten up with worry about it, I know. You're getting nowhere and it's the only thing you want to do. You want to have your chance and so you shall because luckily Anthony Raffish is going to take you beneath his wing. Rather a crippled wing, I'm afraid, but one which still keeps many great talents aloft even if I do say so myself. Now, then, let us walk to my flat where I will ply you with coffee and intrigue you despite your momentary inclination to make a dash for the anonymous security of a Tube train or a *hamburger bar.*' He came down sardonically on the two words as an expression in a foreign language and not in a self-conscious attempt at familiarity with the habits of a younger generation. 'Come, come, my boy, I'm going to make you famous and we start tonight. Don't hang about. But' – he touched the unresisting Zebedee on one elbow and turned him towards Kensington – 'my joints are rather a trial so you'll have to moderate that aggressively youthful pace of yours.'

'Perhaps you should take a taxi.'

'No, walking's good for me. If I didn't walk, I should seize up altogether. It isn't far. So how did you like his Beethoven Two? Not much, to judge from your expression in there.'

'It was very *beautiful.* Very *mellifluous.*'

'But very predictable. Exactly. Nothing jarred but neither did it excite. And the cadenza?'

'I suppose you can't go wrong with Beethoven's own.'

'And what would you have played?'

'Something different. Anything different as long as it was not a vast piece of nineteenth-century pianism, for instance. You might stir up number three with that, but number two's an eighteenth-century concerto. When my teacher was in Paris he met someone editing Saint-Saëns who had unearthed his unpublished cadenzas to all the Beethoven concertos. The one to the B flat is charming. I would have played that if only because nobody would have known it and perhaps they might have been jogged out of that fawning doze he makes all his audiences fall into.'

'Bravo!' said Anthony Raffish again, but this time thoughtfully enough to give the impression that he was commending himself for his own insight as much as Zebedee for his choice. 'I should dearly like to hear it. You shall play to me when we get home.'

'Are you a pianist yourself, Mr Raffish?' asked the student.

'Was, was.' He hefted his arms like a pair of Indian clubs. 'Rheumatoid arthritis. It began forty years ago when I was not much older than you are now. It was another age then, of course, another world, and I don't just mean medically speaking. One went from one ruined city to another playing in the magnificent and unheated old concert-halls of Europe – those still standing, that is. Sometimes there would be great draperies of dust-sheets covering the bomb damage. But it didn't matter; people didn't mind such things then. They came only for the music because they had been so starved of it in the war. When one came out on to the platform they didn't applaud very much by today's standards, perhaps because they were so eager to hear the music they couldn't bear to delay it. My God, how they listened! One night – I'm going to bore you with a reminiscence so you can't say later I didn't warn you – one night I was playing in Lübeck, 1946 it was. And when I went out there they all were still in their utility clothing looking half-starved but immensely serious and Hanseatic. I was going to start with something traditional – a Bach suite or a Haydn sonata, I forget what – but at the last moment I decided against it. Why? I can't say. But I paused on the platform and announced: "Ladies and gentlemen, there is a slight change to the programme. I wish to start with something different." Just like that. Then I sat down and played Mendelssohn's "Variations sérieuses". Do you know them? Of course you do; mavellous music. I didn't say what it was, though, so some of them must have wondered what they were getting. But others knew. I could see people in the first few rows weeping.'

'It's a very grave theme. Plaintive and grave at the same time.'

'Yes, but that wasn't the reason at all. Nor was my exquisite or otherwise playing. No, it was because it was Mendelssohn. It was the first time many of them had heard Mendelssohn in nearly ten years.' The older man might have sensed puzzlement. 'The Nazis had decided Mendelssohn was Jewish music and shouldn't be played, you see. Oh dear, how very young you are and how envious I am. . . . Quite, anyway. Be that as it may, some were meeting an old, long-lost friend again and so they wept. It was proof that civilisation was getting back to normal. And now here we are.' He led the way into a solid Victorian block with a white-pillared portico which had been glassed in with peculiarly thick panes bound with hinges and mountings of brass. 'Arabs,' he said as if that explained everything. 'I've been here since 1947 and never once in all that time did I find it necessary to cut the throat of a sheep in the hall. It never crossed my mind.' He was clumsy with a bunch of keys. 'It's rather shocking, you know, being made to feel conventional after a lifetime's worship of Dionysus. Now, then.'

He ushered Zebedee into a cavernous and slightly shabby suite of rooms. The drawing room felt much larger than it can have been, giving off the splendid gloom of a canyon: high cliffs of shelving on either side plunging towards one another at the bottom in screes of books, papers and music. On the narrow valley floor stood a grand piano.

'Oh, a Bösendorfer.'

'For that you may have not only milk but *sugar* in your coffee,' said Anthony Raffish on his slow way out of the room. 'Yes, Bösendorfer with the real Viennese sound. I dislike all that American horsepower Steinways are putting into their pianos nowadays. Kindly play me your cadenza while I make the coffee. I shall be listening, never fear. If you hear cries of anguish, it will probably not be your playing but my burning myself. I often do.'

'But surely I could make it for you?'

'Never offer to help a cripple, he might take you up on it. My job is to make clumsy coffee and yours is to play – beautifully, mind.'

Left alone the boy sat gingerly down at the piano and gazed up at the rough slopes of bound paper which rose on either hand. Wild horses might not have dragged from him the admission that he *had* had some idea of going to a hamburger bar but he would readily have owned to being nervous, embarrassed, intrigued. Tentatively he played a few bars of the concerto's orchestral opening and then, made confident by the instrument's curious timbre, essayed the soloist's entry which his teacher always referred to as one of the most difficult to bring off in all piano literature. Not the notes, of course; but the stress, the emphasis, the articulation, the dynamics – all were crucial and crucially exposed. He quickly became involved in the music, playing against the concert performance as if setting to rights something improperly done, whole passages followed by lightly sketched-in pages until he reached the cadenza, which turned out well.

'Oh, yes,' said his host, who appeared with a tray at the end.

'Oh, yes, indeed. My dear boy, a little *career*, I think, should be opened unto you. How very much you disliked tonight's performance. I do like your cadenza, incidentally.'

'Well, not mine. Saint-Saëns'.'

'Was it? Was it really?' the murmur implied disbelief; the boy blushed. 'Now, come and have your coffee and we'll talk business.'

'Business?' said his guest warily. 'I thought we were going to talk about music.'

'We are, we are. That *is* our business. Come, we'll talk about you and thus make it easy to forgive what you might think is a certain flirtatiousness and self-congratulation in my manner. There. Sugar *and* milk. My dear wife used to make proper coffee – she was Hungarian, by the way – but sadly she died not long ago.'

'Was she a pianist, too?'

'A very good one. We played together for a short while before I had to stop for good: it was how we got to know each other, how we courted and how we first made love. In those days there were two pianos in here.' Anthony Raffish stared reflectively up at the shadowed cliffs. 'But it's you I want to fix. Let me guess what I think is in your concerto repertoire and then you can tell me I've got second sight. Very slightly off-beat, some of them: Hummel's A minor, Tchaikovsky number *two*, Schumann's Introduction and Allegro, something glittery but not completely trashy like Scharwenka, a Prokofiev, a Bartók, and a neoclassical like von Einem. How am I doing? Then', he said without a pause, 'the standard solo stuff but with oddities thrown in such as Dussek, Moscheles, Alkan, a prelude and fugue by Alfred Lord Tennyson. That sort of thing.'

'*Tennyson?* Did he write one?'

'Good Lord, no, dear boy, I don't suppose so. But I detect an interest in the outré and the bizarre as well as in a personal interpretation of the standard repertoire. Not Tennyson, then; I was being facetious. Lord Berners, perhaps, if we stick to English peers. No doubt a short and merry piece like one of the "Trois Petites Marches funèbres".'

'I'm afraid I've never heard of him.'

'Oh dear, really not? *The Triumph of Neptune* – Diaghilev and Sitwell? No? I knew him well. *Such* a talent; even Stravinsky was impressed. Also a sense of humour. I can quote you exactly what Grove says about those particular pieces: "Of the three funeral marches (for a statesman, a canary and a rich aunt) only that for the canary betrays any genuine feeling." A splendid man. But I digress. Was I not correct in some of my guesses? I can see I was.'

The boy was clearly disconcerted. He was leaning forward, filling his saucer with cold coffee from a cup unwittingly held at an acute angle.

'I don't see how you could have guessed,' he said. 'We don't know each other, Mr Raffish.'

'Anthony. But we do; or at least I do. Let us proceed. The concertos I mentioned, have they not most of them been played here in London over the last six months?'

The boy straightened up, his face pale and anxious. 'You've been following me.'

'Not at all, I assure you. I have been following music: it is my profession. It just so happens you were also present on many occasions. I have not followed you, but whenever you were there I watched you, that I admit.'

'What are you?' Zebedee put the cup down and stood up. 'I'm confused. You're very kind to have invited me home and given me coffee, and I love your piano and everything, but I don't know that anything you have told me about yourself is true.'

'But you do know that everything I have said about *you* is. Very well, then. I am, if you will, a talent scout. I am always at concerts because they are my life-blood and because I am always on the lookout for a certain kind of person. Some months ago I spotted you and thought you were one and now tonight I know that you are. You're not the only one,' he added with maybe an edge of malice. 'There are enough of the others to make me a very comfortable living, but not so many that I don't count them as friends and value them as artists.'

'You're an agent.'

'Yes,' admitted Anthony Raffish, 'I suppose I am. But an agent with a difference. I specialise in lost causes.'

'You haven't the right to say that.' The voice came faintly from the bottom of the canyon as of one already resigned to being crushed.

'Oh, but I have, my dear, I've a perfect right.' He studied the boy calmly, seeing the angry rigidity of the head staring away upwards into the shadows, divining the involuntary flooding of the eyes, knowing the solitary, introspective work. My, but he was vain, this one. 'Like you I am a musician. But, also like you,

I am a performer. We wish for reasons of whatever personal bent to take our private selves out on to a platform. Because I am so much older than you – and no doubt spurred by the bitterness of the performer forced to become a member of the audience – I am a very good judge of spectacle. Already, I suspect, you have a better musical intelligence than I; but I also know that your hoped-for career as a pianist is a lost cause unless. . . .

Unless what? cried the boy inaudibly

. . . unless Anthony Raffish takes you in hand. Antonin Raffawicz will listen to your music but it is Anthony Raffish who will lead you out to play. Now, you will have noticed I have asked nothing about your plans, what your teacher says, not even who he is. I have not enquired about the prizes you have carried off nor the competitions you may or may not have won.'

'I presumed that was because you were too busy telling me how clever you were,' said Zebedee.

'That was to give you confidence. Since I could show you that, although we had never met I already knew a great deal about you just from watching you at some concerts, I imagined we could cut out all the nonsense and the delicacy and get down to helping you.'

'I *like* delicacy. . . . And, anyway, if you're offering to be my agent you'd be helping yourself as well.'

'Granted. But it will be I who take the initial step to bring about the realisation of your fantasy.'

'Fantasy? What fantasy? I have a perfectly realistic ambition to be a professional pianist, that's all. I just want to make a living out of my music.'

'Nonsense,' contradicted Anthony Raffish complacently, 'you want much more than that. You could achieve that by being a *répétiteur* with some teaching and sessions on the side. No, you are ambitious for the spotlight and that doesn't make you any less of a musician. I said fantasy and I meant it. Admit it, now; this is your secret. You go to these concerts fully prepared. And why? Because it is your dream that the soloist will suddenly fall ill and lo! out of the audience steps the unknown Mr Hoyle in the nick of time, sits down among the startled orchestra, gives a nod of assurance to the bewildered conductor, and away goes Rachmaninov Two or Beethoven Five fit to electrify anyone. Especially the critics, hurrying home from the tumultuous applause to write glowing accounts of this new wunderkind

177

who at only a few seconds' notice was able to change for ever the way in which we look at Rachmaninov Two and Beethoven Five. The recording industry ignores him at their peril, the public to their loss, etcetera. And so a great career is launched. By a stroke of fortune a kitten on the keys becomes overnight a lion rampant on fields of ivory. Oh dear me, yes. And why not?'

There was a silence. Then, 'You think you've seen through me, I suppose.'

'Not at all. Your most private depths remain as opaque to me as to you. I merely understand a particular fantasy because it is all bound up with being unable to start your career properly. You're not alone, of course.'

'That's not how it feels.'

'Maybe, but the audiences in the concert-halls and recital-rooms of the world are full of frustrated talents who go mainly because they hope against hope that the million-to-one chance will be given them to step into the breach and shine more brilliantly than the star they're replacing. That is what performers are driven to when they haven't got careers.'

'It's ridiculous. I'm a pianist, an artist, not the sort of spectator who goes to a motor race secretly hoping for blood. I'm not so cold and malicious as to *want* people to fall ill suddenly or drop dead of a heart-attack.'

'I'm sure you're not. But there are only so many concert-halls, so many days in a year, so many occasions for a soloist. It's a highly competitive business nowadays, not a bit unlike sport; and wherever there's competitiveness there's the wish to cut a competitor's throat. In the case of a nice young man like yourself the suppressed wish is to have someone or something *else* do the cutting – luck, fate, circumstance, call it what you like.'

Zebedee had sat down at the piano. Suddenly he began playing Busoni's transcription of Bach's 'Ich ruf' zu dir'. The depressed magnificence of the music rose in the gloom and held everything securely in its place, for it was as if an avalanche had been about to rush down and engulf him utterly. Sustained and sustaining, some echo hung about the canyon's ledges and sills long after the last sound had died. 'I'm not a throat-cutter, it's no good,' he said finally.

'Not even Lipatti played it better than that, dear boy. . . . Why should you be a throat-cutter? That's what agents are for. You are a musician through and through. It is a great crime that the world is so constituted that people like us need to fight in order to be heard. Or at least in order to make a living out of being heard.'

'That's what I tell my teacher. He's always trying to get me to enter competitions. I'm always refusing. I tell him that if I were a poet I wouldn't give readings of my work in pubs, either, not simply to gain an audience. I'm not beery. I'd rather starve than try to be hearty with people I secretly despise.'

'Well, there we are. Nowadays, I'm afraid, one of the unexpected consequences of the television age is that the right kind of exposure can be critical to the success of a performing artist. If American presidents need to be sold on television like soap powder, can a mere instrumentalist hope for a hearing and fame without? It's no good relying on the audience's judgement: they simply don't know enough. What they like is to be able to attach some sort of persona to the performer. You have to be both able and identifiable, and if you're a bad self-publicist you need an agent who can market you in the right way. You need to be managed.'

'Which is where you think you come in.'

'My dear, I know I do. Your name, for a start. "Zeb Hoyle." Whoever heard of a musician being called Zeb Hoyle? It's inconceivable. You sound like a footballer. No, we'll have to find you a stage name. Personally, I like initials; they always sound so distinguished. Either that or a single name like Solomon or Michelangeli, but that would be pretentious for somebody as young as you are. Now, what sort of a name? Nothing too English, I think, something which prompts the faintest of musical associations. Cramer? Yes, I quite like that. "Z. Cramer." No, the "Z" is wrong because the Americans will pronounce it differently. What about "J. S. Cramer"?'

'J. S. Cramer.' Zebedee laughed.

'Perfect,' said Anthony Raffish, his head on one side. 'I especially liked the way you threw back that glossy mane of yours. Looks are extremely important, of course. You're lucky to be so personable. If you were very plain or even downright ugly, we might have had to make you demonic and tousled. As it is, you can be wayward, poetic and *geistig* as the Germans say.'

'I can't believe this,' cried the boy, but there was new colour in his face. 'You sit there and cynically *package* me?'

'Why not? What's wrong with cynicism? I'm not a bit cynical about your playing, which is what counts. As for packaging, you'll need it sooner or later if ever you're going to get out of the dumps you're in. Whatever you do, don't pay any attention to established musicians saying that if you're really worth listening to you'll inevitably be heard. That is a pseudo-worldly vulgarism. You'll find that when people become famous they very much want to believe that all it took was their sheer, unvarnished talent, whereas . . . my dear, the stories I could tell about the wily moves, the astonishing flukes and – yes – the *beds* which have helped many a career on its way. It's enough to make your hair curl.'

Perhaps it was true, thought Zebedee half an hour later on his way back across London to the drab rooms he rented near Archway. It was scarcely the first time he had heard such ideas; usually they made him despondent, even irritable, since he could never be quite sure if they were true and there seemed to be nobody who would give him an answer. The lessons, the regular exams, the years of practice stretched back to his earliest childhood so interwoven with anguish as much as with public praise and private pleasure that they had become the texture of his entire life. So much work and reflection had long since readied him for the public career he knew he had earned and yet now he was to believe he had done only half what was necessary. It was not enough to sell sounds; the marionette in tails who sat on a stool and made those sounds had also to be sold. Candlesticks? Sequins? Lace at the wrists? An eye-catching eccentricity like an inability to play without a glass of water on the piano?

Bitter impatience with such tomfoolery brought his heels hard down on the pavement. Get away from such ideas. Get away, too, from Anthony Raffish. Zebedee was unable to be precise about what he had most disliked in the arthritic musician. Perhaps it was having been at least partially seduced by the man, by the cultured clutter of his rooms, the piano whose tone he could still hear, the urbane bohemianism of the foreign background and cosmopolitan past. Also, of course, Raffish had for a short time enjoyed precisely the success which Zebedee now longed for. But under it all there ran a current of unease like a pool spreading from beneath a lavatory door, and he knew that no matter how much might evaporate in the early light of next morning the defect would still be there.

This turned out to be the case. 'I met the most extraordinary man last night,' he told Antoinette during their hour. Antoinette from Basle had been coming to him for lessons for six months now and she was completely in love with him, which at some level he found quite understandable.

'How extraordinary?' So Zebedee told her. 'I think maybe he is bogus,' she said. 'Watch out. Perhaps you should not see him again.'

But within a week Anthony Raffish lightly knuckled his arm on the way out of a Wigmore Hall recital.

'I didn't see you,' said Zebedee.

'Aha, we were late and crept in at the back at the end.' He indicated a tall, earnest girl with scraped hair. 'This is Sandra Padgett. Sandra, Zebedee. Sandra's a remarkable clarinettist. From Harpenden, but quite brilliant. Come, we will take a taxi to Marble Arch and walk a short while in the Park.'

Zebedee found himself borne along, not quite cursing himself for weakness. Whatever current it had been, sinister or otherwise, it seemed sponged away now by that immediately familiar, open-handed assertiveness.

'We shall talk about musical lost causes,' said the old pianist once they were sauntering across the balding grass, and he spoke irrepressibly of a nineteenth-century Italian named Pietro Raimondi who had written extraordinary works such as three separate oratorios which could be sung one after the other and then combined and sung all three at once. 'A prodigious contrapuntal feat, my dears, but nowadays who can find three orchestras and three choirs for a single performance? A very strange man, quite forgotten, although I seem to remember he composed more than fifty operas. He once wrote a fugue for sixteen four-part choirs, that I do remember. Imagine, a sixty-four-voice fugue. There's a glorious madness there.'

Zebedee glanced from time to time at Sandra, but her eyes were fixed on Anthony Raffish's animated face. The little man made stiff, right-angled gestures to add force to what he was saying.

'There's something very grand about artists, often first-rate artists, with at best a minority appeal utterly refusing to compromise and make their work accessible, isn't there? Or it may be a radical incapacity. Years ago I became friendly with a most strange old half-Indian named Sorabji, a quite astonishing pianist and an even more astonishing composer. He never wrote very much, I don't think, but it's hard to tell because he would allow practically none of it ever to be published or performed. I remember Alfred Cortot telling me how highly he rated one of Sorabji's piano concertos he was allowed to see. A fascinating man; I suppose somewhere must be all those manuscripts of his which I used to beg him to let me see but to no avail. There is one work of his in print which I think Zebedee here might be interested in since it would satisfy any pianist's desire for the outré. It's called "Opus clavicembalisticum" and it goes on for hours and it's so preposterously difficult it makes Busoni look like Grade Five. Now, *there's* a composer who ought to be disinterred, or at least properly examined before being reinterred. But probably a lost cause after all as no doubt he himself wished. One can't help admiring the ferocious pride or stubbornness of people who go to such lengths to scupper all chance of worldly success in order to remain true to their private vision. . . .'

And so he talked and toddled, and so Zebedee's gloom returned at the seeping glitter of menace and corruption he thought to detect somewhere beneath. Was he being warned? 'This young man needs watching.' That was what a reviewer had written about his Wigmore Hall début after first conceding that anyone who includes 'Gaspard' and 'Islamey' in a first recital and plays them with complete technical mastery would merit watching anyway, even were it not for the thoughtfulness of his late Beethoven. *Needs watching*. And what since then? Nothing. No offers, no records, no engagement, nobody watching at all. Happy the man whose private vision can pay the rent.

Abruptly he turned to walk back to Speaker's Corner and catch the Tube. He couldn't think whàt the purpose of this stroll, this conversation was, but hardly doubted there was one.

'You will give me your address,' said Anthony Raffish. He produced an envelope and held a pen in his bunched fingers. 'Yes?' And Zebedee found himself surrendering that part of his life which was comprehended by Archway. As he watched Raffish's painful scrawling he glanced up and found the tall girl's eyes fixed on him with an expression he could not read.

Three days later he received a plain white postcard. *My dear J.S., tomorrow night's Festival Hall concert will, I venture, contain something of interest to you. I think you should be there. Yours ever, A.* Zebedee looked up the programme and failed to see anything immediately suggestive. Among other things a Weber clarinet concerto and – horrors! – a symphony by Ives in the second half.

Rather even Burl than Charles, he told himself, but none the less went.

The clarinettist billed to end the first half was a staunch old virtuoso now moving in stately fashion towards the end of his much-acclaimed career. Indeed, there had been rumours that this might be his last public appearance in England and it was presumably this which accounted for the televising of the first half. As Zebedee watched him come on to an immense ovation he thought he looked ripe for intensive care, let alone retirement. A grey, pained face beneath a strange grey toque of hair, a weird busby which in its way was almost as renowned as the playing of the man beneath it. The concerto started, and Zebedee found his attention wandering. Why was he here? What was the significance of the occasion? In all those serried tiers of seats he failed to spot Anthony Raffish or, indeed, anyone he knew.

A murmur in the audience brought his attention sharply back. Up on the platform something was wrong. The orchestra were nearing the end of a passage which led into a sequence of athletic arpeggios for the soloist, but his clarinet was hanging slackly by his side, held like a stick in its middle while the high grey nest was bending forward as if gravely acknowledging premature applause. His other hand rose to meet it as sudden folds appeared at the knees of his dress trousers. A Second Violin with presence of mind quickly left his desk and moved forward to take the man's elbow and help him backstage. Perhaps mindful of the cameras, which ought at this moment to be switching viewers' attention to a close-up of a cellist's bow or a female horn's *décolletage*, the conductor kept the orchestra together in a way which suggested that like all performers they knew the show must go on. It was all happening so quickly, in any case, that the wobbly virtuoso with his bent back to the podium had only taken a few escorted steps towards the wings when the music reached the soloist's entry. And suddenly, right on cue and from low down in the auditorium, it came.

A tall girl in a long black dress was standing in the aisle between the front rows of seats, clarinet to her mouth. The conductor turned round to face this unexpected source of music, and the girl gave him a visible nod of encouragement. She walked as she played, slowly, statuesquely, down to the edge of the platform and stood to one side of the podium, half-turning to face the audience and the conductor at the same time. And still the dazzling passagework glittered off the little silver keys of her instrument. Coming so soon after the old virtuoso's last notes the comparison was cruelly easy to make. Even the more unmusical among the audience could detect the edged difference in tone the girl produced; instead of the mellow, rounded sounds of the concerto's opening were now an almost nasal brightness and clarity whose excitement gripped players and listeners alike.

It had taken Zebedee several astonished seconds to recognise the girl as the one in whose company he had so recently strolled. He was not particularly startled by her virtuosity, but her punctuality was another matter. He wondered how she had managed to tune up beforehand, let alone keep the reed warm while sitting in the audience. Had she hidden her clarinet under her dress? After an astonishing cadenza the movement ended and spontaneously the audience broke into a great torrent of applause for her impromptu courage, her femaleness, her preparedness, in recognition of her having provided them with a real-live televised *event* and – who knew? – even for her playing, in the middle of which the conductor reached down a brilliant black arm with a white cuff to help her on to the stage. A cheer went up. And it was not until then that certain things began to trouble Zebedee very much indeed. There was something not at all right about this sleighted piece of drama; but time and again he came up against the impossibility of believing it could be the 'something of interest to you' which Anthony Raffish had predicted. How could he have foretold an illness so sudden as to attack a soloist in mid-movement? It was uncanny. But there seemed nothing else suggestive or apposite in the rest of the programme. The concerto itself ended with a standing ovation for the girl whose serious expression unexpectedly yielded to a concerned smile before she handed her instrument to the conductor, exited quickly and, as the cheering continued, re-entered and came to the front of the platform where she raised both hands, very white in the television lights, for silence.

'Ladies and gentlemen,' came her small unamplified voice. 'To set your minds at rest I'm sure you'd all like to know that Julius de Kooning is not seriously ill but is just suffering from sudden faintness brought on by an exhausting schedule. He would like to apologise to us all and promises an entire concerto next time. I'm sure we wish him a speedy recovery. Thank you.'

The applause broke out anew, respectful at first as if for an absent friend and mixed with some relieved laughter, but becoming more frenzied as the unknown girl's interrupted ovation resumed. It seemed to Zebedee quite endless and the next morning he found she was rather famous under the name of 'Alicia Cazenove'. Sandra Padgett had presumably been left in Harpenden, the split chrysalis from which a higher imago had finally emerged to dry her magnificent wings in the springtime heat of the television lights.

Zebedee could predict only too easily the sort of inferences Anthony Raffish might draw for him from this astonishing example of a career taking off and decided to boycott concerts where they might run into one another. He was unable to avoid his own, however, such as the one at the Royal College a week later when he was accompanying a violinist as well as playing some solo works.

'I did enjoy that,' said the familiar voice at his elbow as he left the building afterwards. 'How very well you play Fauré; not many Englishmen can, I find. He demands real subtlety of tone. How right you are not to make his sonorities sentimental as if he were a French Elgar.'

'I don't find Elgar sentimental,' said Zebedee abruptly.

'Quite right, too,' came the imperturbable voice. 'But the English can read sentimentality into anything once they set their minds to it. They treat Elgar like he treated dogs. Now, do I detect *nettlement* in your tone?'

'I've no idea. Not intentionally, perhaps. I shall go home now: I'm giving a lesson later.'

'So busy. What a pity. Oh, J.S., J.S., don't you sometimes feel it all slipping away?'

'I don't quite know what you mean, I'm afraid.'

'You're a silly boy, Zeb,' said Mr Raffish with a glint in his voice, 'and you're much too brilliant to let the silly boy win. Don't worry, I do understand about what happened at the Festival Hall the other night. You're puzzled and faintly alarmed – anyone would be. "How could he have known?" you ask yourself. "Is there something sinister about this arthritic little poseur – for I only have *his* word for it that he could ever play a note himself?" '

This was so precisely the rhetoric with which Zebedee had compulsively been addressing lamp-posts, plates of chips, the bathroom mirror, that he started with a kind of guilt. 'You're unfair, Anthony,' he said; and there was suddenly something so doleful in the ageing face looking up sideways into his through the mauve electric wash of a street-lamp he added, 'But I admit to moments of scepticism. I get those all the time, especially about myself.'

This seemed to defuse things, for when Raffish spoke he was once more all charm and coercion. 'Come,' he said, 'we shall take a taxi and I will prove something to you. And if you're worried about your *pupil*' – again it was like a foreign expression – 'you can ring her from my flat and tell her you will be an hour or so late. This is important to you since it concerns your future. All is not yet lost.'

How Zebedee could once more find himself standing at the bottom of that canyon with the landslides of culture held magically from rushing down and swamping him, he hardly knew. He had willingly come quite against his will, as if to be scrupulously fair to a lover he had already decided to reject. He watched as the older man fumbled in one geological corner of the room and excavated the top of an old radiogram. He switched the machine on with a pop, and the hum of valves warming came from somewhere halfway up the cliffs. He coaxed a record out of its cover and put it on. Out of a crackle of surface noise the two arresting chords of Chopin's B minor Scherzo struck, followed by such a breathtakingly clear torrent that Zebedee was momentarily chilled before undergoing the sensation of being picked up bodily and carried off. In the calm of the central section he was able to cross the room and find the record sleeve. On the front was a black and white photo of a very young man, practically a boy, in that classic musician's dated pose of dreaming face propped on folded hands. The dreaming face was undoubtedly that of the elderly cripple lost somewhere in the shadows of this cavernous room. Zebedee turned the cover over.

A Chopin recital by a pianist who, despite his youth, has been called by no less a maestro than Vladimir Horowitz 'the most astonishing talent of his generation known to me' is a true musical event. Antonin Raffawicz studied in Paris under Nadia Boulanger and Rosina Lhevinne as well as Alfred Cortot in Switzerland. . . .

All should be forgiven, thought Zebedee as the Scherzo ended. *As was intended*, added a cynical observer

186

buried inside him, *as was intended*.

'Well, enough of that,' broke in Anthony Raffish, taking the record off with a harsh scrape. His eyes glistened in the semi-dark. 'All very long ago now. I sometimes wonder myself who he was and what became of him. Such promise, and all that.'

'It was wonderful playing,' Zebedee told him truthfully. 'I've never heard it played like that.'

'Do better yourself, then.' The words were brusquer than the tone. 'Only *do* it, Zebedee. You can now; don't wait until the misery of isolation takes your edge off.'

'But what do you want me to do, damn you?' cried the boy passionately. 'You keep grabbing my arm, tugging my sleeve, saying, "Get on, do it now, don't hang about, it's later than you think," but you don't seem to realise that I know all that already. I worry myself ill about it, my father worries about it, my teacher worries but pretends it doesn't matter being a slow starter. So I hardly need you to tell me what the matter is if you won't also tell me what to do about it. And you can't; getting on is obviously just a matter of dumb luck. Dumb fucking luck.' Disastrously, the adjective came out as youthfully flung in the face of an outmoded and genteel knowledge of the world. Anthony Raffish seemed not to notice.

'My dear, so *change* your luck; don't just sit there being petulant. I've told you before, you need an agent. I have heard you play many times here and there, you know; I told you I was a talent scout. Well, then. I believe in you and I think you have it in you to be a great pianist. Look here. See this?' He pushed a programme into Zebedee's hands. 'See that name? Who do you think is his agent? Or hers?' He found another programme lying about in the general confusion. 'Or his, or his? Or this one? Oh, yes, him, too.' Zebedee's lap flowed over with sheets, playbills, posters, photographs, name after famous name.

'All yours?' he asked at length.

'Mine,' said the old agent. 'Every one of them. Go on, look at them. Him, for example. You don't think that's his original name, do you? Terence Abbott, he used to be, from Sidcup or somewhere. Terry, the south London equivalent of Ovid J. Finkelmeyer. So tell me, does that name go with a black tie and a Guarnerius? And' – some more paper fell to the floor – 'what about her?'

Her was an internationally celebrated contralto pictured in an advertisement torn from *Time*. She was standing holding a sheet of music in one hand (the grey blur of the page could, Zebedee found, be resolved by a musician into – bafflingly – an easy piano version of 'Sheep May Safely Graze') while her other hand rested on a slab of mirror-like black wood, presumably the top of a piano. A gold watch was casually obtrusive. Zebedee glanced at the text. 'Dame Celia finds her DateMatic® an essential part of the hectic, globe-trotting life of a virtuoso. *I'm afraid I find the jet-lag beginning to catch up towards the end of the season*, she admits. *I catch myself thinking that if it's Thursday it must be Puccini but thank goodness I have my DateMatic® to remind me that it's only Wednesday so it must be Meyerbeer. . . .*'

'It stinks, doesn't it?' Anthony Raffish was watching him sagely. 'But out of the stink comes forth sweetness and that's what counts. It's up to you to change your prejudices, I'm afraid. You may think it's something exclusive to the age we live in, but you'd be quite wrong. You don't like the idea of music competitions, either, do you? But they've been around for centuries.'

'Prizes, yes, and contests between famous players; but not those sports events you see on television. Knock-out competitions between wretched children who have been pushed and groomed into empty virtuosity. Half of them haven't an ounce of musicianship in them but it's funny how often the little girls who win seem to have long blonde hair and get all that close camera-work on their lips stretched around their embouchures.'

'Bravo!' said Anthony in delight. 'Quite right, of course; it's a mixture of Young Gymnast of the Year and what I believe they call *soft porn*. But for the winners it's the chance of a career.'

'Yes, and how many of those go on to make one? It's usually the real musicians who come third or who don't get placed at all, and what happens to them? How can anyone begin a career with a nationally viewed public failure into which he was urged for the greater glory of parents or teacher? The whole thing's rotten.' To his embarrassment Zebedee found himself on the edge of tears.

'It's a murky old world,' conceded the agent complacently. 'It's actually rather jolly sniffing out ways of making ends meet. Personally, I never asked to stop creating sounds; but since the matter was decided for me by inscrutable fate I now take the greatest of pleasure in creating careers instead. My only stipulation is that the people I represent are not the products of what Madison Avenue used to call "hype"; they must be genuinely good. You are one such. You want to force me to be specific? Very well, then. In exchange for your signing a contract with me I will undertake to provide you with an opportunity such as you saw young Sandra – or should we say Alicia? – grasp with both hands the other night on nationwide TV.'

There was a long silence. Zebedee was more shocked than he could ever remember. Not even the mawkish pleadings of a schoolteacher years ago had filled him with such a sense of being intolerably presumed upon.

'I can't believe that you can admit to such a thing,' he said at last.

'My dear, I've admitted to nothing. I'm offering you a properly organised career.'

'You've as good as told me you arranged to have Julius de Kooning fall ill the other night. What did you do? Put laxative in his dressing-room coffee?'

'Don't be absurd,' said Mr Raffish sharply. 'I won't have you say such things. That's criminal.'

'I imagine that's what anybody else would say. A newspaper, for instance.'

'My dear Mr Hoyle.' Gone now was the expansiveness of the voice and in its place a glacial remoteness. 'It would be the height of folly to throw up all hope of a career in your chosen profession at the very same moment as becoming embroiled in a nasty and extremely expensive lawsuit.'

A terrifying sense of things having got far out of hand gripped Zebedee. How had they elided so quickly from Chopin to this bristled menace? Was everything really so thin? 'I'm leaving,' was all he could say helplessly. 'You've upset me and I don't quite . . . I'm not sure of anything.'

The bray of laughter from the shadows was one of mockery he had not had directed at him since school.

'You poor little boy. Upset, are we? Deary me, as the English say, we *have* had a sheltered life, practising our scales and keeping our pretty nose clean. The world is too much with us, is that it? Better avoid it altogether while admiring yourself for being uncontaminated? Fine. So when even your precious world of music is revealed as being rather worldly, oh, the hands daintily lifted in horror and, oh, how the first suspicions must be schoolboy ones of skulduggery! The far more likely explanation wouldn't have occurred to you, which is that successful performers like de Kooning get booked solid three years in advance by hard-nosed little agents like me: concerts here, recitals there, recording studios everywhere, aeroplanes, taxis, hotels hotels hotels, and when they reach his age they get tired and maybe even a bit stale and so when that agent comes up to them in private and offers to make a certain arrangement – something non-taxable, let us say, in return for the momentary embarrassment of a public retreat to the dressing room – don't you think they mightn't be glad of a week off? And if the net result of that well-earned little rest taken at no risk whatever to an established career is to give some younger musician a chance are you going to tell me a great moral crime has been committed? Well, are you? So go away, young Mr Hoyle; go away and do some growing up instead of haunting the concert-halls with your scores and your fantasies. I promise you, you'll one day play all the better for acquainting yourself with the world; the great composers were not angels. Go away and swindle somebody or betray someone you love. Yourself, for example. Go and give yourself clap.'

Years later Zebedee never recalled this episode without once more experiencing its vivid shock. Never in all his life had he occasioned such an outburst as this, and at the time he but dimly grasped how it could have happened. In his mind's ear he could still hear the bitter tone but never the words themselves. On the other hand he found it easy to recall a conversation some months afterwards with a fellow-musician, an oboist with whom desultory chat before a recital had revealed they had an acquaintance in common.

'You're not with him, are you?' the oboist asked when Anthony's name had cropped up. 'Are you with Raffish?'

'Absolutely not.' Zebedee must have betrayed a vehemence which the other picked up at once.

'Ah, you went through that mill, did you? No doubt a brilliant man but a nasty little queen for all that.' Then, catching the blank look on Zebedee's face, 'You don't mean he didn't make a pass at you?'

'Good heavens, no,' said Zebedee, but with more assurance than he felt.

'Surely you didn't believe all that crap about his wife?'

'The Hungarian pianist?'

The oboist laughed. 'Hungarian pianist, was she? French oboist, the night he met me. For my money she never existed at all; she was a useful fiction. I admit I never liked him so I was glad he lost all interest in me when he discovered I already had an agent. In fact I gather he's first-rate. He certainly knows how to spot talent. He goes to every concert that ever is, knows all the managements intimately. He's got a sort of *carte blanche* to wander around the dressing rooms and hobnob with people. There was a time when I couldn't play anywhere without him popping up from behind box offices and stage doors. I suppose that's what you have to do, just *know* everybody, and it seems to have paid off in his case. There are lots of famous names with Anthony Raffish and there's apparently nothing he won't do for his musicians. But watch out if you cross him – they do say he can be pretty catty and spiteful, although I've no intention of finding out.'

About eight months after that Zebedee was approached by an American recording company, one of whose talent scouts had been impressed by a recital he had given in London. He had been flown to Pasadena and there had recorded a programme of piano music by Gottschalk which, coming as it did at a time of increasing interest in nineteenth-century American music, had a considerable success. This led to a contract to record a MacDowell concerto, and suddenly he was being billed as an up-and-coming exponent of American music, living in America for months at a stretch, travelling about that continent from hall to hall and from studio to studio. On his twenty-eighth birthday Zebedee found himself, with some degree of irony, signing a contract to record Ives's 'Concord' sonata. How differently things had turned out, he wryly thought, from what he had once imagined or even wanted. Not 'J. S. Cramer' playing limpid Viennese classics but Zeb Hoyle playing Ives and being paid handsomely to do so.

Shortly after that he crossed the Atlantic for one of his rare visits to Europe to fulfil an engagement at a Promenade Concert where he was booked to play Rachmaninov Two. His appearances in England were now infrequent enough for it to be a real pleasure to return. In the earlier part of his transatlantic exile he had commuted a good deal between Boston and Basle, for the young wife he had taken with him to America had failed to adjust to life there and by the time she came to deliver their child Antoinette had gone home to her parents. It often struck Zebedee how odd it was to have a Swiss son; but then, that whole episode of marrying and parenting now seemed part of a previous period in his life, even to belong to a person who no longer quite existed, someone who had once been deeply unhappy in north London.

In fact he found the pleasure of being back in London undercut more than expected by the memories it evoked. How pungently it returned, that atmosphere of despondency and dreaming; of endless hours at the keyboard in rented rooms, of lonely walks to all-night fast-food bars, of concerts and recitals from which he had gone home rancorous with envy. A particular stench of memory still clung around that brief episode with Anthony Raffish, he admitted. How did those few meetings of a long time ago still retain the power to make him feel awkward, even guilty? He had of course been very young then. . . . Had he betrayed himself in some way? He could no longer quite remember. Anyway, it hardly mattered now as he sat in his dressing room, clearing his mind in a professional manner of all but the music itself.

For almost an hour he sat in stiff collar and shirtsleeves quietly reading the score and sipping black coffee until the bell went. The walk onstage afforded him considerable pleasure: it was only the second time he had played in the Albert Hall, and it was still something of a novelty to view the scene of his former yearning pilgrimages from the performer's side of the platform. With a sense now of pleasurably relaxed homecoming he softly began the first of the eight chords which opened the concerto.

Rachmaninov's Second is a busy work for the soloist. In the first movement, at any rate, there are few of those moments common in concertos of a century earlier when he can sit back from time to time and let the orchestra introduce or develop its own material. Thus it was that Zebedee was too occupied to notice that all was not well with him until a good way into the first movement. The pain suddenly became acute enough to force itself on his attention and in so doing reminded him that it had been there in his stomach practically since the moment he had come onstage. He noticed the conductor watching him with concern; the keyboard became slippery. More and more his mind was diverted into holding himself together until the movement's end while his fingers mechanically, professionally, played the notes. At last they were into the accelerando of the coda whose increasing pace and excitement made it easier for him to disguise and appease the pain by swaying his body, shifting position.

Zebedee came to his feet almost as he played the final chord. On his hurried way across the platform to the exit he was conscious of little but gesturing vaguely to the conductor as he left, half-seeing on the other side the white fields of upturned faces like a hillside of moonflowers. Outside a St John's Ambulance Brigade volunteer sat dozing on a canvas chair. Zebedee passed him at a run.

Inside the lavatory and in something like blessed relief he let himself lean panting against one wall with his eyes shut while the external world came filtering back. There was a soft knock on the door and a man's voice – the ambulanceman? – asked discreetly if he were all right.

'I'm OK,' Zebedee told the back of the door weakly. 'I can't go on again but I'm OK. Something I ate. You'd better tell someone.'

He listened to the man's footsteps recede. From his stomach and spreading to the rest of his body the pain of disappointment suffused him. The triumphant return was spoilt. He had played less than a quarter of the time spent beforehand reading the score in anticipation and so sudden and confusing had been the sickness it was difficult to believe that for him, at least, tonight's concert was already over. Then almost immediately there came the distant sound of the concerto's slightly delayed second movement starting. As he sat letting the anguish drain slowly out of him he wondered whom they had found as an understudy at such short notice. The movement was half over before Zebedee could slip out, a handkerchief pressed to his face.

On the way to his dressing room he could not resist peeping in through the curtained entry on to the platform. There at the piano in the glare of the light sat a blond young man of melting good looks, albeit of a rather dated and foppish kind. He was in jeans and a sweater and was contriving to wring the music of its last romantic drops. These spattered his rapt audience as refreshing spring rain, but for Zebedee behind his curtain they flowed together into a certain once-familiar runnel of unease.

At the sudden touch on his arm and the whisper he turned abruptly. But it was only the ambulanceman asking if he were all right.

'Where did that boy come from?'

'Lord knows, sir. Just popped up out of nowhere. Stepped

into the breach in the nick of time, though, didn't he?'

And as Zebedee lay showered and weak on the settee in his dressing room the distant surf which was the sound of someone else's wild applause oozed through the walls.

At Even Ere the Sun Was Set

The road towards dusk became full of the mauvish air which was sliding down from the mountains. On one side the sea with its groups of people picking their food from among the corals exposed by low tide; on the other the tall hot glooms of forest: wax trees, statue trees, palamandrons and the hollow cries of parrots. The road itself was dusty, a decaying patchwork of tarmac and concrete and rutted stretches of gravel which was an archaeological record of botched contracts, official indifference and local self-interest.

Along this road towards dusk there now appeared a stringy old brown man in an unravelling frond hat pushing a cart which was principally a circular metal tub on two wheels. The wheels were of solid wood, nearly round and rimmed with strips cut from tyres. Without bearings the holes at their centres had worn so that the wheels flopped now this way, now that, groaning at all angles. By the man's right hand as he pushed the cart was a small brass bell which he rang every few steps as punctuation to his cry: 'Soup! Delicious! Fresh! Excrement soup!'

Sauntering towards this old man was a figure in the utmost contrast, a man from another planet maybe: tall, blond, in a cool white shirt with a crimson silk scarf at his throat. In an apparent concession to local custom he had on his bare feet a pair of cheap rubber sandals. He was ambling as if entranced by the dusk, the peaceful breathing of the ocean, the evening calls and fireflies floating out of the trees, the early bats flittering their irregular circuits. Certainly at this moment and in this land he was at one with all other people slowly moving about while not going anywhere. For a moment a delicate member of the jonquil family caught his attention at the roadside. When he straightened up the oncoming old man with the cart was only a few yards away.

'Excrement soup!'

'Good evening, father,' called out the stranger. At least, thought the old man, he speaks a bit of our language even if his accent is funny.

'Good evening, sir.' The stranger was relieved to find that he could at least communicate with the old bastard, not like that idiot from the south who had made such a fool of him in the market that morning, although he was still not at all sure about what this one was selling. 'What's that?' he pointed at the cart.

'Soup. Excrement soup. It's delicious.'

'Delicious. Hot, is it?'

'God's-teeth-and-buttocks, of course it's not hot, you stupid fool,' said the old man to himself. To this foreigner he said: 'Cold, sir, with lots of ice as is the custom here. It's delicious. Very refreshing, sir. Try some?' He reached for the stained ladle which dangled from one shaft of the cart's handle.

The foreigner shook his blond mane with self-deprecating humour. 'For a moment there I thought you said "excrement".'

The old man did not smile.

'Quite right, sir. Excrement.'

'You mean – I want to get this right – *shit soup*?'

'Precisely. I believe in the south they call it that. But we're a bit more sophisticated round here, sir. We call it excrement soup. Besides, it's more than mere shit: there's vanilla and good white sugar and, of course, the ice.'

'Delicious indeed.' The stranger was nodding with serious anthropological interest, thinking: Christ's-lights-and-bladder, why can't I understand this sodding language by now? What *can* this stuff be that he's selling? 'Do you buy it ready-made, father? Er, bulk import?'

'Dear me, no,' the old man said, and his frond hat unwound a bit at his vehemence. 'The very idea. No, I make it myself, fresh each morning, just like my mother did and her mother before her. This is original to our family. It's genuine. Oh, I don't blame your being sceptical, young man. One hears such stories nowadays. They say that in the City the excrement soup there –

if you can find any, and it's a big If – is practically all bogus. Chemicals and what-not. They say they put that monosodium glutamate in it to make up for the lack of flavour, as well as commercial vanilla essence. Can you imagine? There's a kilo of home-grown vanilla pods in there.' He pointed to the battered tin tureen with an ornate knob which covered the top of the tub like a grey alloy bell. 'Excrement soup!' he called towards the nearest knot of low-tiders and sent a brassy tinkle pealing down to the shore. It seemed to mark a temporary loss of momentum in the conversation.

The blond foreigner still wore a friendly expression of grave interest and easygoing humour, but this was now being eroded from within by a puzzlement which might develop into further self-deprecation or into extreme tetchiness; only time would tell. Meanwhile the forest exhaled a spicy stink of hot rot. 'Hot,' he said conventionally and mopped his face with a floppy white handkerchief. For his part the old man flicked a long yellow fingernail against the alloy tureen with an irritating clacking sound.

'Listen,' he said and shook the handle of the cart. From within the tub came a dull clunking and bobbling as of hard and soft nodules in slow agitation. 'That's ice you can hear.'

'I know, father.'

Now was the time to go, a decisive bidding of good night, the onward and no less decisive walk. But at that impeccably judged moment the old man said: 'You speak our language very well indeed, if I may say so, sir. How many years have you lived in our country?'

'No, I don't, only a little. Oh, about six months now.' The moment was gone.

'Six months only? I don't believe it, sir. Why, I've met foreigners who have married one of our lovely girls and settled down here and at the end of ten years they still can't speak more than a few words. And most of those are commands.'

'It's not right.'

'It's not right. So you must be very clever and hard-working.'

'Good lord, no.'

'Now, I', the old man said, 'am not at all clever, but I *am* hard-working. Every day up at four to make the soup. That takes nearly two hours to get it right – depending on the contributions I collect from family and friends. Then at five-thirty the block of ice arrives from the ice-plant, and I have to saw it up. By the time I get on the road it's past six and here I've been all day.'

'Heavens. It must be a hard life, father.'

'Too right. You have to be an excrement soup-seller to appreciate just how hard making an honest livelihood is nowadays.'

'Well, for example, how much have you sold today?'

'About half.' The old man joggled the shafts again and the knobbly sloshing could be heard. 'Say, three gallons. Oy! Soup!' He turned to the group on the foreshore, some of whom were now drifting towards the road. One or two boats were putting out behind them, unlit pressure-lamps suspended above their prows, turning towards the evening star. The flat calm, the immoderate tranquillity overlaid everything and produced in the foreigner a sudden feeling of equable resignation, albeit with a lingering residue of utter rage.

'So what' – he found himself asking without the least idea of how interested he actually was in knowing the answer – 'what do you do with what's left over at the end of the day? Keep it until tomorrow and mix it in with the new soup?'

'Sacred pus, what kind of a question's that?' demanded the old man of himself. 'Dear me, no, sir,' he heard himself saying, 'that would never do. No, I give it to the pigs. It fattens them up beautifully, does excrement soup. Lots of good nourishment there.'

By now some of the low-tiders had reached the cart and were gathering round, staring at the foreigner with not unfriendly curiosity, the children silent but easily induced to giggle at a jab from a companion's sharp little elbow.

'So the whole lot's fresh each morning?'

'Exactly. The whole lot's fresh each day, as I told you.'

'He speaks our language,' announced a boy in a T-shirt washed into holes. He was carrying a small octopus impaled on a short length of wire.

'No, I don't; only a little.' Oh, the formulaic nature of his life's conversations. He once more mopped his face.

'Ah, but you do; you're doing it now,' a young man assured him wisely. Then, 'You must be very rich.'

'No, I'm not. Well, here I'm rich but not in my own country.' Christ-on-a-rubber-crutch, did it never end?

'Rich enough for some good excrement soup,' observed the old man.

'Look, father,' said the blond foreigner, 'I want to get this

198

straight once and for all. In here' – he tapped the tin tureen –
'you have a soup made of, let's see, excrement . . . ?'

'Excrement.'

'Vanilla pods?'

'Vanilla pods.'

'White sugar?'

'White sugar.'

'And ice?'

'Plenty of ice.'

'What else?'

The old man shook his head, and his hat further unwound.
'Aha,' he said. 'Now, that's a trade secret. If everybody knew all
the ingredients, they'd go off and make their own and I'd be out
of business. Now, what I *can* tell you is that there's a little bit of
fruit mixed up in it, but I'm not saying what.'

'Tamarinds,' hazarded one of the onlookers.

'Mangoes.'

'Bananas.'

'Jackfruit.'

'Not saying,' said the old man.

'Well, it sounds delicious,' said the agreeable foreigner.

'Delicious,' came a chorus of voices. 'It really is delicious.'
There fell a short silence.

'Er, how much is it?' A collective sigh acknowledged that a
fresh stage had been reached.

'Now,' said the old man, 'it's the end of the day and I can't
pretend it's *exactly* as fresh as it was at five-thirty this morning.
Also, of course, some of the ice has melted and it's a bit runnier
than it was. So' – he paused and glanced up at the now deep
violet sky well thronged with bats – 'let's say forty *piku* a glass.'
He reached forward to a rack between the shafts which held a
selection of brown tumblers made from beer-bottles with their
necks cut off, then paused. 'On the other hand, sir' – and he
looked straight into the young foreigner's face with the
implacability of a vampire – 'my life is very hard. . . .'

'Very hard,' echoed the mesmerised stranger.

'. . . and for you and as a special offer I should like to express
my pleasure that you have taken the trouble to learn our
language so well. . . .'

'No, I don't; only a little.'

'. . . and give you the opportunity of tasting our national
speciality which so many guests in our country refuse to try, in

199

my humble opinion very rudely.'

'Very rudely.' The tall figure, whose white shirt glimmered in the gathering night like the robe of a saint, bent its head.

'So', concluded the old man, 'for only four *dankals* I'm going to give you a full half-gallon pitcher.'

A general murmur at the generosity and fairness of this offer surrounded the young stranger.

'Oh. Thank you. Thank you many times, father.'

'Don't mention it.' The old face set itself into an expression of remorseless pleasure as he lifted the tureen-like cover, dipped deeply in with the ladle and swirled the tub's contents around. From a hook on the side of the cart he took a red polythene pitcher. 'You can let me have this back tomorrow. Or leave it with any of these people here. They'll return it. See?' He up-ended the pitcher and displayed a hieroglyph in paint on the bottom. 'Now, then. Smell that.'

The stranger in the martyr's shift leaned forward over the tub. Dear Christ, it really *was* that all along; there's no mistake. Well, there is but it's not down to vocabulary.

Up came the ladle full of blackish broth and ochre smears which plopped into the pitcher.

'Delicious,' said somebody.

'Delicious.' I don't believe this.

Now chunks of ice knocked against each other, but softly, padded by the thick slops. The stranger tried a joke.

'Like diarrhoea.'

The old man's ladle paused and he shook his head severely.

'No, sir. There's no diarrhoea in *my* soup. That's the cheap way out. Only good solids in this; but, as I said, during the course of the day the ice has melted a bit, which has thinned it all out. But it's based on properly formed motions.' The ladle dipped back in and resumed its unhurried transfer of the national delicacy. Soon his thin old wrist was ridged with tendons and trembling with the strain of holding half a gallon of his soup. He added another dollop and let the ladle fall back into the tub with a distant splosh. The red pitcher was brimful. Several rounded objects the size of gooseberries floated in the scum at its lip. 'There we are, sir. Only four *dankals*. And I'll throw these in as well for nothing' – and he scrabbled in a box, coming up with half a dozen toothpicks.

The foreigner reached into his pocket and produced a five-*dankal* note.

'I'm sorry, father,' he said, 'I'm afraid I have no change.'

'Neither have I,' said the old man from his vampire face.

'Filthy-lying-old-sod,' yelled the foreigner inwardly. 'Has anybody got any change?' he addressed the onlookers without hope. After a moment he laid the five-*dankal* note mutely on top of the cart.

As he did so there came an evening breeze from the forest which breathed such incense across the road as momentarily to embalm the group gathered round the cart. Some hidden tropic flower of incredible sweetness had mixed its scent with all kinds of resinous, humidor odours and sent olfactible tendrils out into the dusk. They ensnared the foreigner, rooting him like an ungainly Gulliver to the spot before unravelling away, curling and uncurling invisibly. The boy with the spiked octopus began walking back down to the shore, somehow signalling a general drift from a node of momentary interest. The foreigner in his glimmering shirt found himself, too, following them down to the sea bearing before him his brimming plastic grail with meekly belligerent gratitude.

Why to the sea? As if, having sensitively waited for the last of the locals to disappear into the darkness, he could cast both pitcher and contents into the cleansing wastes? Or was there still more of this dreadful public rite of unmerited penance to perform? Behind him he heard the squeak of the flopping wooden wheels as the old man pushed his cart away along the road amid the swirl of bats and fireflies. The little brassy tinkle followed the voice into the distance: 'Soup! Delicious! Fresh! Excrement soup!' Maybe the *faintest* chuckle?

Awkwardly he stood on the shore in an expectant knot of fisher-folk.

'Delicious,' one of them said.

'Delicious indeed. Do have some.' Ingeniously he offered the plastic pitcher to the group at large, hoping to strike some vein of hospitality which custom would forbid them to refuse. They smiled charmingly and nodded their negation, leaving him standing helplessly on a beach in fading light holding two litres of unthinkable substance for which he had paid, was paying, would always pay.

'Thank you,' said one, 'but we've already eaten. We're full now.'

'Yes, full now,' came the voices with an inclusive, excluding certitude of those whose lives are righteously governed by properly observed rituals. 'It's night now.'

And the moon soared up like a bouncing singalong ball preparing to take humanity through one more of its best-loved choruses.